THE FARM

Harrowing

H.G. Merritt

The harrowing of the soul can be like the harrowing of the soil;
to increase the yield, things are turned upside down.

NEAL A. MAXWELL

CONTENTS

2020

Lexi's story is fiction, although many of the locations mentioned are real. The characters in the book are also fictional and any similarities to real people, not intended.

However, during this unprecedented year, all of us have our own pandemic story to tell. Sadly many did not survive. Their stories must need be told by others. Throughout our world, people succumbed to this invisible predator and governments struggled to protect their people, not to mention their economies. Ah, yes, their economies.

Like Lexi, we struggled, perhaps not with a sheepdog puppy in tow or carrying our trusty crossbow, but we struggled nonetheless. Hoarding became a pastime and many worked from home, rather like the old cottage industries of the industrial revolution, except now the work involved laptops, desktops and phones. Children were forced to stay home, using technology that many parents might have been trying to wean them away from only weeks earlier. We lost friends, and relatives, and we waited to see the daily statistics rise and fall.

Villains emerged, trying to cross boarders, refusing facemasks, crowding beaches and using their mobiles to promote themselves. Greater villains hid in the shadows; poverty, ideology, racism, sexism, religious intolerance, nationalism and the cult of self. The Earth continued to warm and our inability to focus on that particular malady received little attention.

We were too involved in our lockdowns and our loss of the socalled freedoms to which we were entitled. In the background, in more places than we could imagine, skirmishes, bombs and mortar fire continued to prevail side by side with the race to set up testing stations, treatment centres and dig graves.

In the small Pacific haven of New Zealand, cooperation and adherence to the strict guidelines presented by experts, the people won out. In the State of Victoria, Australia they looked forward to when the only waves they recognised are those on the beaches.

1. THE END

Everybody has a different story about what happened. I can only tell you mine. Not that I'm especially qualified to tell you, or that my story is unique, but it's my story and you wanted to know it.

No one knows for sure the exact date, I mean, it kind of crept into existence without most people paying too much attention, but it crept fast, one hundred meters sprint fast. It didn't start in some remote corner of the world, a place that people had vaguely heard of, and then swept across the globe. This monster roared across the Earth and landed like many meteorites, everywhere, at once. No one had time to think. There was an election looming, the news was full of sports, the Olympics or some other sporting event and a couple of big scandals, as well as the assassination of the United States President, so no one was paying attention until sometime in May. At least that's what I can recall.

My brother, David, was sharing his apartment with me. It wasn't anywhere close to ideal, but when you're between jobs and broke, a good brother is just what you need, and he was a good brother, even when he was lecturing me about turning my life around. I hadn't always been like that, not even after the divorce, when cheap wine and TV filled the gap that had once been a husband and kids. The kids had gone their own way long ago. I'd expected that. But the husband, the charming-to-a-fault Derick, moving to Italy with my cousin, that was a shock, and a story, and not worth the telling. I'd made my own new life in Brussels, teaching again. That's where I met Anton Dufort. He was a Catholic, had a wife and was a government minister. So, we had an affair. Then I became his mistress. It was all very civilised. His wife Ingrid knew all about it. We were friends. We even went clothes shopping and on holidays together. Then the story broke in the newspapers. It was frightening to be named and recognised as his mistress. My private life was spread out for friends and colleagues to pick over. Anton attempted suicide. In less than a week Ingrid went into hiding and I lost my job. A month later, David came to Belgium, got me sober enough to pass through customs and brought me home.

I was David's flat mate, which was lucky for me, because when the head went woozy and my flu turned nasty, he carried me to bed and became my nurse. I was so far from reality, drifting in and out of vague consciousness, that I don't remember much except his face and being wiped with a damp cloth.

I woke up again on May the 20th. I know that because David was obsessed with using a calendar. He was also a compulsive note writer. The big pink Post-it said he'd gone off to shop for food and more painkillers. He thought he was coming down with my flu. I never saw him again. By mid-afternoon that day I began to worry. After taking the last of his paracetamol I decided to find him. He always shopped at the same supermarket. A creature of habit was David. He joked that he had a crush on one of the girls working there. Well, maybe it wasn't a joke, but it wouldn't have been one of the girls either. The streets were quiet, but I figured that was probably due to the rain, buckets of it, and by the time I got to the supermarket my hair was soaked and the place was closed.

'Too many staff are sick I expect.' A bloke stood beside me looking in like I was, not knowing what to do next. 'Don't try around the corner. They're shut an' all. Government should have had a lock-down, like they did last time. Happened too quick, I'm guessing. Reckon I'll try the take-away.' He slouched off down the street, hand in pockets, collar up.

2

What the man told me concerned me. I went back to the apartment and switched on the TV. The news was full of reports of some new virus, so new it hadn't got a name yet. People were being asked to stay at home because the hospitals and doctors couldn't cope. Even the presenter looked less than healthy. I had clearly missed a lot while I had been resting at David's place.

I wondered how my kids were coping. My youngest, Ben, never answered his mobile. Too busy balancing his studies and social life I expect. I left a message telling him where I was, how I was, and asking him to call me when he could. Ben had been my easiest child, both in his birth and from then, ever after. He'd handled school without the angst or competitiveness of his siblings and still managed to land a place on the engineering course he'd wanted in Bologna. I didn't even have my eldest son's telephone number. Marcus was in Switzerland somewhere. I tried to call his sister Olivia, in France. I asked her to contact me. My eldest two children were very much leading their own lives and they didn't have much contact with me or their father, particularly their father. I hoped at least one of them might ring back soon. They didn't. It got to eight o'clock, so I locked the door and went back to bed, with my phone beside me. David had his own key. He'd let himself in.

I managed to sleep throughout the next day, and when I did wake up and wander into the dining kitchen, David hadn't come back. I tried his mobile but there was no service, which was strange. I took myself back to the supermarket, but it was still closed, and the one around the corner was the same, except the automatic glass doors had been smashed. I went in, even called out, but the whole place was deserted. It was clear that someone had been in and helped themselves. Potato chips packets were scattered on the floor and someone had cleared the place of cola. The surveillance cameras were off, so I helped myself to painkillers and instant meals from the freezer. I know David might have written a note, or left the cash at the checkout, but I wasn't feeling public spirited. I went back to the flat and cooked my pizza.

The next morning, I woke to the muffled voice of a mobile loud-speaker van driving slowly down the road. I opened the window to hear it more clearly, but it made no sense. People were being asked to stay indoors and pray. Great! I decided to drop in at the local police station to report my missing brother only to be yelled at by a hairy old copper trying to keep the place running while every other cop was down with the virus, except he called it 'the sickness'. Sickness, contagion, pandemic, no one had the time to name the damn thing. It still doesn't have a name, but eventually it became known as 'the virus'. I didn't even get to tell the duty sergeant about David. The poor bugger erupted into a fit of coughing and was red in the face. He waved me away. That afternoon I binged on junk food and then I fell asleep on the sofa.

When I woke up the following day the phones, the TV and the internet were all down. I felt marooned. David hadn't had much to do with his neighbours, but he'd introduced me to the guy across the corridor, Bill, and an old lady on the floor above. I'd forgotten her name. She'd chatted to me a couple of times when I got the mail. I needed to find out what was happening and maybe get back to the police station. Perhaps there would be more staff on. I knocked on Bill's door but got no answer, so I went upstairs and knocked on every door because I didn't know the old woman's flat number. Her door was the only one that opened.

'Come in luv.' She pulled me inside and then locked the door behind me. While she made a pot of tea, she told me she'd seen people breaking into shops and even fighting each other on the streets. 'Not a police car in sight!' She shook her head. I told her about the police station. 'I've been praying,' she confided as she poured the tea. 'I went to church, but it's locked, and I tried to see the priest, but his house was locked an' all. Have you got any food?' She asked me.

'Not much but I'll share with you. People had broken into the supermarket and people were just taking what they wanted. We could go down there together.' Perhaps it was her fear of being alone, or just that her freezer was empty, but she was quite enthusiastic about leaving her flat with me. She suggested we go sooner rather than later.

We crept along the deserted streets, unnerved by the quiet. She lagged behind me once we got to the store, but as soon as I started tipping stuff into my trolley, she was quick to follow. By the time we pushed our load back to the apartment building she'd brightened a lot. I invited her to eat with me, but she said that the trudge back, and the anxiety of stealing from the supermarket had left her tired. We promised to see each other the following day.

 The police station was open but deserted. I called out, rang the bell, but no one answered. By now I was worried. I felt so isolated. I just wanted my brother home. I needed to talk to someone, to find out if they knew anything. I returned to the apartment building and tried Bill's door again. I remember thanking God that the electricity was still on.

It's weird looking back because I remember some things very clearly, but in those early weeks some days merged together. I wandered about for a couple of days, looking for my brother. Each day being outside became more frightening. There were plenty of bodies about and people, quite clearly ill, huddled in doorways or laid on park benches. I hurried on past, consoling myself with the idea that I didn't know any of them, and besides, there really wasn't anything I could do. Frightened faces looked out at the world from their windows. One guy was reading the Bible out loud as I passed and suddenly burst into "Jerusalem", singing in between coughing.

I found Bill's spare key in David's kitchen, hung up neatly with a plastic label. I knocked on the door louder than ever and shouted his name, and when I got no answer I opened the door and was met by the loud buzz of insects. They turned out to be blow flies. Bill, or what was left of him, was sitting on his sofa, wrapped in a blanket. He smelt like he'd been dead for years. I rushed back out and locked him in with his flies. I sat down on the staircase outside and tried to control my urge to vomit. That same day I went up to the old woman's place with hot coffee to share. She had her door latch on and told me that I'd better keep away. She'd started to feel ill the night before and was feeling so weak she was staying in bed.

You and me both know what the upshot of this is luv. If I were you, I'd get as far away from town as you can, before you get it.'

'But I've had it.' I told her, pressing my face close to the narrow opening. 'Some people must be surviving. You could. Here, please take the coffee, it's warming! I'll let you get back to sleep and I'll check on you in the morning.' She took the jug, thanked me, then repeated her advice before locking her door. It was the last time I saw her. When I banged on her door the following day, she didn't answer. I think I must have panicked a bit then and ran from floor to floor knocking on all the doors. None of them opened, and after hearing that god-awful buzzing behind some doors, I hurried back to David's apartment.

❊ ❊ ❊

It was time to make plans. I knew I could not remain in the apartment building, surrounded by the dead and dying. Outside, it was clear that a kind of lawlessness was beginning to spread. I needed to do something, to be proactive. I dug out David's maps, packed all the food I could find, hunted for his spare car keys and went down to the garage to load the car. David had been a keen camper in his youth, so I took his tiny tent, a sleeping bag and a couple of blankets. I was so pleased with myself for remembering the matches and a tin opener. The electricity went off halfway through cooking my TV meal, which I took as confirmation that it was time to leave.

 The following morning, I set off with no particular destination in mind, just the idea that heading towards Derbyshire should be safer than staying in the city. There were cabins, mobile homes and probably even holiday homes that might be easy to occupy. I left David a note telling him where I was going. I filled up with petrol at the nearest shopping mall and hid the car among other parked vehicles that had clearly been there for a while. One had a body in it. Someone had been dying when they did their last shop. Taking 'shop 'til you drop' very literally.

You're wondering how I can talk about it so glibly, as if it was an adventure. I wonder myself sometimes. Of course, it wasn't an adventure, more like sustained, full on panic that drove me into action, and while ever I was moving, doing stuff, I didn't have to think. Thinking brought worry. Where were my children? Were they safe? Were they alive? Why the hell did David go out for painkillers?

* * *

There were others in the mall, I could hear them before I saw them. Young men, taking their frustration out by smashing shop front windows and stealing guitars from the music shop. I hurried past them. Occasional furtive figures dived in and out of the empty corridors. There was maybe a handful of people in the mall, a strange and eerie place with only the safety lights on. Most people, like me, were not acknowledging anyone else. We were all strangers with no business being there. A woman did speak to me at the clothing store. She'd got several very expensive dresses in her trolley and asked me what I thought of the beach wear she was holding. What can you say? Miles from the coast in a scene from a zombie movie, and you're looking at a one piece with secret support! I grabbed my new, very sensible undies and hurried to the outdoor pursuit shop for boots, socks and a few fleece tops.

While I was getting a backpack for my goodies, a man stumbled into the store. He brought down a whole rack of anoraks as he coughed and spluttered. He was in a bad way, gasping as he lay on his back too weak to get up. Snot and saliva covered his chin. His shirt, grubby from days of wear tucked half in and out of his trousers, and from the smell he'd soiled himself. He pleaded at me to help him, but what could I do?

I hurried away, intent on reaching David's car, hating myself for being a coward, when something stopped me in my tracks. In the echoey mall, the plaintive wail of an animal was coming from the darkened pet store. It had an 'up for adoption' section, strays that the local shelter had placed here to find a home. Most of the poor creatures were lying limp, except for a small black and white puppy who began to leap at the glass when she saw me approaching. I saw an opportunity to help a vulnerable, but living animal, and took it.

Heading for the exit there was one other place I wanted to check out before we left. The sports equipment store had a section that I'd been very familiar with, a few years ago. At the end of the store, behind a secure grill, now wrenched from its mounts, was the sports shooting section. Most of the guns and rifles were gone. I didn't want them anyway. Instead, I chose a crossbow, arrows and quiver, and a handful of spare parts. It had been a long time since my husband had introduced me to archery and at the time my preference for a crossbow had annoyed the purist in him. I had no idea where my old weapon had gone but I had a feeling this one might prove useful.

* * *

The puppy slept on the front seat as we climbed out of the city and headed for the open moorland. Only later did I remember the dog would want water, so I broke into a convenience store for half a dozen bottles. By the time we rolled into Bakewell, which was as silent as the city I had just left, the boot was well and truly full. I parked in the half empty municipal car park, fed the dog and myself, took her for a walk by the river and locked us both in the car as night fell. She slept like a baby and I cried. I opened my handbag. The contents of my purse had become completely bloody useless. I was guessing that my credit cards and driver's license were unusable, and I had more loyalty cards than notes of money. I closed the purse and dug through the rest of my handbag. Even my passport seemed irrelevant. I looked at the photo of my younger self inside, I had always looked quite young for my age. My short, straight blonde hair with wispy ends with just a little bit of grey hadn't changed, except perhaps the percentage of grey had increased. In a plastic display wallet, I had pictures of the kids, and David. There he was grinning like a maniac in a red beret on our weekend in Paris. The pictures of my kids were old, not quite school days but nearly, Marcus in his doctoral gown, Olivia looking glamourous on her twentieth birthday, her blond hair streaked with purple to match her dress and young Ben, standing in the snow on a mountain top.

Sitting alone in the car, the enormity of my situation washed over me. What the hell was I doing? How was I going to survive? Where was David? I should have stayed in the city and waited for him. A flood of regrets and fears tormented me until dawn.

* * *

In the early morning light, I thought I saw someone across the river, and slid further down in my seat. The man was carrying a rifle. He passed out of my sight, into the town. I wasn't ready to meet anyone carrying a weapon, with or without my crossbow.

I knew there was a visitor's centre in Castleton, and someone had already broken in, so it was easy for me to collect as many brochures and lists of accommodation as I wanted. The dog and I sat on a bench in the sun, flicking through the materials trying to find somewhere we could stay. The first campsite we came to looked ideal, being beside a river, but the owners had locked the gates and a pair of hungry dogs were patrolling. We crossed that off our list. Maybe we would come back if we were desperate but the idea of shooting a pair of Dobermans to get a bed would mean I had to be feeling very desperate.

The road that weaved through the Hope Valley was deserted, not a car, a bike, or even a tractor in sight. As I drove through the villages wishing that someone would appear, I half regretted not calling out to the lone rifleman I'd seen in Bakewell, and as we rolled back into the same carpark for the night, I was heartened to see two men walking across the bridge with a woman. Only when they got nearer could I see clearly that she wasn't walking along with them, in fact her shoes were dragging along the ground, her head bent. They had not seen me and paused at the edge of the lawns by the river. The shorter man took hold of the woman and tossed her to the ground. Her face was badly bruised, and she did nothing to defend herself as he lifted her dress and took down her undies. I could feel the fear and bile rising in my throat. While the taller man knelt on her hair, his hands pressing down on her arms, the short man began to rape her. I started to put the lead on the puppy, my hands shaking as I reached for the crossbow. The men might have seen the movement in my car if it had not been for the guy running towards them across the bridge, his rifle lifted. The men seemed undecided, while the woman suddenly started to vomit and cough, in the face of her rapist. Both men released the woman and turned their attention to the rifleman who had paused, facing them, his weapon ready.

'You can't shoot us both, and she's sick anyway.' I heard the taller man shout.

'Then you'll both be dead. Leave her be and get away before I send one of you to your maker.'

'You'll be a dead man if you do, 'cos, I'll crush your skull. Get back to your pub and leave this alone, old man. You're not up to it.'

'He might not be up to it, but I am.' Was that really me, walking towards them with my crossbow loaded? I had gone completely mad, surely?

'You're not going to use that!' The big man came towards me, his lips twisting in an unpleasant smile. His expression changed to surprise. A crossbow arrow planted firmly in his chest. He toppled and hit the ground with a thud. The small man didn't wait to see if his friend was alive. He pulled up his trousers as he escaped across the bridge, and we could hear a car engine starting up somewhere in the town. I dropped the crossbow and couldn't stop shaking. The rifleman looked down at the woman and then came over to me.

'She's not going to make it, and that little sod who attacked her probably won't either. Are you all right?' The landlord of the

Red Lion took me across the road to his pub and gave me a stiff brandy. He even fed the puppy. He had been a paramedic in the army, and he must have treated a few shocked individuals in his time. 'That woman, she was the wife of a friend. One of the last people alive here, now it's just me and the wife. She's an invalid. I'll go and let her know what's happened. Stay here tonight, if you want. We can make a bed up for you.' I don't think I had ever felt so grateful for a stranger's kindness as I did that day.

✳ ✳ ✳

It was a time when lots of stuff was 'the last', and that night I thought I was having my last pub meal, liver and onions, washed down with a glass of beer and with good company. The landlord and his wife were interested in what news I could give them, which wasn't much. They told me how the population of the market town had been decimated in less than a fortnight. They'd decided to stay, figuring it was probably safer in the country, and they had nowhere else to go. With the death of the woman, a local estate agent, only three homes were now occupied and two of those had the sickness. The landlord had stolen a generator from a campsite nearby and made sure they were well stocked for fuel and food for the time being. None of us were thinking much about long term in those days.

I slept well that night, the puppy curled at the bottom of the bed. In the morning I left, promising to let them know where I would be staying and to visit them again when I could. The landlord presented me with a clean arrow. He'd retrieved it for me. As I drove back over the bridge, I noticed the woman and the tall man had been buried where they had died.

2. TOM

While most of the country, and the rest of the world, was reeling from the deaths of a large part of the population, I was looking for somewhere to live. From time to time I thought about my killing of the unknown man with my crossbow, and the probable deaths of my family while I drove up and down the Peak District searching for somewhere unoccupied that I could take over. Every so often, the reality would overwhelm me, when I saw bodies, or let my thoughts stray to my brother, my children, even my rat of a husband, but somehow the enormity of it all hadn't really sunk in, as I concentrated on my task of finding a roof over my head.

Of course, there were any number of available homes that contained their dead owners, but I wasn't prepared to dispose of bodies and disinfect furnishings before I could move in. I wasn't that desperate, yet. The puppy was good company and having to care for her made me aware that I had to feed myself too. I was so busy looking for a small holiday cottage that I allowed my petrol to run low. I remembered a small station that I'd passed a while ago, and as we were a little off the beaten track I decided to double back.

As I started to fill up, to my surprise, the pump stopped working and the door of the garage opened. An old man raced out yelling at me. 'It's not free yer know. You still have to pay for it!'

'I will.' I reached for my bag inside the car.

'Money's no good, woman, not anymore!' His eyes were too close together, and he seemed to be looking me up and down.

'Then what are you expecting me to pay with?'

'Well,' he leered, 'you could be nice to me, maybe keep me company for a while. Not many folk left. You could do a lot worse than shack up with me.'

I swore at him before I climbed back into the car and drove off. Dirty old sod! In my anger, I took off up a narrow, barely tarmacked lane seething at the man's cheek and wishing the next customer he propositioned would infect him with the virus. My grannie always warned me against wishing ill on others. I should have known better. I took a corner a little quickly and found myself sliding across the road and into a ditch. As the car thumped against the earth embankment I felt one of the tyres blow. We weren't going anywhere.

I filled the backpack with as much as I could and then packed David's pull-along shopping bag, now casual suitcase, with the tent, sleeping bag and as much as I could cram in there. The waterproof anorak felt bulky, so it was easier to wear than to carry. I was grateful that the weather was fine, with grey monotonous cloud cover overhead and it was cool. David would have called it walking weather. It was late in the afternoon by the time I locked the car and with the torch and the puppy lead in one hand and the pull-along in the other, I headed off along the road, which according to the map eventually fed into a wider road that ran along the valley bottom to a small town.

When it got too gloomy to go on, I left the road, climbed into a field and made camp for the night. I was thankful that David had chosen a small tent that was easy to erect, as it kind of flicked into place. I just hoped I'd remember how to twist it back in the morning. The dog and I ate outside, trying hard to ignore the bites from spring midges. Then with a blanket on the tent floor to protect it from puppy claws we crawled inside. I lit the torch and as I slithered into the sleeping bag, the pup curled up on the bottom. I slept better than I would have imagined, perhaps because I was exhausted.

My watch had run out of juice, so I had no idea what time we woke and ate, dog biscuits for her and the last of my bananas for me. I packed, and we began our march towards the distant road, stopping occasionally for the puppy whose little legs were willing but far from able. I had no idea how old the little thing was, so by the afternoon I was carrying her. Then it began to rain and for a second time we made camp, this time in a wood below the road. It was still light by the time the tent was up but neither the dog nor I wanted to eat outside. We were both still itching from the midge bites. Trying to ignore our dampness, we shut out the evening, looking through the gloom from the small mesh window at the empty valley below. I cried and told the puppy about all the things we should be grateful for, including being alive. The puppy was curled into a tight ball next to me, totally oblivious to our dire situation. Just as I was about to sleep I heard a car coming up the road, the headlights flashed through the tent as it passed. I hoped they hadn't noticed us. I saw their lights, but we were in darkness and surrounded by trees. As they didn't slow or return I knew they hadn't spotted us. We slept safely, protected from the storm outside.

By morning the storm had blown itself out and we resumed our tramp towards the road. Checking the map, I'd been annoyed how little progress we'd made. The wheels on the pull-along were showing a lot of wear and tear from the unmade road and the puppy was eager to be carried long before we stopped for lunch. I'd only been carrying her for a short time when one of the wheels of the pull-along cracked, and the two halves rolled away down the road. Carrying the pull along like a suitcase soon tired me out too and the pair of us must have looked quite dejected as we chewed our lunch, sitting near the road. It took a lot of self-talk to get me up and on the road again. Thankfully the pup helped, rejuvenated by her healthy dog food, she was eager to be off and for a good hour it was her pulling at the lead and me struggling forward with the hated ex-pull-along. Just as her enthusiasm was beginning to subside I heard the singing of a strong, deep male voice giving a stirring rendition of 'If I Were a Rich Man' accompanied by the thud of something being beaten.

We must have looked a sorry sight, bedraggled, dirty, stumbling along the road, our battered pull-along clattering over the rough stones, as I had reverted to dragging it along on one wheel. There was a long moment when we all regarded each other before he spoke. I was weighing up in my mind how fast I could run, with the puppy, if this guy turned out to be a nutcase. He was possibly in his sixties and large framed. He looked quite surprised to see me, and at first made no attempt to come nearer, which I took as a good sign.

'Oh dear, what's happened to you? Are you alright?' It was a voice of sincere concern.

I don't remember exactly what I said, but I recounted as best I could the days since my brother's disappearance. It all came flooding out of my mouth at the same time as the tears welled up and filled my eyes. As he listened he put down his wooden mallet, a frown on his face.

'Would you like something to drink?' He picked up a small flask and began to pour out the hot tea. He took the puppy so I could hold the mug. It was warm and comforting. While I drank he introduced himself as Tom. 'We've had the virus out here too. It's a terrible thing. I'd heard reports about the violence. So, people are leaving the cities now?'

I shook my head. 'I don't know. I just knew I couldn't stay there.'

Tom asked me when I'd had my last warm meal. 'Would you like to come in for a bit? The house is just up the drive. I could make you a nice lunch.' I agreed to his invite. Fatigue and hunger won out over my fear of him being a stranger. He took charge of the pull-along.

And that was how I met Tom Gresham. Old, wise, bear-like Tom, who gently shepherded me up to his house, made me lunch and sat me down for a good long chat. I found myself revealing more about my life but in such a jumbled way, I'm sure he could never have followed it. It didn't seem to matter.

'So, where are you headed next? Have you got family around here?'

'I don't have any family, I came out here to find some vacant holiday place I could use.'

'Well, we have chalets here.' He pointed out the window to a row of wooden buildings at the end of a path. 'You could use one of those if you like. Or there's the B and B rooms up the corridor.' He saw the doubt in my mind. 'There are locks on all the doors.'

'Are you sure? I wouldn't want to impose or anything. I could pay for my stay. I wouldn't have to stay long.'

'Oh, don't worry about the money. No one else is going to be using them right now. I haven't seen another living soul since....' His voice tapered away, then he brightened. 'To tell you truth Lexi I'd really appreciate the company. I should be paying you! Now, I should warn you that the chalets haven't been used in a while, so would you prefer to have a room inside the house tonight or would you prefer to move into a chalet straightaway?'

'Oh, a room in the house would be fine, thanks Tom.' I didn't want to seem rude after all his hospitality, even if I was a little nervous.

'I could drive you back to your car and you could get all your other things, if you like. And you can stay as long as you like.'

Along with his kindness, Tom was practical too, and before I knew it, he was showing me the bathroom, with a solar-heated shower and a cupboard full of men's shampoo and shower gel. When I came back out to his warm kitchen the puppy was tucking into diced pet food.

Tom was a man of his word. We collected everything from the car, including the tyre, which he thought he could fix. He gave the crossbow a strange look but said nothing. Once back at the house he ushered me into a delightful bedroom, all folksy, with a patchwork quilt and dried flowers, and told me to make myself comfy. I sat on the bed for a while but hearing him banging about in the kitchen drew me back out there. He was making a meat pie and when I asked if I could help, I was given the vegetables to peel and chop. A rice pudding, all ready to bake, was sitting on the bench beside the cooker. The puppy had already made herself at home, curling into a tight ball in her bed next to the open fire, burning low now as the day was warmer. After the meal, we sat on the two sofas beside the large fireplace.

'It was my brother's place,' he explained. 'Used to be a good little business during the summer, but as he got older it all became too much, so he did B and B for a while, then stopped altogether. He's been a bit of a recluse for the last five years.'

'Where is he now?'

Tom pointed, his face suddenly ashen, 'Out there. I buried him two weeks ago.' Then he sniffed. 'I'd been laid up myself for a while, and when I finally got up, he was gone, stone cold, out there in the paddock. Must have died shortly after I'd taken ill. His face was all gone. Insects, I expect.' His face crumpled. 'I'm sorry, you didn't need to hear that.'

'Oh, I've seen my fair share of dead bodies myself Tom. My brother just went out and never came back.'

'Before the TV stopped, they said that people died quickly once the illness took them, or like you and me they recovered.' Tom stared into the fire. The man exuded honesty and warmth like a woollen blanket. 'As far as I know there's not many of us, one in so many thousand, they said.' He stood. 'I think the people you've met might have been the ones who just kept out of the way until the sickness died down.'

Curled up in bed later that evening, with the puppy at my feet, looking out into the night, at the stars, through the dark trees that circled the house, I thought about my brother David again. I remembered how he'd always been there for me when we were children and later, when Derick abandoned me, David phoned frequently to check to see that his little sister was coping. He hadn't had it easy, but he was always thoughtful towards me. I felt guilty for leaving without him but deep down I knew he would have told me it was the sensible thing to do. He'd want me to be safe, and I was safe, for the moment at least. Tom's company had restored my spirits. I no longer felt that I was rushing headlong towards some unknown, terrible fate. He'd said we could talk about my plans at breakfast, but I had no plans. How could we all survive when the world we knew was over? I looked at my mobile phone, positioned as usual beside the bed. It was dead and not likely to be of any use, but I kept it, nevertheless. My watch had disappeared from my wrist, somewhere along our hike up the dirt road. I hadn't missed it. Tom told me that although the normal electricity was no longer working, the house used solar energy and a back-up generator for power.

We had no way of contacting anyone. That wonderful, easy to use world we'd come to depend on was gone. We were on our own. Tears fell as I realised how much I missed my brother, my children, my old life. Scattered across the globe I did not know if or when I would see any of them again. I was worried that they were experiencing their own unravelling. The misery was overwhelming.

* * *

Sunlight playing on my face woke me. The puppy was whining. I suspected she needed to pee, so I let her out of the bedroom intending to dress and follow her. I could hear Tom talking to her in the kitchen, and then the back door opening and closing. He was taking her out for a walk. By the time I was dressed they were both back and Tom was at his stove. Bacon and eggs for breakfast was a luxury I'd begun to think would never happen again.

'Our mother always insisted on a good, big breakfast,' he said. 'Fried bread?'

'Where are you getting all your supplies?' I perched on the stool at the kitchen bench.

'My brother always kept himself well stocked, but I am running low on some things. You said the supermarkets have been broken into?' He deftly flipped the bread over.

'Big time! It was like kids at a candy store when I was there, but not many people, just mad people collecting stuff. Some of the food would be going off by now.'

He started to put the food on two plates. 'There are two big chest freezers in the shed. We probably need to stock up. We could go to one of the bigger supermarkets in Chesterfield, or there's a Co-op in Bakewell.'

'I was thinking,' I began cautiously. I didn't want him to think I was being rude or pushy. 'You've got enough land here, haven't you? You should think about growing your own food. We don't know exactly how food production has been affected, but with everything going the way it is we could run out of food soon. The last time I was in a supermarket there was virtually no fresh food left and most of the freezers were empty.'

'We've...' He checked himself. 'I've got fifty acres, all told. Arthur used to have cattle, then deer, before he had the chalets built. That's why there's the big fences all the way around, used to be electrified. It cost him a fortune to put it in, but the deer didn't do as well as he'd expected. There are a few of them left up in the top wood.'

'Venison!' I tucked into breakfast and the conversation ceased for a while.

'We could check out the farming stores. We'd need supplies from there and perhaps some heavy equipment. I've only got a small tractor and a sit-on mower. We'd need something to plough the land, probably some manure to enrich it and seeds, and the like. We could try it.' Tom was getting keen but then he stopped and put down his fork. 'I am sorry. I was saying, 'we' but you've probably planned to leave, head off to wherever you were going.'

I shrugged. 'I wasn't going anywhere. In fact, I wasn't sure what I was doing except getting out of the city. It was bad there and likely to get worse.' I looked down at the plate. I'd demolished the breakfast in record time. I'd been ravenous. 'In fact, if you don't mind Tom, I'd like to stay. I can help you. You're right, we should plant our own veggies but when you mentioned the deer, I was wondering what other animals we could keep here. Have you been in contact with any of your neighbours? We should check on them, but if they're gone, we could bring their animals back here. Chickens would be good, maybe even pigs, but I'd not fancy slaughtering them.'

Tom looked at me in amazement. 'I've no idea who's alive. I haven't been off the property for weeks, even before the sickness.' He spooned coffee grounds into his old coffee pot. He looked up and after a moment, he quietly said, 'I was staying with my brother...to dry out.'

I took a deep breath and looked at his earnest, anxious face. 'Your brother sounds a lot like mine, the caring kind. I'm not here to judge you Tom. No one's perfect.' I stood up. 'We should head off to get our stuff and maybe later we could check on your neighbours.'

It was a unique shopping experience. We travelled in Arthur's very nice Range Rover. Clearly the chalets had been more profitable than the deer. At the almost deserted supermarket we joined three other people in raiding the shelves. While they took everything from cook-at-home bread to frozen meals, we concentrated on things like tea, coffee, sugar, stuff we couldn't readily produce ourselves and as much flour, butter, lard and cooking oil as we could carry. Tom insisted on our collecting some of the frozen meat and we each grabbed handfuls of chocolate bars. The deserted farm produce and equipment store was a more serious adventure, starting with equipping us both with a set of tools and boots for me, gathering up seed packets, plus every possible aid to growing plants, from fertilisers to pest control. Outside, Tom hooked the Range Rover to a shiny new horse float where we stacked our treasure, then he gave me the bad news.

'You drive the car back and I'll follow you in this.' He pointed at a very large, green and yellow tractor, which came, he said, with a host of attachments he'd come back for later. I had never driven anything as large as a Range Rover and now I was pulling a horse-float too. Thankfully no one else was on the road as we trundled our way through the deserted valley and back to the house. When we got there, I did pose him another problem. Petrol! How were we going to drive the monstrous tractor without fuel? He'd filled up at the farm store but how long would it be before we ran out.

'Then we'll have to pull it ourselves!' he countered, flicking through the instruction manual. I laughed at the imagery. It was a rare instance of Tom not thinking practically. He was infatuated with his man-toy.

'Or we could just find some horses!' I suggested.

Among our treasures that we'd 'liberated' were overalls, mostly the blue, car-mechanic type, but also the cover-all suits used by decorators, and scene-of-crime pathologists. Together with face masks, they proved useful. That afternoon we drove to the top of the road, where it met the main road, and began a disturbing experience.

We developed a routine. First, we knocked at the door, then we toured the outside of the house peering through windows. This sometimes told us all that we needed to know. The dead were long gone. We left the house undisturbed. Arthur's desk had provided Tom with a list of his neighbours, an invitation list compiled by a certain Mrs Hebden, for a distant Harvest Festival party that would no longer happen. The Pettigrews, at the first house, were dead on their couch. They had no live animals and so we moved on. We found Mrs Hebden in bed, dead, but not dead long as she was untouched by maggots. As Tom had known the old woman well, he carried her out to the lawn where we gave a her a Viking funeral on her favourite chair, fuelled by several wooden chairs and a side table. She had six brown chickens, in a neat little pen.

'How do we get them back home and where do we put them?' Tom and I were watching the flames rising, both of us doubting that we had the stomach for any further visits that day. I had noticed some mobile 'A' frame hutches at the farm store, I should have mentioned them at the time, I confessed. 'Maybe we could get those?'

Tom drove back to the store with the horse float. He would be gone for well over an hour, so I walked down to the next home, a hobby farm, where I found four goats roaming in the neat vegetable garden and a calm horse who came to the fence as soon as she saw me. According to Arthur's list, this was the Davidson's home. The front door was unlocked, and I found an old man dead in the hallway. His wife, also dead, was wrapped in a quilt lying on the sofa. The other rooms downstairs were empty. I was about to leave when I heard a weak voice asking who was there. A middle-aged woman was sitting on the bed. She was sick but still able to move about. I took off my face mask and told her I was helping one of their neighbours to check on everyone.

'Are there any others alive?' She coughed into a handkerchief.

'We don't know yet. The Pettigrews and Mrs Hebden are dead, and I'm afraid...'

'My parents are both dead, I know. I should bury them, but I don't feel strong enough. I'm going to die, aren't I?'

'I don't know,' I sat beside her on the bed. 'I didn't and Tom didn't. Maybe you'll recover.' I looked back through the open door to her mother's room. 'We burnt Mrs Hebden's body. It's the safest way. Would you like me to help you with your parents? You don't have to watch but it will take two of us to get them outside.'

She'd been sitting on the bed for a long time, perhaps ever since her mother had died, and she followed my instructions mechanically as we carried the old lady outside. She struggled to get back inside the house, but I told her I could do the rest. I watched her sit on the empty sofa before I went back outside. They had a good log pile ready for winter, so I stacked the wood under the bed quilt her mother was wrapped in. Then I hefted the bodies side by side onto the quilt. I was glad she wasn't watching because manhandling them wasn't pretty. I threw the remnants of some petrol I'd found in their garage over the bodies and lit the fire. It roared into life but quickly settled. I went back inside to tell her and found her sitting on the bed.

'Have they gone yet?'

'Not yet. Give it a couple of hours before you go out. If I was you, I'd get to bed and try to sleep. I think sleeping helped me. You need your rest. Have you eaten?'

She nodded and began to climb the stairs. After three steps, she stopped and looked back at me. 'Who will burn my body if I die? I don't want the maggots to eat me away.'

'I will come back tomorrow and see how you are. If you like, I could come back later with some soup. We have solar energy, and you should have some hot food. Would you like soup?'

She sighed. 'Come back tomorrow. I don't think I could stomach soup right now. You're right, I think I need to sleep.' She started to climb again, and the effort was almost too much for her.

'Look, when Tom gets here why don't you come back with us. It's warm and comfortable there and we could look after you.'

Her eyes were dull and even looking at me was an effort. She thanked me but assured me she really just wanted to get some sleep. She knew, she said, she'd be better in her own bed and as she climbed, she added, 'It's better to die in your own bed, isn't it? Please come back and burn me. That's all I ask.'

I didn't even know her name. She must have been visiting her parents because she was not on Arthur's Christmas list, and when Tom and I cremated her the following day, I wished that I'd at least asked her name.

Before we ate that first night of our search, we had constructed not only the 'A' frame hutches but also a free-standing, top-of-the-range chicken shed to house Mrs Hebden's chickens. Tom had found a metallic labelling gadget in Arthur's desk and in a very Tom-like gesture he began labelling every item of livestock housing and equipment we appropriated with their previous owners' names. He wanted to honour the memories of their previous owners. On the second day, after Ms Davidson's Viking funeral, we transported the Davidson's goats in the horse float to the farm and settled them into a new shed and wired enclosure. Tom brought their horse, Pippa, along as well. But it was on the third day that our most valuable and perhaps most difficult acquisitions were found.

Two properties remained to investigate up the road. One was a large farm, the Conway's, with more equipment in their shed than we knew how to use. We noted it but left it where it was. There were two sheds facing the house and no sign of anyone until we broke in and found several people dead in their beds. Before we left the house, Tom noticed a small room with a desk and two bookcases full of factual books about animal husbandry and farming methods. We loaded the Rover up with nearly all of them. Inside the sheds, unhappy at being confined, we found several alpacas. Neither of us had any idea of how to handle these particular creatures, and we were debating how to treat them, when one dark brown animal spat into Tom's face. Surprised, Tom staggered back leaving the animals just enough room to force their way out of the shed and into the paddock. Within moments they were calm and eating grass as peacefully as sheep.

'We might come back for them.' Tom sounded doubtful as he wiped his face. 'The wool's good but I think we should read some of those books before we try to do anything.'

There was a quaint wooden house between the Conway's and Arthur's property bordered on one side by a stream and on the other by a rocky outcrop that naturally separated it from Arthur's land. In between, a low, wooden building with matching outhouses belonged to a Doctor Grint, a retired surgeon, who we could not locate anywhere, in or outside his house. From his bookcase and the magazines scattered through his untidy living room, it appeared that the good doctor was a keen organic gardener. His books covered everything from natural pesticides and companion planting to Lovelock's Gaia hypothesis. He had a lot of books about bee keeping.

'Can you see any hives outside?' I called to Tom who was checking the kitchen cabinets for anything useful. If Dr Grint was alive, he was pretty relaxed, leaving his door unlocked. We suspected the worst, but just in case he came home and thought he'd been burgled Tom left him a note on the kitchen table. As we left we noticed six beehives in a sheltered cove of the outcrop and we also saw Doctor Grint, on the ground beside one of his hives. We both marched up to retrieve his body, Tom lighting the smoker by the side of the doctor to pacify the bees who were becoming interested. As we lifted the man, he groaned, and we quickly carried him away from the hives to where we could remove his net protection.

'I'm sorry, did I call out when I fell? Do I know you?' The doctor's face was blotchy, red and swollen. He didn't seem to have any of the virus symptoms.

'Tom Gresham, I'm Arthur's brother and this is Lexi. We thought you were dead.'

'Might well have been if my girls weren't kind.' He looked back at the hives. 'I sneezed and lost my balance. Tipped straight into the hive and set them off. A couple must have got into my net and stung me. I was feeling so weak, I couldn't seem to get up.' We helped him back to his house.

'Has there been developments in the epidemic?' He looked confused when we told him that everyone who lived nearby was dead. 'What day is it?' It was June the third. Our answer confused him more. He got up shakily and checked his calendar on the fridge. Then he tried to turn on the TV. Doctor Grint and Tom talked while I made tea and carefully replaced all the groceries we'd taken from his kitchen.

'He's been up there on the ground for nearly three days, and he was sick in bed for a week before that.' Tom explained to me quietly. We watched as the doctor drank a third glass of water before he attempted the tea.

'I hadn't been feeling well but I thought I was over it when I went up to check on the girls, my bees. I don't remember much after that until you both woke me.' The doctor polished his spectacles and looked down at his knees. 'It's been bad then?' Tom told him just how bad, and I was able to recount what I had seen before I left the city. The doctor seemed mystified and saddened. 'What shall we all do now?' He asked no one in particular.

'We don't know about any other survivors but we're trying to get ourselves organised to live as well as we can. We've checked all the homes between here and the main road and brought any livestock we could back to my brother's property. We intend to learn how to live off the land and care for the animals.' Tom made it sound exciting.
'How is Arthur?' The doctor drank his tea.

'Dead, I'm afraid. Many people haven't survived.'

'I'm sorry. He was a good man. What are the authorities doing?'

Tom's lips tightened. 'As far as we know, no one's left in charge.' I told the doctor about the police station and we both explained that the electricity and other services had stopped.

'Someone must be doing something. They'll sort it out soon enough. Shops are being looted you say?' He stood slowly and shuffled to a small cabinet, taking out a bottle of whisky and pouring himself a very large glass. Remembering his manners, he apologised and offered to pour us a drink. We both declined. The doctor gulped his down in two swallows and Tom's throat mimicked the action.

'Don't worry, we'll see it through. We've already made a start in planning and getting what we need to survive. Perhaps we could exchange some of our eggs or vegetables for your honey.' Tom was doing his best to put on a brave face.

'I don't know how you can be so optimistic. What happens if we fall ill? What happens if some lawless thugs from the city come this way and take all our food? This is just terrible. How can we deal with it?' He went back to his bottle of whisky and poured another stiff one. 'The authorities must take charge,' he reassured himself. 'Of course, they will.' He returned to his seat. 'We just have to sit and wait for them to arrive. Cheers.'

Tom and I left him still trying to fiddle with his laptop although it had run its battery down long ago. The doctor had a small generator, still in its box, and Tom offered to show him how to use it, but the man simply waved us away, thanking us for our concern.

'I'm worried about him,' Tom confided as we closed the gates and started up the drive.

When we got back to the farm the puppy was furiously wagging her tail, mouth open and yapping with excitement to see us. I promised her that we would take her with us when we next went out. That didn't happen but not because I changed my mind.

Sometime after midnight, we were both shaken awake by the distinct sound of a gunshot in the still night.

3. ADDING TO THE COLLECTION

Doctor Grint left us a note. He'd addressed it to us and placed it in the centre of his tidy desk.

'What does it say?' I asked Tom.

Tom tutted with a small, wry smile on his face as he read. 'He says he can't face the uncertainty of the future and begs us to take care of his girls.' Tom shook his head. 'Just one sentence on why he committed suicide and three whole pages of instructions on how to look after bees!' He waved the paper at me. 'The old bloke must have been writing this for a while before he shot himself, either that or he'd prepared these notes beforehand.'

I took the note from Tom. 'I suppose we'll never know. This first page of his suicide note is in a different ink to the instructions. I think we've got some reading to do about those bees before we do anything. I wonder where he kept his bee gear?'

Back at the farm, we knuckled down to finding out about our animals. We each ploughed through all the books we could find on one sort of animal, beginning with the chickens because they were already scratching in the dirt of their enclosure. Tom reckoned he should try and get six more and search for a cockerel too for the next generation of chickens. I thought we might find more birds down the road, so we set off in the afternoon on another search.

We did find more hens, a cockerel, some ducks and three quite friendly geese, well friendly once I found they ate grass and led them out of their dirt pen and into the horse float to a pile of grass. They didn't much like the luxury chicken pen we'd built next to the first pen and instead took over the stable next to Pippa. Tom's brother had a new stable block built when the chalets were paying well, so that guests could go on horse treks in the valley. During our search we also found a second horse, a fine shire horse that had been used to pull a small carriage. As neither Tom nor I knew how to hitch a horse to anything the carriage stayed where it was for the time being, but the horse Tom named Galahad, came to keep Pippa company. The owners, sadly, had been badly mauled by their own dogs, a pair of German shepherds who had been locked in the house with their dying masters. They were waiting for us as we went around looking through the windows. Neither of us felt the urge to let them out, so we left them barking and growling. I might have been tempted to put them out of their misery with an arrow but after hitting one of them, the other might have got me. The more animals we collected, the more I felt we were doing the right thing for the animals, otherwise more of them would have succumbed to the fate of those dogs.

We needed two more trips with the horse float to collect a dozen sheep, and although neither of us had any idea of what we could do with them, four small piglets came back to the house that day. We found no one alive and the last two homes were deserted, locked up with dust covers on everything. Tom wasn't sure if they were holiday homes or not, but it seemed likely.

'Hmm, just need to get some petrol before we get back.' He turned the farm's old Land Rover into the forecourt of the very same station that I'd been to the last time. I sat in the car while Tom got out to fill the tank. The old man came racing out just as he had with me, demanding payment. Tom tried reasoning with him, but the old fella wouldn't budge.

I got out of the car and collected my crossbow from the back. 'Tom! Tom! I'll handle this.'

The garage attendant was hurrying back inside to operate the electronic lock on the door, but I was too quick for him and he'd succeeded only in locking us both in. He turned to face me. 'It's the last delivery you know. It's worth something.'

I lifted the crossbow. 'I'll tell you what's going to happen. You will allow my friend outside to fill up our tank with petrol. Later, one of us will return with food. Food that we will deliver in exchange for the petrol.'

He blinked. 'I don't believe you'd use that thing' His tone changed. 'Come on lady, I was just messing around.'

'I'm not. Turn the pump on.'

Sullenly, he gave Tom the signal to fill up and went to the counter to make the pump available. I made for the door.

As we drove off Tom gave me an inquiring look.

'I promised to trade him food for petrol.' I explained. 'But in the future, I think you should do the filling up Tom.' Tom appeared to understand because he nodded.

Back at the farm I started to make an omelette mix, while Tom went off to put a box of food together for the garage. Omelettes were something David and I used to make when our parents fought. We ate omelettes a lot. I heard Tom drive off in the Range Rover back to the petrol station to deliver our food.

When Tom returned later he told me of the brief conversation he had with the garage attendant, Frank. Tom had been curious and asked him what he was going to do when all of his petrol had run out and the frozen food had all gone.

'He told me that he'd probably head into Chesterfield.' Tom shrugged. 'Because he thought that they ought to have sorted everything out by then. The problem with Frank's idea about things being sorted out is there's probably nobody left to sort it out.'

'Well, we don't strictly know that.' I replied. 'We're just assuming that no one has taken control. Perhaps the cities and towns are being brought back to life.' I said it but I had my doubts. I remembered how far life had changed in those few short weeks of the virus and how no one seemed to be trying to keep control of anything.

'I doubt there's been much change since you left, except it's probably worse now.' Tom was looking out of the window at the moonlight. 'I think we're right to be doing what we are and I'm glad you suggested it. I might still be living off left-overs like Frank.' He turned to face me. 'Thank you for staying. Now, don't we have some serious studying to do before it gets too late tonight?'

For the rest of the evening we poured over a book about alpaca management. We made plans and a long list of equipment we thought we'd need.

When morning came, we set off to collect equipment from the Conways' farm and to guide the alpacas to their new home. The alpacas were calmer than I'd expected. Once they were housed I helped Tom to build more fences to partition our little zoo. It was a pleasure to see the deer appear before sunset, and Tom fed them some of the deer pellets he'd spotted at the produce store. We spent that evening trying to decide what to do about finding a horse drawn plough when the petrol finally did disappear.

Before I got up the following day, an idea had been stirring in my head, which I shared with Tom during breakfast. 'I think we should get to a library Tom, to find more books on animal care and agriculture, like the ones at the Conways' and in Doctor Grint's study.'

'I'd thought that too. We could do with some basic first aid information, handyman stuff, oh, there's a whole load of books we need. We could turn Arthur's office upstairs into our reference library.'

I was brushing the puppy. She'd raced into the barn after a rat and found every spider's web she could. She didn't find the rat. 'I know Sheffield has a good library, but I don't want to go back there yet.'

'Chesterfield then! We could try there. Perhaps it wouldn't be as dangerous.' He'd just finished arranging the halters and grooming equipment for the alpacas on the wall of their stable. He stepped back to admire his handy work. 'We could go and see if normal life has been restored.'

I gave him a wry look. 'I think I'll take my crossbow anyway.'

We detoured via Bakewell, which was still deserted, and I feared that when we stopped at the Red Lion, the landlord and his wife would be dead, but they weren't. They greeted us like long lost friends and insisted that we ate with them before we went on to Chesterfield.

'We'd love to have any honey you have spare; my husband has a sweet tooth. I'm just not sure we can trade anything.' Donna, the landlord's wife, was sitting in her newly acquired wheelchair hugging her Doctor Who mug. 'If you think of anything let us know.'

I shook my head. 'I doubt there'll be any honey from us this year. We're both cowards, so we won't be interfering with the hive until one of us makes friends with the bees. However, when that momentous event happens, we're happy to share, won't we Tom?' He agreed and repeated the word momentous as if to emphasise how remote our coming to grips with the bees might be.

He gave me a quick glance. He was about to broach a topic we'd discussed together earlier. Then he leaned towards the landlord. 'Vince, you could both come up to our place and live with us, you know. We've got plenty of space and you'd be very welcome. I'm not getting any younger and I'd appreciate another hand. Lexi's a marvel but ...'

'But I'm useless when it comes to the jobs that need brawn.' I didn't mind admitting it, and although Tom would appreciate Vince's help around the place, he was more concerned that the Carters had no one in an emergency and they might also enjoy the company.

'We appreciate the invite, but we're good here. The place was modified for Donna and we've got a vegetable garden out back. We could do with some chickens though, so if you happen to find some more, we'd be grateful, and don't forget we've got a cellar full of wine to share.' Vince put his hand on his wife's knee. 'Donna's got me putting her loom back together, and I've collected all the wool I could find in town, so when winter comes, we might be able to trade some woollen pullovers.'

'Be warned though,' Donna cautioned, 'they won't be fashion items but hopefully they'll keep us all warm. Did you say you had alpacas?'

'Still reading up on them, but yes.' Tom finished his cup of tea. 'Do you know anyone who can spin?'

Vince started to collect the dishes. 'I could try my hand. There's a spinning wheel at the craft shop and they wouldn't sell that without some sort of manual. You could bring us your wool and we could give you clothes. Sounds like a good swap.'

When we left Bakewell, we were in high spirits and so were the Carters. Tom had been to the local craft shop with Vince, and they'd returned with carding equipment, a spinning wheel and five books on spinning and weaving. It was clear how they were going to spend their evenings. Now we had our own mission to conduct in the Chesterfield library.

The marketplace in Chesterfield was deserted and we parked in the cobbled precinct outside the market hall, usually bustling with crowds under the brightly coloured awnings of the stalls, now silent and deserted. We came across two bodies outside the fast-food outlet. Someone had already broken into the red brick building, smashing one of the glass panels, so I suspected we were too late, but apart from paper scattered across the floor, children's books thrown everywhere, and some foul words scrawled on walls, the reference section appeared to have escaped destruction.

We separated, each with our list of the types of books we wanted, each grabbing a trolley as we went. I could hear Tom singing to himself, The Sound of Music this time, and muttering occasionally when he found something useful. As I got involved in what I was doing, I realised just how much I'd have to read to be able to handle even a couple of the animals we'd collected. The horse books filled a whole bookcase, so I ignored the ones on riding and concentrated on husbandry and handling. Poultry keeping seemed almost as complicated. I was about to push my collection in Tom's direction when movement behind the stacks stopped me. I automatically reached for the crossbow on my back.

'Whose there? Come on out!' I waited. Nothing stirred. 'I don't want to hurt anyone by mistake. Come on, let's see each other.'

They both came to the end of the stack, their arms raised.

'Heard you shout. What's going on? Oh! Hello!' Tom came rumbling down the main aisle.

The young man was tall, thickset, and had probably played rugby at some stage of his life. His thin brown hair was already receding while his beard was healthy and ragged. He looked anxious as his dark brown eyes glanced first at Tom and then me. 'Someone had broken in here already.'

'We just wanted somewhere to hide, somewhere safe. We thought no one would come to the library.' The young woman was stocky, with a round face and large, soft blue eyes under a mop of unruly red curls. She clutched her companion's arm as she tried to avoid looking at the crossbow. They both looked as if they were somewhere in their mid to late twenties.

'We just came here for something to read!' Tom beamed at them and introduced us.

'I'm Peggy and this is William.' We shook their hands awkwardly. 'We've been sleeping in here.' She pointed at a couple of neatly packed sleeping bags stashed in the corner. 'It was so scary out there and we daren't break in anywhere because of...' Peggy's voice faded, and William put his arm around her.

'We've seen too many dead bodies,' William explained 'and the living aren't much better. The ones who are left are like wild animals, killing each other for cans of baked beans. We didn't know what to do.' I could see the strain in his face, the dark rings under his eyes.

'When did you last eat?' Tom asked. It reminded me of when I first met him. He was taking charge again. He got them to help us stack the books in the back of the car and then invited them back to the farm for some food. As we drove out of the town, we narrowly missed a crowd of people ransacking a house. Two women screamed at each other as they tugged on a blanket while a group of men kicked and punched each other, but we never knew the cause of the violence. Sat in the backseat Peggy looked around anxiously.

Before we turned off beyond Bakewell Tom asked our new friends to sit on the floor and to use the scarves he'd put on the back seat to cover their eyes. 'I'm sorry to ask you to do this,' he explained, 'but you've seen how little you can trust strangers and we want to keep the location of our place secret for as long as we can.' They glanced silently at each other before donning the blindfolds, and I saw William gently reach out for Peggy's hand.

Peggy was delighted at what she saw when Tom took off her blindfold and ushered her into the house. He was already explaining that we'd make up a bed for them if they wanted to stay the night, or longer, and that there was plenty of accommodation if they wanted it. Peggy told Tom that she loved the cosiness of the fireplace with its stone surround and brass fire dogs. She ran her hand along the top of the old leather sofas and paused to look across at the open kitchen with utensils hanging from the ceiling.

Tom brewed tea while I made up the double bed in the third bedroom. There had been an uncomfortable moment when we'd shown them the bed and asked if they needed two rooms.

'My parents never knew we'd already slept together,' Peggy

blushed, 'we've been engaged for six months, but I still live at home.' She inhaled a quick breath, correcting herself. 'I lived at home and we were going to live there, with my parents, after the wedding.'

'You'd fixed a date?' Tom raced to ask the question, trying to move Peggy's thoughts about what might have been.

'In a month!' She dissolved into tears. 'It's not fair and I hate this.'

What could I say? I could understand her feelings. We let her sob in William's arms. His unshaven face was full of apologies. We left them together, while we pottered over chores.

A little time later when we had all regathered Tom moved purposely to the kitchen and asked if either William or Peggy were vegetarian. Peggy's eyes were still red, but she had recovered and asked if she could help Tom with the meal. William and I had finished stacking all the books on the shelves in Arthur's office by the time the meal was ready. The smell of thick vegetable broth, warm bread and apple pie filled the kitchen.

'This soup is delicious Peggy!' Tom tore into the bread and distributed it to us all.

'Well, I was a chef.' Peggy revealed. She rolled her eyes as William reached for the salt, and he gave her a cheeky grin.

'Really? Well, a good cook is always appreciated.' Tom enthused.

'Who's the cook in your house, Tom, you or your wife?' Tom and I were both quick to explain that we were not married. I told them how I'd been wandering aimlessly when Tom took me in.

'So, what did you do before, you know, before the illness?' Peggy had begun to relax.

'I was in London, semi-retired from the civil service.' Tom cut into the apple pie.

'That must have been interesting,' William began to pass around the servings. 'Did you travel a lot?'

'A fair bit.' Tom dug his spoon into his pie, then paused. 'But you know, after a while you get tired of it. Forever packing up your belongings and moving to the next posting. I was a lot happier in a permanent post in London.'

'Where did you live, abroad, I mean?' Peggy asked. To please her he recounted a few of the countries he'd worked in. The list was impressive.

I started to collect the dirty bowls as I told them about my pre-sickness life. 'I was teaching in Europe but home for a long break.' I didn't tell them I'd had a disastrous affair with a minor Belgian politician after my divorce and was hiding in my brother's apartment trying to put my life back together. 'Where were you working as a chef?'

'Petro Aglino at the new hotel in Sheffield. I was so lucky to get it, so we could finally get married.'

Tom waved his spoon. 'And you, William?'

I'm a butcher, was a butcher, I suppose.'

'There'll always be a need for butchers.'

'He's being modest.' Peggy gave William a proud smile. 'He was a butcher, but he's been working as a sashimi specialist for Petro. He trained for three years in Japan.'

While I washed dishes, Tom took them on a tour of the place, and they were eager to help him with the evening feed routine and locking up the poultry for the night. He was deep into explanations about sheep when they came back. We talked long into the night until our eyes became heavy and drove us to our beds.

'Lexi!' In the morning, Tom poked his head around the door of my bedroom. 'Can you smell burning?' I could smell something, but I didn't think it was burning. I dressed quickly and tiptoed past our visitor's room to check the kitchen.

'Morning!' Peggy looked up from the stove.

'Bacon and eggs, and pancakes!' Tom took a deep breath and savoured the smell.

'Just me, wanting to thank you for last night.' She'd set the table and was ready to put the food on plates. 'Let William know, will you Tom, he's checking your pigs for their sexes. He thinks he should help you get them into more secure pens.' Tom was off out to the barn at a trot.

'You really didn't have to do all this,' I told Peggy. 'We're just happy to have you here.'

She sat beside me, her face suddenly grave. 'You know what Tom said last night about us staying here, was he serious? Could we really stay?'

Of course, they could stay. It was obvious to us all that they'd both be assets to us with the skills they had. Peggy was eager to be put in charge of food preparation and by mid-afternoon she'd scoured the pantry and the vegetable garden, picked through our packets of seeds and sent me off to plant things. William was excited to be working with live animals, while Tom and I made no secret of the fact that neither of us had wanted to contemplate killing our stock for food, the inevitable would have to happen sooner or later, and William was capable of dispatching them humanely.

As soon as we could clear out the first chalet, William and Peggy moved in, and a new routine emerged which gave us all more time to plan and construct the enclosures and pens we needed. We also began to discover which animals we particularly liked. I had warmed towards the alpacas and although I retained some of my initial fear, I found that the bees were fascinating to watch. It was still a long way off, but perhaps Doctor Grint's girls might, someday, become my girls. Rather than trying to move the hives, Tom and William made a gate in the tall fence that encircled Arthur's place and effectively increased the size of our property. We also burnt what was left of the doctor. Neither of us had wanted to move him after his suicide. We'd covered him in his own duvet and left him in his study. William and Tom carried him out, and when it was over we scattered his remains in the flower garden closest to the bees. When we had time, we continued our search of properties close by, finding more chickens, which we gave to the Carters. We also found two more vehicles.

One afternoon Peggy and William went for a walk over the hill of the property and came racing back, excited because they'd spotted a man working in a vegetable garden in the rather grand house that stood in the lea of the hill. Tom and William immediately drove off to investigate and returned with a new dinner guest.

'I had no idea that anyone else was alive here and after seeing what it was like in the towns, I'd just accepted that I'd live out my days eating eggs and vegetables.' Giles Montgomery was a soft-spoken man in his early forties, thin-faced, clean shaven with dark-brown hair, whose smile creased the corners of his face and brought a twinkle to his blue eyes. It was hard not to like Giles. He was amiable, unassuming and slightly old-fashioned.

He kept us entertained with stories of his life as a former travel writer then slept on the couch until breakfast. He had been invited to stay with us, but he confessed to enjoying his own company and private space after years of living in close proximity to others. He promised to visit often, which he did, and I drove him back to his home in the afternoon.

It was the first time I'd seen Merton Grange and I fell in love with it immediately. Ivy covered the stone walls, framing the casement windows which diminished in size as they climbed further up the house. On one corner of the house was a tower, the remnant of an earlier building, now integrated into the home that Sir Grantham Merton had built for himself in the seventeenth century. Giles took me on the grand tour, pointing out the family art treasures, the quirky African souvenirs acquired by his grandfather and Egyptian artefacts collected by his great uncle.

'Funny old lot, the Merton's, either stiff upper lip or completely batty!' We were facing a large wooden mask used in Dogon funerals, according to the label on the case. He had his hands on his hips, a slightly lop-sided grin on his face.

'So, which are you?' I moved on to the next display cabinet.

'A complete waste of space, according to my father.' He peered down at the collection of necklaces, some of which appeared to be teeth. 'Of course he was an excellent judge of character. Sadly for him, he was not able to produce further progeny to succeed him.'

We talked until it was dark, about everything and nothing, and we might have gone on talking if I hadn't felt guilty about being away for so long. I drove back feeling strangely elated. I had really enjoyed spending time with Giles, and the afternoon had swept by far too quickly. Even when I reasoned that I had not had a break from the daily chores since arriving at Arthur's place, and could take some time away, I was uneasy and defensive when I got back.

Everyone else had already eaten but Peggy had saved some vegetable pie for me. I was grateful, more so when I tasted it. It would have been sad to miss it. When Peggy and William went off to their chalet, Tom asked me how things had gone with our new neighbour.

'I was beginning to worry that something might have had happened to you.' Tom joked.

'I'm sorry I didn't get back earlier, but I was having a lovely time. Merton Grange is so beautiful, and Giles is a very entertaining host. He's got an Egyptian sarcophagus and some very precious Blue John vases. It's like visiting a small version of Chatsworth.'

'Like a private museum from the 19th century.' Tom stretched by the fire. 'The house is enormous. Maybe I could get Giles to show me around inside one day. I'd love to see it. Any suits of armour in the hallways?'

'None that I saw.' I sat down next to him. 'You should ask him. I'm sure he'd be happy to invite you inside.'

'You know it's funny since I managed to sober up and I've been back here working on the farm I've come to realise how much I took this place for granted. How little I really explored the area or took notice of it. I couldn't wait to leave for university and to move beyond my rural upbringing. I never visited the grange, or even gave it that much thought.'

'Was it really that bad growing up here?'

'Arthur and I were so different. He grew up always knowing the farm would go to him, because he was the eldest. From a young age I had the added angst of knowing that if I stayed here I would be working for my brother, so seeking further horizons was my only option.' He looked up at the photograph of them both outside the house, two young men, both alike in looks but one in work trousers and an open-necked shirt, the other in a suit. 'That was taken just before I left the farm, off to join the civil service. I think Arthur was glad that I was going. It meant that the farm would be his and I'd be out of his hair. And there was the girl we both liked.'

'A girl?'

'Try not to sound so surprised. Arthur asked her to marry him, but she turned him down. I think he blamed me. I think Arthur believed that she preferred me.'

'Highly unlikely,' I smiled. Tom laughed.

'What about you and your brother, Lexi? Were you close growing up?'

'Yes, he wasn't a bad big brother. And actually, Giles this afternoon reminded me of David quite a lot.' I went into the kitchen to warm some milk for our cocoa.

'Why, because you instantly felt an affinity with him?'

I turned to face him. 'I suppose, but more so because my brother was gay, and so is Giles Montgomery.'

4. RESCUE AND FIRST AID

According to Giles, he'd spent far too much precious time in his past, trying to reciprocate the love that several women had heaped upon him. I could well imagine women finding him attractive, I did. He was slim and handsome to look at, charming and easy with his conversation, thoughtful and caring, and had the obvious advantage of wealth thrown in. Once he had acknowledged his true nature however, friends, male and female, had dwindled away. My gregarious, out-going brother had been surrounded by supportive friends and an eventual partner who adored him. Sadly, his beloved Lawrence had an undiagnosed heart condition and he had left us all far too early.

After two more expeditions to search for survivors or untended livestock, the Range Rover required more petrol. We had all but retired the old Land Rover workhorse that was probably as old as Tom, but we had gained a second Land Rover. When the petrol in the district ran out, both would be useless, so Tom was delighted to find a second friendly shire horse whose owners had operated a wedding carriage business. We waited anxiously for Tom and the horse to arrive at the farm. Tom looked very pleased with himself behind the horse, and in a vehicle that might have been used in any number of popular movies.

Tom and I headed back to the petrol station, crossbow in the back seat for good measure. Frank was sitting on a chair reading a magazine when we entered. Once he saw who had arrived he folded his reading material and slowly stood up.

'There's not much petrol left, you know.' He examined the box of provisions, carefully organised by Peggy to provide sustenance for at least three weeks.

'Petrol Frank, we don't have all day.' Holding the crossbow was quite empowering.

'Hello! What's going on here then?' Tom and I swung around to see Giles standing behind us. He was taking in the scene. His eyes rested on the crossbow, a deep frown on his face.

'It's all good.' Frank rested his hands on the box of produce.

'Just paying for petrol.' I explained, suddenly feeling very self-conscious about the crossbow. 'Strikes a hard bargain this guy.'

'I take it you're exchanging food for petrol. By rights, I should be the one enjoying that lot.' Giles gestured towards the box, then fixed the old man with a quizzical stare. 'Frank works for me. This place is mine, and so is the petrol.'

'Ah, well. We could always provide food to you Giles. We had no idea you owned the place.' Tom offered.

'No need Tom. And as for Frank here, he's already getting food from me.' I gave Frank a hard look, but he was too busy putting the box behind the counter. Giles escorted me to the door. 'That's quite a nasty looking weapon you've got there Lexi.'

As Giles filled up the car for me I told him about my first encounter with Frank. 'I'm so sorry about that. I wish I'd known. I've been happy to have Frank living here because not having anyone here leaves it free for someone to damage the place or burn the petrol, and besides, Frank had nowhere else to go.'

Tom and I climbed into the cab and Giles spoke to us through the window. 'From now on the petrol for you is free, until it runs out. I will go back in there and give him a piece of my mind, in fact several pieces of my mind.' Tom and I gave Giles our thanks before he headed back inside.

* * *

'Now we've got the chickens organised and the pigs separated, the horses all stabled, and the alpacas and goats taken care of, we should try and get a couple more freezers and perhaps a bigger generator. What do you think Tom?' After our evening meal we'd started to spend time planning for the long term.

'Could we also get some warmer clothes, I don't have anything for the cold months?' Peggy asked. Tom wasn't too keen to visit Chesterfield, so despite some misgivings I suggested we head towards Sheffield. The huge shopping mall, north of the city, might have a better selection of clothes left, and the home and handyman stores close by could give us our generator and fridges.

Bright and early we hitched the horse float and drove north east to the outskirts of Sheffield. The outer suburbs were very quiet, and we saw no one as we passed through. At Norton, we spotted a lone figure hurrying away as we slowed down. A pack of lean dogs crossed our path near the Parkway and a house was burning at Darnall, but we saw no other people. We didn't speak much as we watched the silent streets pass by. Litter flapped at us from the pavement, sometimes the garbage was undistinguishable from the remnants of bodies by the roadside. Tom paused the car at Meadowhall, sighing as he looked across the valley at the deserted viaduct beyond the shopping mall.

'I wonder what this will all look like in ten years' time.' He shook his head. It had been a long time since any of us had thought about the long, distant future of the world. Since the coming of the virus, it was the cities that had changed the most. Life in the rural areas had always moved at a slower pace. I had seen with my own eyes the life of the streets vanish rapidly, as the bodies and the rubbish took over the cityscape. Tom was right, in the years to come, what would the buildings and modern structures look like? Would the natural world take them over? It was a sobering reminder of losing more of the familiar.

On our shopping excursion we found two good sized fridges and another generator in the deserted home and handyman centre, as well as stocking up on work gloves, overalls, wellington boots, small tools and two trollies to transport our finds. Tom parked in a delivery alley and we were feeling like we'd had a productive trip as we headed for the mall.

'Hold on! What d'you want?' In the entrance, we were stopped by two scruffy young men, each carrying a lead pipe and an array of other weapons. Behind them, we could see the mall was lit by firelight as well as small industrial lighting. People were obviously living here.

'Just getting some warm clothes for winter. I see you're making sure everything is distributed in an orderly fashion. Well done, you!' Tom smiled at the young thugs who were doing their best to look tough.

'Not so fast! What can you trade? We don't let anyone in there, you know.' Three smaller, younger boys hovered in the shadows watching us.

Quick as a flash Peggy thrust her huge tote-bag at them. 'Apples and some fresh bread!' It had been Peggy's idea to bring goods to trade with people on our trips out. Our experience with Frank in particular had shown us how valuable our fresh food could be, even those with food seemed greedy for more.

The boy's mouth was visibly watering as he smelt the bread. 'Yeah, that'll do!' He nodded. 'Give your stuff to the old woman sitting at the fire.' They each took an apple and let us pass. 'Nice crossbow,' one of them said, 'can you use it?'

'Oh yes, she certainly can, young man!' Tom led off towards the open fire in the central court. Even from this distance I could smell meat roasting, I wasn't sure what it was until we saw the carcass of a large dog on an improvised spit.

'Greyhound kennels up the hill.' A woman whose dress might once have been blue held out her hand and Tom mistakenly shook it. 'Nice manners but I wanted the barter. If it's good enough you can share a pot of tea before you shop. If it isn't, then you'll be sent up and given half an hour max.'

Peggy handed over the bag with the bread and fruit but insisted she got her bag back.

'No probs, sweetheart!' The woman emptied the contents of the bag into a large plastic laundry basket. 'You're good! Stan, tea for our guests. Sit down and take the load off. Where you from? Not round here! Them apples are fresh and mmm, I can smell that bread from here.'

'West of here,' Tom told her. 'Are you in charge here?'

'Of this bunch?' She chuckled. She was probably in her sixties or older, with wrinkles in her cheeks and the corners of her eyes. Her hair had been scraped back into a bun that was slowly un-ravelling itself into a ponytail. 'Not likely! They wanted someone to cook for 'em and I was hiding in the Tesco, so they elected me, and here I am.'

Her face softened. 'They come over all tough but they're shit-scared, like the rest of us. Stan there, he was sleeping rough before everything went belly up. They wouldn't let him sleep inside, when this place was open. He slept in the charity bins in the car park. Now he's sleeping on the top of the range double bed in the furniture store.' Stan grinned at her through broken teeth and started to pour out the tea in delicate china cups, rescued from gathering dust in some homeware store.

'I'm just pointing them in the right direction, like the greyhounds. We've got boys up there looking after the dogs and once a week we slaughter one of the old ones for meat. The kennels were breeding them for racing, now we're breeding them for meat. The lads are on the lookout for other breeds. We can't handle breeding anything big yet. We send regular search parties to look for livestock. We've got a horse up at the kennels and last week we found three chickens, so we're hoping for eggs.'

Tom nursed his delicate cup. 'You're all doing well here. How many people are there?'

'Fifteen.' The woman opened a half empty tin of biscuits and passed them around. We were obviously welcome visitors and she pressed us to return if we had more produce to barter. Tom promised to not only bring food but to keep his eyes open for any livestock they might want.

'I'm Marie, by the way. I used to be a cook at the school up the hill. I knew most of these little buggers when they were growing up. Now we've become the only family any of us are likely to see. Rough as guts most of 'em, but all willing to work together to survive.'

With Marie's blessing, one of her boys escorted us up to the clothing stores, and we started collecting our winter wardrobes. The boy, whose name was Troy, followed William around offering helpful hints about what was useful. He explained that he'd been on a camp to Scotland in his final year of school and picked up a lot about keeping alive in cold temperatures. It was while he was helping Peggy pick new boots that the commotion began downstairs, and William was first to get to the low wall that overlooked the food court below. He signalled for us to drop low and be quiet. The crossbow came off my back as I joined him.

There was a lot of shouting going on, sounds of someone barking instructions, scuffles and screamed protests. Marie and her boys had been rounded up, the camp ransacked and half a dozen men in dark pseudo-military-style clothes and black woollen hats like commandos were trying to move them to the exit despite their complaints. As we watched, Marie again lashed out at one of the men and received a savage punch in the face. She crumpled and it was all William could do to stop Troy crying out and rushing to help her. Two of her boys carried her and the rest were pushed and manhandled towards the main exit. Troy beckoned us to follow him. He knew the building well and guided us to some of the offices that overlooked the entrance. From there we could see four large trucks, old police vans used for riots.

'Man, we got to help 'em!' Troy whispered, his eyes were desperate.

'How can we? There are too many of them and they've got truncheons or something.' Tom never moved his eyes from the scene as the black hats began loading the resistant squatters into one of the vans. They appeared to be using batons on the more stubborn prisoners. The other vehicles already contained people who were banging desperately on the inside of the vans. More people were being dragged from nearby buildings. A neatly dressed man in a grey suit, with dark brown skin and short black facial hair, struggled to free himself, while a teenage girl, her long blond hair flying in her face as she screamed, was slung over one of the black hats' shoulders. He gave her a firm thump on her bottom and told her to be quiet.

Suddenly, Marie's van erupted. The boys weren't going to be taken anywhere they didn't want to go. Three of them leapt back out and were immediately set upon. Another man, thin and wiry built, also jumped free, but instead of making a bid for freedom he went to help the man in the grey suit who had been knocked to the ground and kicked. The girl was dumped on the asphalt as the black hats recognised that the situation was getting out of hand. Two of them brought down the would-be rescuer, giving him a brutal beating with their weapons while the boys had been knocked senseless and dragged back to the vans.

Detached from the violence, the man who appeared to be supervising the operation, every inch of him suggesting a lifetime in the army, now had a pistol of some sort in his hand, which he fired into the air. That got his prisoners attention, and mine, as he then advanced on the three remaining escapees. The girl was curled in a ball. She was sobbing, her hair completely covering her face. While the man in the suit was trying to crawl away, the man who had been brave enough to help him was lying still on the ground.

'He's going to shoot him!' Peggy gripped William's arm as three of the vans started to leave.

'No, he's not!' I'd already got the crossbow on the window ledge and fired it through the broken window. The black hat staggered back, dropping the gun, the arrow going clear through his arm. He was yelling with pain and two of his men dragged him back to the van. For a second, he looked up and I knew he'd seen me. His companions followed his gaze, looking nervously up at the building, but we had crouched low enough to hide. At this point they headed for their vans and drove off. My heart was pounding inside my chest so fast I had to take a few moments before standing up again. I had never seen anything like that before. Who were those people, and where were they taking their prisoners? I thought about poor Marie and wished we all had crossbows.

'Awesome!' Troy gasped. 'Great shot!'

I stood slowly. 'Not really, I was aiming for his chest.'

Tom went off to get the Rover and horse float. We had no idea if they would come back, but we went down to see if we could help. The man in the suit was standing shakily, holding his arm. The teenage girl dissolved into Peggy's arms, trembling violently, her face smeared with dirt and snot. Troy had raced off and returned with three blankets that we wrapped around them. William and I knelt beside the injured man. His face was covered in blood and he was moaning softly.

'I don't know if we should move him,' William looked anxiously across at me. 'I don't know much first aid.'

'We've got to move him and get out of here fast.' I urged, thankful to see the green Range Rover creeping around the corner.

'But if he's got internal injuries, we could make it worse.'

'Well, we can't leave him here!'

'Just bloody well get me out of here. There's no bones broken.' The man opened his eyes and winced as he moved. His eyes closed again, and we thought he'd passed out.

Tom and William lifted him into the back of the car, which wasn't easy as the float was hitched. 'I don't know that we should be moving him Tom.' William was shaking his head. 'I don't think we can take his word for it that no bones are broken.'

The man's eyes opened once more. In his Scottish accent he stammered, 'I wouldn't let you move me if it was dangerous. Trust me, I'm a doctor!' Then he lost consciousness.

I rode with him in the back, trying to keep his body as still as possible, wishing we'd got something I could use to clean him up. Troy sat on the floor beside me, his face close to the back window and quieter now, possibly replaying the events in his mind. Tom drove with William beside him. The grey suited man sat on one side of Peggy, who had her arm around the young woman, shushing her gently and pushing her hair out of her face. No one spoke until the man in the suit leaned forward to thank us for helping them all.

'You're welcome. Do you want us to drop you off somewhere?' Tom offered.

'I haven't thought. I've been living in one of the warehouses near the mall, because the supermarkets still had some tin food, but I don't want to be around here anymore.' He gave Peggy a smile. 'The name's Ashton.' He leaned again towards Tom. 'Where are you heading?'

Tom was usually very cautious about telling strangers where we lived so he simply said, 'Derbyshire.'
'Maybe you could drop me at the edge of the city. I'll see if I can find somewhere there.'

'Don't you have family or friends that survived?' William turned around to see him better.

'My wife died in our bed. I just locked the door and started walking.' I couldn't see his face, but Ashton's voice held so much pain that I didn't need to.

'Well, you could all come and live with us. Couldn't they?' Tom added the last question in a sheepish voice. As if any of us would object to him adding to our number. More hands would certainly make lighter work, and it was Tom's farm anyway. We all agreed, as Tom added his usual qualifier, 'Of course you can leave whenever you want, but we'd hope you'd stay. There's plenty of room.'

'Does that invite include me?' Troy was suddenly taking notice again.

'Naturally, young man, you don't think we'd leave you behind.' Tom looked at him through the driving mirror.

Troy pushed his mop of blond hair back with his hand and gave me a sidelong glance. 'As well as looking after animals, would you teach me to use that crossbow? I could go hunting for us.'

'Maybe.' I wasn't about to get into any of that. I'd seen Troy pocket the black hat's gun when we were busy trying to get everyone into the Range Rover. I hadn't said anything, but I intended to keep an eye on him, until I was sure he'd listen to reason and give the gun up to Tom, for safe keeping.

Although she was quieter now, the young woman was still too shocked to make any comment whatsoever about coming to the farm and neither could my patient, who occasionally moaned but had no real say in the matter. Even with all their trauma, Tom asked them to wear the blindfolds. I think the shock of the violence against Marie and her boys had highlighted to him that although we were far safer than others, our little valley could also be invaded. We were all at risk.

We put my patient into my bed as soon as we arrived, then set about preparing rooms and beds for our new guests. Peggy didn't want the girl to be alone, at least for her first night, so Peggy moved back into the guest bedroom in the main house with her. She helped William and Tom prepare another chalet for Ashton and Troy, then reheated soup for us all. Meanwhile, Tom had helped me dress our patient in a pair of Arthur's pyjamas, after applying antiseptic to the bruises on his body. Thankfully he was out for most of our inexperienced manhandling. I managed to clean the cuts and bruises on his face, which would certainly be painful when he did wake. He had a lean, weatherworn look about his face and body, like a man who enjoyed walking or some other outdoor activity. He had a thin, handsome face, with a slightly hooked nose, dark brown hair and deep-set eyes. He wore the now universal unkept beard, but one that had been well-managed. Small wrinkles near his mouth and lower cheeks hinted that his face was used to smiling.

'Soup's ready!' Tom popped his head around the door. 'How's the patient?'

'Out for the count, still.' I stood and went to join him. 'He's going to be in a heap of pain when he does wake up.'

'Lucky my brother was a hypochondriac.' He handed me full packets of paracetamol and codeine tablets. 'Lots more where they came from.' He watched me put them on the top of the dressing table, and when I came back to him, he spoke quietly. 'If he's in here, do you want us to make up a chalet for you?'

'I think I'd better stay in here with him, at least for tonight.' I was anxious about leaving him alone. I'd never had to deal with someone in such a state. I think I was hoping he might wake and then I could take the blanket and sleep on the sofa.

'Of course, of course.' He followed me down the hall.

'Maybe we can put him in a chalet tomorrow, I'm not about to give up my gorgeous little room that easily.'

'It's going to be a change to have so many people here. I do hope we're doing the right thing.'

'What else could we do, and you said yourself that we could do more if there were more of us.'

The house had suddenly become noisier that was for sure. A small party of people now gathered at the table to eat. Tom declared that the soup smelt wonderful, and then sat next to Troy with the cheerful bluster of a host in his element. He kept the conversation light telling our new guests about the farm and how we'd collected all the livestock. He recounted how he had first cast eyes on me with the puppy and the broken pull-along. I wondered how desperate my actions looked to the others, driving out of the city to find some kind of sanctuary in the country, but no one seemed the slightest bit surprised.

Later that evening when the house was quiet, I sat in the armchair beside the stranger in my bed, listening to the disturbed sleep of a teenage girl who had still not spoken, and the snores of a man who had decided to share his farm with strangers. As the night drew on, I wrapped myself in the blankets and sat in the armchair, trying not to think, longing for sleep. I looked at the stranger's profile in the moonlight and allowed my eyelids to close.

I woke with the sun on my face.

'Good morning!' He tried to turn towards me but gave up. The bruises no doubt instantly reminding him of why he was in the bed in the first place. 'That was a wee bit stupid of me.'

'Good morning!' I stood up and went to the edge of the bed so he could see me better. 'How do you feel?'

'Like six thugs kicked the life out of me, and I'm sorry, I think I lied to you yesterday,' he looked up at me.

'So, you aren't a doctor, after all.'

'No, that bit's true, but I lied when I said nothing was broken. I think I've got a couple of cracked ribs.'

I sat up. 'What should we do? Should we strap it?'

'No, nothing. They just have to heal. No lifting or straining.' He was in quite a lot of pain, so I went around to the dresser and got him the painkillers and poured him a glass of water from beside the bed. It was a struggle to get him sitting up enough to drink and after he'd swallowed the pills he fell back against the stacked pillows. 'Did you sleep there, all night?'

'My bed,' I explained, 'and you looked like you were in very bad shape, so I thought someone should keep an eye on you.'

'Thanks for the loan of your bed.' He looked amused. 'I suppose it would be an idea to know each other's names. I'm Andrew Mac-intyre.' He offered me a bruised hand and then withdrew it.

'I'm Lexi. We don't go in for surnames around here.'

'And where is 'around here' exactly?'

'The depths of Derbyshire!' Tom's cheerful broad voice entered the room before him. 'I heard voices, so I knew you were awake. How do you feel?'

The doctor suddenly looked confused. 'Have my senses been damaged or can I smell bacon?'

'Your senses are working well. Bacon is indeed cooking. Would you like something to eat?' The doctor's facial bruises were making talking difficult, but he assured us that eating couldn't be any worse. He asked if he could try something.

Ashton was tucking into a hearty meal, looking more relaxed with his jacket off, and Peggy was making a plate up to take to the girl. 'She still hasn't spoken, and she kept waking up and sobbing. I just hope there's no permanent damage to her, she such a scared little rabbit. How's your patient?'

'Multicoloured, and I suspect he'll turn purple before he heals.' I began to put a few things on his plate. I nodded to Ashton. 'How are you feeling today?'

'Like I've won the lottery. Tom has asked me to stay.'

I piled scrambled eggs beside the bacon. 'Has anyone seen Troy?'

Peggy grinned. 'Already out with William. He's mad keen on horses, apparently. Eats like one too!'

We both delivered food to our patients and while Peggy stayed with hers, Tom seemed intent on monopolising Doctor Macintyre, so I went back to the kitchen to eat with Ashton.

'Lexi, I'd like to stay here if I can, but I've never worked with animals.' He folded his arms. 'I suppose I could help with the general chores and I could learn the gardening stuff.'

'What did you do before?' I reached for the tomato sauce.

'Real estate.' We both looked blankly at each other and then burst out laughing. 'I know, really useful skill set, haven't I? What about you?'

'Teacher,' I said.

'Troy said you were the one who fired the crossbow. That's not a skill you needed for teaching was it?'

'Misspent youth. Although, I know a few young miscreants who might have behaved better if I'd pointed my crossbow at them.' I took a drink of coffee. 'If you like, I'll give you a tour of the farm.'

Ashton had probably been very good at his job. He was relaxed and easy to talk to, a people person, who must have been very lonely during his time wandering aimlessly through the stricken city. We found William and Troy in the stables, brushing down the horses. Troy was eager to tell us that he'd already helped with the morning feeds, let the chickens out, fed the pigs and made friends with the puppy. In fact, he had named her Gypsy. All those able to work spent the rest of the morning in the vegetable garden weeding and were ravenously hungry by the time Peggy called us in for lunch.

I looked in on my patient before going back out to help pick soft fruit for Peggy's jam making. There were sleeping-beauty-high brambles running outside the boundary fence and Peggy was eager for us to get as many early blackberries as we could, before the birds beat us to them. It was almost teatime when Ashton and I strolled back up the drive with our plastic tubs of shining fruit. It was early in the season, but a warm spell had encouraged them to fruit. Ashton had also found something he could contribute to the farm in addition to his tasks as general labourer. He was a natural organiser. He'd listened to William's routines for the pigs and began to recognise that for the farm to run efficiently we should keep careful records. Tom loved the idea of someone taking over the schedules and general management of the farm. With only four of us there had been no need for keeping track of what everyone was doing, but that was about to change. Tom immediately installed Ashton in his brother's office which had also become our library.

Everyone wanted an early night, so after eating we began to drift off to bed, Troy and Ashton to their bachelor pad, William to his lonely chalet, Peggy to her silent girl, leaving Tom and I alone. He stood and stretched.

'I had a very lazy day today, chatting to the doctor and trying to get through to Peggy's patient, but you know, I'm dog tired. Would you mind if I went off to bed? We didn't make up a chalet for you did we? Would you like my bed? I can sleep on the sofa.'

I gave him a sour look. 'Tom, look at the sofa and then you and me. Who do you think would fit better on it? I'll be fine. And I get to sleep near the fire.'

'Are you sure?' He waited for my nod. 'Then I'll see you in the morning.' I watched him amble towards the bedroom while I checked in on Andrew Macintyre.

'You're looking better,' I said, holding the glass of water while he took a night's dose of painkillers.

'Colourful!' He agreed in his soft, lilting Scottish accent. 'There's going to be a bit more swelling for a few days before that goes and the bruises come out. I'm grateful for the medication. Tom tells me that it was you who stopped them kicking me to death.'

'I was the one with a crossbow. Anyone would have done it. I'm just glad we got you and ourselves out of there safely. Were you picked up at the mall?'

He sighed. 'I was driving south on the motorway and I decided to top up with petrol. They got me at the petrol station. My medical bag and all my things are still in the car. I was heading to Birmingham.'

'You have family or friends in Birmingham?' I took the glass from him.

'No. Everyone I cared about died back in Scotland. My parents died long ago, and then my sister and her husband in the epidemic. I was coming south to the new administrative centre being set up in Birmingham.'

'What new administrative centre?' This was news to us.

He shifted on his pillows. 'Someone is establishing a centre of operations if you like in Birmingham. No idea who's in charge or how it is being handled but I thought I could be useful. I explained to Tom today I'm a surgeon, and apparently not many of us are left. Before the internet crashed, Durham University sent out emails to a whole list of people who were asked to go south, if they were able. I've no idea if anyone actually went to Birmingham but I decided to go anyway. I tried telling this to the goons with the trucks, but they didn't seem to know anything. They wouldn't even let me go back for my medical bag.'

'I wonder why they haven't done something like that in London?'

'I've heard the capital is a dangerous, volatile place to be right now. Anyone who could get out apparently did.'

'Oh.' I had images in my mind of London as a frontier town, complete with rolling tumbleweed. I had been getting used to the idea of cities in our area being lawless wastelands, but it was strange to think our nation's capital had become just as hazardous. 'Do you still want to go to Birmingham?'

'If there is an administration of sorts in the Midlands, then they're not doing a very good job. I think for now I'll be accepting Tom's kind offer of a place here. He says there are a few people left around Derbyshire who would appreciate having a doctor.'

'Of course, we would. Now try and get some sleep. As soon as you can walk, I'll give you a tour of the farm. Oh! And I'll take you back to the petrol station for your things.' I turned to go but he delayed me.

'Thanks again,' he said. I smiled and patted his unbruised shoulder, telling him to sleep tight, before making my way to the sofa. I wrapped the wool blanket around me and organised the cushions. As I watched the fire slowly dying, I found myself thinking about Belgium and the log fires in Anton's forest cottage. He had a thing for tartans. His seating had been covered in a subtle green plaid and we'd sit there in the evening drinking wine and talking about the problems of the world. Sometimes, we slept there too, naked on the fur carpet, wrapped in his tartan blankets. It was a long way from the old leather couch and Tom's occasional snore.

5. GATHERING

'I'm impressed, and all this since the virus?' Macintyre leaned on the wall of the barn, and I worried that I'd made him walk too far. He'd asked for a tour in the afternoon, but after visiting the pigs, goats and alpacas, he looked a little tired.

'The only animals on the farm to begin with were deer. William and Tom made most of the pens for the animals we collected. There's still a lot to do, and we're only beginning to learn how to look after them all properly. I don't suppose you know anything about looking after bees?'

'I'm afraid not.' He pushed himself off the wall, lost his balance and staggered a little. I caught him. 'Hmm, not as sturdy as I thought I was. Do you think we could go back? I might need to take it easy for a while.' We linked arms and I helped him to shuffle to the house, where he was returned to his bed by a concerned Tom.

'Those cracked ribs are going to be a problem for him for a while,' Tom said joining the rest of us on veggie peeling duty in the kitchen.

Ashton reached for another potato. 'Has the young lady spoken yet?'

'Not yet.' Tom dropped a carrot on the chopping board and began to attack it. 'I worry about her.' He paused and his face creased into his familiar grin. 'But Peggy says she is eating now, so that's something, at least.'

I took the doctor his supper and met Peggy. 'The girl's name is Zoe,' she whispered. 'She thanked me for the food and asked me my name.'

'That's great news Peggy!'

'Lexi, she was attacked and beaten long before the round up we witnessed. Both her parents died while she was out at work, and when she got back she just panicked and ran out of her house, looking for help. She's no idea where she went. Some bastard offered her shelter then locked her in his house and ...' Peggie's voice trailed away.

'Poor girl. No wonder she's traumatised. Did you tell her where she is and that she's safe here?'

'I concentrated on the safe part. She's not ready to meet anyone else yet, but when she is, I think another woman might be best. She seemed a bit frightened by Tom.' She tapped my arm, as I was the only candidate.

We did talk, but I sensed she preferred Peggy, whose warmth and youth were more what she needed. I did serve one purpose, explaining about how the farm worked and describing who lived there and how they had arrived. She asked me about my experiences living in other countries and told me that she wanted to travel. Zoe's experiences made me realise how particularly disruptive this upending had been to young people. At least I had lived quite a few decades of normal life before the world turned upside down. I came away from our chats saddened not only by what had happened to her, but also about young people like her whose lives had been so abruptly changed.

Sometimes the human spirit can be very resilient, or perhaps it was Peggy's natural mothering instincts, but within a week Zoe was up and helping about the house. Once they knew her history, the men went to great pains to make her feel comfortable, but each in their own way. Tom made her laugh and William spent time showing her the farm or telling her his own stories. Ashton, or Ash as she called him, spent the most time with her, explaining his new recording system and even sitting with her as she started to read books from our library. She asked to see the doctor, to thank him for what he did.

Summer was a busy time, but the long days meant there was always time for other things. Some of us started to explore beyond our boundaries, hiking to the River Wye and admiring the stunning architecture of Haddon Hall. Riding became another popular pastime, although it was basic riding lessons from Giles for most of us. Giles also offered his tennis court at the back of his home, and one afternoon he organised a tournament, collecting the Carters to join in the fun.

'It's funny but I thought I caught sight of someone when I drove through Nether Haddon this morning. I knew there was a tennis net there, in better repair than mine, so I fetched it and I'm sure I saw the back of someone heading towards the river. I called out but no one answered. Whoever I saw clearly didn't want to talk with me.' Giles was leaning against a tree and I was sat with Donna Carter next to a table of drinks as we watched Troy and Ashton knocking balls backwards and forwards. Troy's slight frame was floundering against his more enthusiastic and powerful opponent.

'Sometimes I think I can hear people, outside, in the street, at night.' Donna Carter allowed Mac to pour her more wine. 'Just my imagination!'

'Scary thought!' Giles mused. He looked back at his house and smiled wistfully. 'This old place is full of creaks and groans, probably a few ghosts too.'

His hit-up finished, Troy was helping himself to the punch. I gave him my disapproving adult look, which prompted him to knock back the first glass and reach for a second. Troy took his refill, gave me a wane smile and walked off to find Zoe.

'Come on sunshine, your turn. I organised a match for the entertainment of our guests. The Merton Marvels.' Giles gestured to the pair of us. 'Against the Meadowhall Monsters!' Ashton and Mac were already on their way to the court.

I glared at Giles. 'I'll get you for this!' I grimaced. 'I'm hopeless at tennis.'

Giles leaned against the outer net of the court. Giles had a habit of draping himself against immovable objects. 'Well, the competition is warming up. There could be serious pressure here!' He turned his attention to the two preparing to face us, both doing preparatory racket swings and jumping into the air a few times.

'Don't worry, my treasure!' Giles put his arm around me. 'I'll protect you against these powerful players!'

'Who's going to protect you from her?' Mac chipped in. 'Make sure she leaves the crossbow at home!' They laughed and Giles gave my arm a squeeze.

As he started a knock-up with Ash, Giles said, 'You and the good doctor seem to be getting on well.'

'And what's that supposed to mean?' I crouched down trying to look as if I knew what I was doing.

'Pure observation, my love!' He called over his shoulder as he ran to hit another ball. The ball shot over Ashton's head and Giles strolled back towards me. 'I like him, and I think you do too. Is he still talking about going to Birmingham or has he decided to stay? A doctor in the district would be a very comforting thing. You'll have to work your feminine wiles on him.'

'I have no intention of doing anything of the kind, Giles Montgomery!'

In less than five minutes, the game was over, and I was sitting on the ground. In cartoons, it's often birds or some such thing spinning around the head. I can assure you there were no tweeting birds, just a sickening pain in my head and a slight wooziness. Ash had landed a sharp little volley right on my forehead. I clearly saw the concern on his face as I fell and then legs rushing towards me. I vomited down the doctor's shirt front and I vaguely remember Mac and Giles helping me all the way back to the grange.

'There's going to be a big egg there for a while, but no permanent damage.' Mac handed me two painkillers and a glass of water. I had been gently ushered to Giles' sitting room and draped across his beautiful red velvet sofa. The doctor spoke to Giles. 'We should take her home and we'll need to monitor her for the next few hours, just in case of concussion.'

'I thought you said no damage?' I swallowed the second pill.

'I said no permanent damage. There's always a slight chance of concussion.' Mac turned to Giles. 'I'll keep her under observation.' Mac began to help me stand.

'Good.' I heard Giles reply. 'Will you stay with her overnight?' Giles looked down at me. 'I want the doctor to stay with you. Can't be too careful.'

So, that's how I came to be in the same bedroom that the good doctor and I had shared that first night, except that this time I was in the bed and he was in the chair.

* * *

A cold snap in early September turned the trees golden and copper red. We began to prepare for the winter in earnest. The two barns could house most of our animals. Tom, Mac and William did the best they could to harvest what they could from neighbourhood properties, and everyone pitched in with our own vegetable and fruit gathering. For the first time in our lives we had to anticipate our needs for the coming winter and prepare for them. There were no holidays, no weekends when we could spend time checking emails, posting photographs or even watch TV. We were active every day, often from dawn until dusk. We hardly ever had trouble sleeping and our bodies were becoming fitter through the exercise and the healthier food.

We all helped Giles gather his apples and he helped us to collect as much of our crops as we could. Just to make certain that we wouldn't starve there was another trip to a supermarket in Chesterfield. We raided shelves for bottling jars. I remembered seeing bottling and jam making equipment in the Pettigrews' house, so we went back and collected all there was. Peggy and Zoe set about preserving and pickling with one eye on their produce and the other on the instructions. All of this work was being guided by instructions we found in our library or through Tom's vague recollections of what was done on the farm before he had left for university. We planned to share our bounty with the Carters in Bakewell, and it was Zoe's idea to have a celebration where we could all come together and eat.

'I don't mean like a Harvest Festival with hymns and like, prayers, but just to celebrate that we're ready for winter.' Zoe was slowly coming out of her shell after her trauma and easing into the life on the farm. She was gradually accepting friendship and enjoyed spending time with the animals. The eighteen-year-old had not wished to talk about her life before the events at the shopping mall but she was beginning to enjoy the simple pleasures that life at the farm could offer. She enjoyed helping around the kitchen, trying to learn everything Peggy could teach her. On a few occasions she'd also asked Mac to teach her some basic first aid. Occasionally, I would find her sitting in the library, not tearful but staring into space, her mind lost in thought. So, when she suggested celebrating the harvest we all wanted to make the festival a success.

'We could bring Donna and Vince to us. We have the room. They could stay the night.' Tom also felt we needed a celebration. It had been a tough few months.

'Better still, why not ask them if we could use their place for the celebration?' William suggested. That would save them having to drive here and we could organise everything.'

The Carters loved the idea. 'I've got a cellar full of beer that needs drinking, not to mention a freezer full of bar snacks that Donna and me are sick of eating.' Vince was very enthusiastic. 'It's a bit lonely here and we'd love to entertain once more. We miss it. I just wish there were more people we could invite.'

Giles offered to do a little search of the area to see who else he could find. The rest of us focused on the food for the event. Giles spared William from slaughtering a pig, as he already had one in his freezer. Peggy made a list of things that she wanted from the nearest professional kitchens, and Mac and I got the job of finding them. We started by checking Arthur's old guide to Derbyshire, with its list of restaurants.

✳ ✳ ✳

'Is this a bain marie?' He held up a long metal dish, the kind that hotel restaurants use for serving breakfasts. We were in one of the pubs that only a few months ago I'd been in with my brother and his friends. It was strange to be back there when it was dusty and completely deserted.

'Could be, but I thought it was something like this.' I held up a steamer pan. David had one like it.

'Let's take both.' He checked the list. 'Just about done! Want anything from the bar before we go?'

I shook my head gathering up our treasures and then stopped. 'Would it be silly to take a bottle or two of champagne?'

'Sounds like a great idea!' Mac beamed a mischievous smile. I made a mental note about Tom. He'd been around alcohol since his drying out period, particularly when we visited the Red Lion, but I knew I would have to help him avoid the temptation he might be faced with. As far as I could tell he had been coping quite well so far. We stuffed everything into large plastic boxes we'd found in the kitchen and were about to leave when we heard a door creak open upstairs. My crossbow was in the car, so I wasn't staying around and hurried to the front door with my white plastic container.

'Who's there?' A woman's quavering voice called out, 'we're armed!'

'We aren't,' Mac yelled back. I put my stolen property on the floor and went to join him. 'We've been stealing cooking equipment from your kitchen. We're having a wee celebration. Mind if we borrowed them?'

'Are you Scotch?' The woman had a strong eastern-European

accent. We saw a pair of runners and then denim jeans coming down the first few steps.

'Scots, yes! Scotch is the drink.'

'Sorry! My English is not so good.' My first impression of Inga reminded me of the pictures of an Amazon, or perhaps a Scandinavian shield maiden, all broad shoulders, magnificent breasts and strong Nordic features. She was holding up one of the decorative swords from the wall display and appeared very ready to use it. Behind her was Fay, most of her body hidden on the other side of the fake shield that had accompanied the sword on the wall.

Fay set the shield down and patted her friend on her arm. 'I don't think we'll need that dear.' Fay was slightly older and shorter than Inga. She had short brown hair, thin lips, a snub nose supporting large gold-framed glasses and she had aa slim frame. She reminded me of a local librarian. She introduced herself and her friend, explaining that they had been staying at the pub when the illness killed everyone else. They'd barricaded themselves in their room when the landlord became violent after the death of his wife. He was already showing signs of infection and wanted them to help him, but they were afraid. They'd survived on the well-stocked minibar until they were certain the sick couple had died. They'd cremated them both and raided the nearest shop until it was almost empty.

'You have food to cook?' Inga inquired.

'We do and you're very welcome to come and stay with us. We're a sort of collective farm.' Mac did our introductions.

'It's been very frightening here.' Fay looked as if she might cry but fought against it with a swallow or two. 'A gang of young thugs came through. They'd escaped the city, but the sickness caught up with most of them. Since then we've hardly seen anyone, except for the big police truck that went past a few days ago. It came from Chesterfield and headed towards Sheffield. There must be people in the city but we're afraid to go. You can keep the kitchen things. They're not ours.'

'Fay and I are partners by the way. Just so that there can be no misunderstandings, you understand?' Inga picked up the plastic container at my feet as if it weighed nothing.

'We understand.' Mac told them and we waited for them to pack their suitcases. He poured us both a small whiskey. 'Scared the pants off me. Thought I was in for another bashing.'

'I know what you mean, and I'd left the crossbow in the car. I hadn't expected us to meet with anyone. I hope Tom doesn't mind us inviting new people to the farm.'

'He won't mind. Old Tom's generous, and besides, I think he likes the company.'

Mac looked up the staircase, where frantic noises and the sound of suitcase zippers hinted that they would be down soon. 'I'm thankful that I was invited to stay. I've really enjoyed being at the farm, and I like the people there. I like it when we get to work together,' he told the staircase, 'I think we make a good team.'

We moved apart as our new guests thumped down the stairs with their luggage. Somehow, we managed to get everything into the boot. Inga and Fay were cheerful and being starved of any other company for so long they were eager to lead the conversation. The blindfolds went on after we'd explained their purpose. Inga told us it reminded her of sleeping on long-haul flights.

Back at the farm we learnt more of about Inga and Fay. They had been on holiday in Derbyshire when the sickness started. They were both keen hikers and had met initially while staying at a hostel in Snowdonia. Fay sold women's dresses in her own little boutique by day and in the evening and weekends she painted for pleasure. Inga worked for an investment bank in London and lived on a houseboat near Windsor. Both were enthusiastic cooks and overcrowded the kitchen, helping Peggy with the evening meal, until she sweetly told them that they were guests and should sit back and enjoy someone looking after them. Peggy was the kitchen boss, and she guarded her space.

After dinner, Tom suggested his favourite game of charades. Inga was an eager player although no one could interpret what she was doing. She laughed and yelled answers along with everyone else. Fay preferred to watch, but she smiled and clapped appreciatively at the performers. Afterwards I showed our new guests to their chalet, which I'd prepared before dinner. I was getting used to preparing rooms. I once joked with Peggy that if ever life returned to something like normal, we could run a small hotel together.

Days later Zoe's Harvest Festival was a great success and better attended than any of us expected. As well as everyone at the farm, and the Carters, Giles brought new people from his drive around to find survivors. Giles presented a middle-aged couple from a hobby farm outside Hope, Madge and Peter Clifton. He also showed up with a young policeman from Hathersage and two families, the Boyles from Castleton and the Laughtons from Froggatt. Both the Boyles and the Laughtons were newcomers to the area. None of them had been aware of the survival of anyone else until Giles had knocked on their doors. Each of them had managed their survival in their own ways.

It was a very optimistic and light-hearted evening. Giles and Vince had furnished sufficient alcohol to encourage conversation and eventually dancing. Tom, on fruit juice, was an unofficial master of ceremonies. Later, when we were driving back to the farm, Fay and Inga told us they'd decided to move to the Red Lion as guests. Their loneliness and that of the Carters had drawn Donna to suggest the move. The move would also be useful because, after talking to the Carters, Fay and Inga had decided they would try reopening a bakery in Bakewell. It had always been Fay's dream. Now, fate had presented her with several premises and equipment to make her dream a reality. There was broad enthusiasm for the idea, and an agreement that the farm could then trade produce for the bread. Fay knew she would have to investigate flour substitutes and Ashton offered to help with their research.

Gradually the party started to wind down, until there were just a handful of us left inside the Red Lion. We were all offering our solutions as to how to reorganise the cities, in that languid and slightly incoherent state people get to, between being cheerfully inebriated and nodding off to sleep. During a long diatribe by Mac on the inadequacies of the health system to cope with viral epidemics, Ash fell asleep.

'I wonder what is happening in the cities, right now. What's happening to all those people they put into the trucks?' I pondered while looking at Ash who was dozing, his head resting on the corner of the settle. I was remembering the events at the mall.

'Population control.' Mac poured himself the last of Giles' bottle of whiskey. 'They can keep them alive, feed them, control them better if they're all contained. That's probably why they were rounding up people.'

'A bit heavy-handed though.'

He nodded. 'I'm guessing the people involved are police, army, even security companies. They had a certain amount of co-ordination about them, but they also didn't seem to have much of an idea about what was going on. The impression I got was that they were expecting resistance, prepared for violence, but they weren't going to back down from getting people into those trucks.'

'Won't bringing a whole lot of people together cause more problems?' Vince was standing, leaning against the settle where Ash and I were sitting. 'How can they feed them? Where will they put them? What about more people getting sick and spreading the virus?'

Mac inhaled before he spoke. 'All good questions but think of the logistics of trying to track a population if you let it continue to live in isolation. This way they can have a head count, provide care and some form of shelter for a large number of survivors.'

'Sounds like a dictatorship to me. And from the way they were treating you, not a particularly benign one either.' I still couldn't get the images of violence out of my head.

'Perhaps the authorities behind the roundups have genuinely good intentions. This could be their first step in returning some order to life and gaining a handle on the situation. Just because their front-line workers were aggressive doesn't mean we should judge the policy a bad one.'

'At the very least they needed to explain what they were doing, where they were taking you and why. These authorities you talk about need to understand that people are scared and uncertain enough as it is, without living in fear of violence from the ones sent to help them. If you ask me it was all very odd.' I shook my head.

Ash jolted awake. 'Sorry what did I miss?' He rubbed his eyes.

'Not a lot,' I told him, 'just Mac trying to make excuses for the way he was treated at the shopping mall.' Mac raised his hands in a shrug with a lopsided grin on his face.

'Right!' Ash looked bleary eyed as he carefully stood. 'High time I went off to bed. Night!'

Giles, who had been nodding but not saying much stood too and wished everyone a good night, Vince moved behind the bar, stacking glasses.

Mac was on his feet. 'It's just hypothetical speculation anyway Lexi. As you said, we don't know who those men were, or who they are really working for. It just might be nice to think for once that someone, somewhere is responsible for us, and taking steps for us to eventually return to normal. Who doesn't need that right now?' He faced me with his eyebrows raised. I agreed with him.

The atmosphere was subdued the following morning. Inga and Fay surfaced with sore heads and bleary eyes, but with an eagerness to investigate the properties that the Carters had listed for them. We all gradually made our way back to the farm and did what was necessary for that day.

I threw myself into farm chores, and by lunchtime I was aching but made the effort to climb up the hill to visit Giles. He was gathering vegetables from his garden and I helped him to carry armfuls of beans and the last of his summer fruit into his extensive kitchen where he was all ready to start preparing jams, chutney and bottled fruits. He gave me the task of washing the fruit and then putting some in containers for freezing.

'So, the ladies have gone to find a bakery, how wonderful!' He poured tea while I buttered the scones that he'd set out for us.

'The doctor was telling me last evening that he'd probably be resuming his journey to Birmingham when he was feeling well.' He led the way to his sitting room, which overlooked the valley beyond, where the River Bradford snaked its way towards the village of Youlgrave, hidden in the valley spurs beyond.

'He told us about that.' I searched for something that could change the subject. I didn't know he still intended to leave. 'So, are you continuing your search for more survivors?'

'Probably, I've enlisted Ashton to make a list of the people we know about, and I thought I'd drop off copies to everyone, so we all know. My petrol won't last forever, although I've instructed Frank not to give it away anymore, except to the farm. God knows if he'll stick to that instruction, but I can check the usage at the bowser. Tom tells me he's trying to get people to use the horses you've collected.'

'He's not been too successful with that, so far. The cars don't threaten to bite you when you try to saddle them up. I suppose we should all be using horses, shouldn't we?' Giles made great scones. I suggested he could go into business with Fay and Inga.

While walking back over the hill I saw a sudden flash of light from the hillside. I didn't automatically respond. It took a moment for me to realise that something bright had shone in my direction for a second. I might have gone to investigate but William was riding towards me with an unfamiliar horse in tow. It was actually a Welsh Mountain pony, but that distinction was not apparent to me at the time. Anything with a mane, tail, teeth and went 'neigh' was a horse.

'Vince Carter dropped by. He's got a horse float now and while he was on his way home this young fella started to follow his car. He said you'd told him last night that you wanted a horse so he's giving it to you. It comes with a saddle and a bridle, so you'll be ready to ride it. Vince thinks it recognised the float, so he went to the stables and collected some gear. There are still three horses alive there, in a paddock, so I'm heading back there now with our float to take a look.' William had been a keen rider in his youth before other pursuits had attracted his attention. He dismounted and helped me up. As we rode, he told me his family had owned a small field at the back of their green grocers where he'd kept a pony, and then a horse. I could imagine him riding across the moors above Ringinglow, where his parents had lived.

'Used to terrorise the sheep!' he confessed, ''Cept at lambing time, of course. It didn't take long to get into Derbyshire from there and I reckon that old gelding of mine used to love it as much as I did.'

'Did you and Peggy go riding?'

He guffawed. 'Never in a million years. Peggy's scared to death of horses, even little uns, Nah, she'd hate it. You won't find her any-where near the stables.' It didn't seem to matter to him. I liked William. He might not be as clever as some but if you needed help he'd be there, and if you asked his opinion you'd get an hon-est answer.

We rode the boundaries of Arthur's property, mostly at a gentle walk, then ambled back to the stables together. I kept my eye on the hill but never saw any other sign of the light.

Mac was in the stable when we got back putting new hay down. 'Had a good ride?' He asked both of us. I told him we had and that he should come riding with us sometime. 'I'd like that,' he said simply. He helped me brush the pony down until we heard the sound of Giles' car churning up the dirt driveway. He was in a hurry.

Inside the car was a mess of dirty clothes, blood and two old, withered hands. It was Frank.

Giles opened the back door. 'I met him staggering up the road to-wards my house. Someone's beaten him, badly!'

Mac set off towards his chalet to collect his bag while William reached in to get Frank. 'Let's get him to the house.'

6. WILD THINGS

The petrol station appeared deserted. William and Giles had moved in opposite wide circles to spot any movement, but there was none. We waited, hiding behind a large oil tank, and as the time passed I tried not to think about what was in the tank, and if it was flammable. There were plenty of places to use for cover, the carcasses of two old cars, discarded crates and wooden pallets. I wondered how such a tidy man as Giles could allow this much clutter behind his petrol station.

It was a cold day, promising rain, the sky full of scudding clouds. I was chilled to the bone and ready to suggest that whoever had attacked Frank had moved on, when the back door opened, and two young men tumbled out. They were drunk. They staggered slightly, laughing at each other and yelling, although we couldn't make out what they said. We were alarmed to see that one of them was wielding a handgun. I felt Giles stiffen beside me. William muttered, 'Christ!' under his breath. To everyone's surprise, including the two youths, the gun went off. It stopped their messing around for a moment, before they burst into fits of laughter, continuing their drunken meander towards the picnic tables behind the carpark. A crate of wine bottles was on the bench seat, and they began to arrange the bottles in a row across the length of the table with the exaggerated precision of the sozzled.

'My bloody wine shipment! Frank told me it never arrived. I'll kill that old devil when I see him!' The outrage on Giles's face made me wonder how much those bottles of French wine cost him, then another shot brought our attention back to the improvised shooting range.

The boys were no marksmen. Two shots later and they hadn't shattered a bottle. Giles gave me a nod. My arrow shattered a Burgundy bottle. It sobered the young hooligans instantly. Stopped in their tracks, they looked around. The bottle shot gave me confidence. My aim was improving. I wasn't up to my old competition standard but getting there. A second arrow hit the table, through the gap between the two boys.

Giles moved closer but remained behind a pile of tyres for protection. He yelled, 'Put the gun down and hold your hands up, or the next arrow will get one of you!' For a second the boy holding the gun considered aiming it, but his friend pushed his arm down and took the gun. He threw it away from them, towards the tyres. The shooter didn't object.

'We surrender!' Both put their hands up.

The crossbow was empty, but I kept it up as we approached, keeping one eye on the boys and one on the gun. They looked so scared that I doubt they noticed the empty bow. It was a relief when William bent down and picked up the weapon.

'You're not the law! You're trespassing! This is our place.' The shooter wasn't about to surrender meekly.

'Wrong!' Giles took the gun from William and pointed it at them, his handsome face suddenly strong and chillingly hard. 'It's my place. You're the trespassers, maybe killers too.'

'We didn't kill nobody!' The boy stood his ground. His friend sat down on the bench.

'So, where's the old man who manages this place?' Giles took a step nearer to the boy.

'I dunno! No one was here when we arrived.'

Giles lowered his voice, and it was ominously calm. 'There was an old man working here.'

The shooter became agitated. 'The old bastard tried to kill us. He hit my brother over the head with a cricket bat, and I've got bruises all over my back where he hit me!'

The silent brother looked up at me. 'It's true! He was wild like. He caught me with my hand in the till and whacked me on the back of my head. You can see.' He bent his head towards me. The blood was dry. The wound hadn't been washed or tended. I nodded at Giles.

'So, you clobbered him! He's an old man. You could've killed him.' It was William, his large frame blocking the faint sun from the shooter as he loomed over him.

'Just got the bat off him and gave him his own medicine. We just wanted to get some cash and some food. We haven't eaten for days.' The shooter sat beside his brother. 'Honest! We don't know what happened to him, he ran off. He was bleeding. I might have broken a few bones, but I didn't want to kill him.' He looked down and muttered. 'We were just so bloody hungry.'

'And after my booze! By the looks of you!' Giles voice softened. 'You're lucky, the old man's alive and being treated by a doctor, which is what your brother needs too.' Giles looked at William and me. 'Beats me what we're going to do with them! We could hand them over to the black hats in the vans.'

The two boys spoke at once, the younger one begging us not to do that, the older one challenging by assuring us that the black hats would take us too. They'd seen them rounding up people in Chesterfield.

'You!' Giles turned on the older boy. 'You've said enough. Too much already!' He addressed the younger brother. 'What's your name?'

'Barry!' It was little more than a mutter, and Barry was beginning to look pale.

'Well Barry, what do you think we should do with you? You've broken into my garage, stolen and drunk my property, and severely injured an old man. In normal times you'd be up for a long custodial sentence, even at your age.' Giles folded his arms.

'I dunno.' Barry's colour had drained from his face and a second later he was vomiting over the grass. No one did anything much while the older brother rubbed Barry's back and told him everything was going to be fine. Barry groaned and wiped his mouth on his sleeve. When we were certain that Barry had finished regurgitating red wine and chocolate, we blindfolded them before squashing them into the car.

'We do it to any strangers.' William assured the shivering Barry. 'When we get there, our doctor can take a look at you both. Then,' he brought his face nearer to them, and in the sternest voice I'd ever heard William use he said, 'you're going to apologise to the old man. Then, we'll consider what your punishment should be.'

* * *

At the farm the two boys faced Frank, who had been allowed to sit in the armchair, provided he kept silent. I wondered how long that would last. Barry wiped his nose on the same sleeve that had mopped up his vomit. Giles presented his evidence and a fragile but unbroken Frank listened. Once, he tried to interject but Giles silenced him with a glare and a promise to discuss the missing wine order at a later date. It was clear to all of us that the horrendous attackers, with murder in their hearts, were nothing more than two lawless but frightened teenagers, who were as ill-prepared for what had happened to them as we had all been. We could all associate with that. Neither of the boys had seen their parents since the day their father had raced to the betting office to place a bet before the whole place closed. Their mother disappeared two days later. She went out to shop and never returned.

William took the boys outside towards Mac's chalet to get Barry looked at while the rest of us discussed the teenagers.

'Clearly, we can't surrender them to the appropriate authorities because we've seen what purports to be that authority, and it's certainly not appropriate.' Giles began.

'They could have killed me!' Frank whined.

'I could have killed you myself on several occasions, and I don't think I'm alone.' Giles looked to me, as I nodded. I noticed Tom nodding too from his seat on the sofa.

'I think we offer them the opportunity to stay here,' Ash suggested. Frank opened his mouth to protest but both Giles and Tom glared at him. 'They are both minors by the looks and they need somewhere to stay. The young one at least seems to be a reasonable boy. Frank probably would welcome some help protecting the petrol station, and the two lads could help him in exchange for food and somewhere to stay. We could keep an eye on them.'

'I think that's reasonable.' Tom agreed. 'Thoughts everyone?'

Some were doubtful that the boys would accept the proposal, and Frank said he'd not feel safe in his own bed, but after considering the risks of forcing them to coexist and help each other, it was settled. I had expected his older brother to speak for them and fiercely object, but it was Barry who spoke and agreed to our terms. They had one night's stay at the farm in a chalet, after eating a huge meal of beef stew and dumplings. Mac had cleaned and checked Barry's wound. He couldn't say for certain if the boy was concussed but he showed no signs of it. He made Barry promise to tell Frank if he felt ill or faint, and Giles threatened Frank that if anything happened to the boy, he'd blame Frank.

The following morning, blindfolded again, all three were returned to the petrol station, along with a month's supply of Peggy's frozen meals. Giles warned them that the woman with the crossbow would hunt them down if anyone got injured.

We spent a few days discussing the incident and how to improve our own defences. Ash proposed a manned gate house where we could operate the fence and gate with a warning system to the house. Restoring the power to the fence would also be a good idea, if we could find an electrician. Meanwhile we'd be more vigilant on checking for any gaps in the fence.

✳ ✳ ✳

Throughout the autumn Ashton had been typing his newsletters to the local survivors that Giles had uncovered. They numbered less than fifty, including children. Some were transient, heading north or south, back to their homes. Most of them were walking, but a few had transport, mostly bicycles or cars with petrol that might take them on to their next unclaimed vehicle. Hardly any had horses. We were never afraid of losing ours because the animals required food and water, as well as all the equipment to ride or drive them. Only those intending to stay acquired live transport. Our own stables were full and so were the stables at Merton. Thanks to Giles, who was a skilled horseman and a good teacher, I'd progressed from enduring painful trotting to spending afternoons with him, following bridle ways and footpaths. I now felt a lot more confident handling as well as riding horses thanks to him. He was convinced it was a skill we would all need to perfect eventually, except for the very fortunate who had acquired electric cars and the means to charge them. Even those vehicles would age with no replacements coming off obsolete production lines. Horses had been replacing themselves quite naturally for a long time, was Tom's opinion.

In October, the winds and torrents of rain halted all of our excursions. We were confined to the farm and hurried through any tasks that required stepping out beyond the house. Heaters were acquired from a hardware store on the outskirts of Chesterfield and on the same day we equipped everyone for the winter. Not everything was miserable. We began to reap the rewards of Tom and Peggy's careful management of our food, fuel and apparel supplies. Evenings were spent in the house, huddled around the fire, reading, playing games and talking.

'So, what did you teach?' Mac asked me one night when the others were playing cards. We'd moved to the library office because their raucous cries of triumph and defeat were distracting.

I was tempted to say children, but I could see he'd actually put down his Russian classic and appeared genuinely interested. 'Mostly history and literature, but in Belgium I taught upper primary classes.'

'Why the change?'

'Job opportunity I suppose, and I needed a change. My family didn't exist anymore and there were too many memories.'

'What do you mean your family didn't exist anymore? Don't you have children?' He asked.

'Grown and gone.' I explained. 'They were never very good at keeping in touch, except for the odd email and photo, but I knew they were doing fine, just not around anymore.' I had to add. 'Like my husband, he'd taken himself off to Italy with a younger partner, both of them eager to start producing progeny of their own, so when a job came up in Brussels I thought why not.'

'Did you enjoy it?'

'Very much. At that age, most kids don't have hang-ups or teen-age attitude. They really want to learn.'

'So, what happened? How did you finish up in Sheffield?'

How indeed! I was cautious despite his apparent interest and empathy, but I couldn't bring myself to tell him the whole unvarnished story. Perhaps I wanted his good opinion.

I began cautiously, starting with the children moving on, Derek's ridiculous fling with someone a quarter his age, their romantic dash to Italy and my retreat to Belgium. I slid over my guilt about falling in love with a married man. Of course, the normal excuses came tripping out about his wife's approval and our civilised ménage à trois, which became very uncivil when the truth came out. When I'd finished he was quiet, and I immediately regretted every word. Of all the people to tell! He was a judgmental, opinionated surgeon, whose life had probably never faltered from the path he'd set himself.

He looked unwaveringly into my eyes. 'You've had a tough one there. I suppose my relationships have never been particularly deep because my work comes first. My hours are long and there is always more work to catch up on and keeping current on surgical practice takes all my free time.'

'Surgery seems like pretty intense work to me.'

'It is, but it is also very rewarding. Just last year in Germany I was involved in an arm transplant, one of the first of its kind in the world. It took four surgical teams to make it happen, but the result was astonishing. I'd never felt so alive.'

'Were you on the frontline in the early days of the virus at all?'

Mac looked like he was about to say something but hesitated before recalling. 'Everything happened very quickly where I was. After the initial outbreak I worked for a few days in general admissions before the hospital ground to a halt. We had doctors and nurses dying every hour at one stage, and the rest of us lived with the knowledge that we could catch the virus at any time.' Mac closed his eyes momentarily. 'It was hard to lose so many colleagues in such a short space of time. We battled an invisible enemy.'

'What about before the virus? What kind of life did Doctor Macintyre have then?'

Mac smiled. 'I was halfway through getting my pilot's license when the virus struck, and I was really looking forward to getting it. I already part-owned a Piper Cherokee plane similar to the one I've been training in, and I've been dreaming about taking that thing up.'

I smiled as Mac spoke enthusiastically about his flying lessons. It was another side of Mac I had not seen before.

* * *

'I have an invitation for you all,' Tom said on his return from Bakewell. He'd been collecting our winter woollens, spun and woven by the Carters, from our own alpaca and sheep. In return Tom had taken them some of our home-grown meat and vegetables. 'Fay and Inga have moved from the pub to their new bakery store, and they're inviting everyone to a grand opening next week, if the weather holds. The Carters can put everyone up for the night if we provide our own bedding or sleeping bags. It's probably the last time everyone will be together once winter weather hits.'

It was a sobering evening for us all, and I don't mean there was no alcohol. Giles and the Carters had done their best to provide punch, wine and even fruit juice for the children. The apples from Giles' orchard had needed William's strength to operate the grange press to turn them into juice. Fay and Inga's spread was enough to feed all the invited guests, and that was the problem. There were people missing. Frank and the wild boys had not been invited, but we'd agreed to take the leftovers down to them. Ashton checked his list and found that most of the families were not there. As the Nevins had settled just outside Bakewell, off the road to Over Haddon, Vince Carter and Giles went to see if they were well and took them one of Fay's pies. What they found sent more search parties out to check on everyone who was missing.

Vince told us that the Nevins' front door had been open. It was hanging off its hinges, indicating a forced entry. The place was a mess, suggesting that people had not been removed willingly.

Little Kayla Nevin's toy bear lay on the floor where she'd dropped it. Mrs Nevin had been in the middle of writing her diary. She'd managed to scrawl HEL before she was taken.

William and I found much the same at the Boyles' place in Castleton. They'd occupied a larger building that had once been the Cheshire Cheese pub. There were signs of panic and struggle everywhere. A pottery vase was in pieces and there was blood on some of the shards. We were about to leave when William heard a faint noise. We stopped to listen. It was coming from the kitchen, but when we went in there was silence. The kitchen floor was littered with pots and pans. It looked like the Boyles had thrown everything at their attackers, including a large pan of stew, its contents congealed down the wall.

I called out. 'Hello? Is anyone here? It's Lexi and William from Merton Low Farm. You came to the Harvest celebration?' We waited. 'Do you remember playing with Gypsy, the dog?'

There was a whimper. It came from one of the cupboards by the sink. We had to step carefully over broken crockery that someone had scattered across the floor in front of the cupboard. When we opened the door, we understood why. Tamsin, the youngest of the Boyle's children was crouched inside, hugging a pink felt cat, her little face was white, and her fine curly hair matted to her head. William let out a long breath before reaching down and lifting the child safely over the crockery. The Boyles had tried to save at least one of their children.

'Harry's in the roof!' Tamsin blubbered before she buried her face in William's shoulder. Sure enough Harry, her older brother, was in the loft, which had no visible means of access except the small inspection panel. We called to Harry and watched as he carefully removed the hatch from inside and peered down at us.

'Have they gone?' He told us that his parents had heard the truck coming and hidden their children. He'd listened to the screams of their mother and the vase breaking. Harry hoped it was on one of the 'black hats' heads. He said he would have got down out of the loft in the morning and rescued his sister, because he knew where she was hidden. As we drove the children back to Bakewell, I couldn't help admiring the quick thinking of Mr and Mrs Boyle.

There were other escapes. The young policeman had seen the truck and hid in the graveyard. Not very original he confessed, but it worked. The two Laughton girls had hidden among the rocks on Froggatt Edge, the gritstone escarpment above their home. Fearful, they'd watched from that distance as their parents were dragged into a van. Only the sound of Tom's gravelly, singsong voice had brought them out of hiding and into his torchlight.

* * *

Back at the Red Lion, supper was ready for those who had been searching. 'How did the vans know where to go?' Tom scratched his chin as we waited in line for our piece of pie. 'Most people have blacked-out their homes. They couldn't see the lights. It couldn't be by chance that they were found.' The thought that the vans might come to the farm frightened me.

We all drew to eat around a large oak table in the centre of the pub's dining room. The sudden abductions of people in our local community had jolted all of us. As far as we knew this was the first large scale black hat operation that had taken place in our area.

'I would say they were simply targeting particular areas for rounding people up, but this appears to be a targeted roundup over a wide area, not limited to a particular town.' Mac mused. 'They seemed to have only gone to certain properties.'

'It's a mystery!' Donna Carter waved her fork before using it to tuck into her pie. 'It's as if someone had given them a list.'

'Oh! My God!' Ashton dropped his fork. 'The list!' His eyes were wide open. He spun around to face Giles. 'Somehow they've got our list and they're working through it.'

'Can't be that simple.' Giles put a steadying hand on Ashton's shoulder. 'We purposely didn't put addresses on the lists we distributed, only on our master file, and that's on Tom's computer. We all know that Tom won't let that leave his office.'

Lucy Laughton looked down at her hands and muttered, 'There was another list. My parents put it together so all the families with children knew where to find each other. They were going to share babysitting and birthday parties, stuff like that.' She burst into tears, apologising.

'But they came for me!' The policeman was confused.

'You were on the list too.' Lucy stopped crying long enough to take a breath and gave him a quick glance. 'Because you were a policeman.' She turned to Mac. 'You were going to go on the list too, but my parents didn't know what kind of doctor you were, they said.' Her words filled me with dread and relief in quick succession. Mac was not on the list.

Night was almost over. The pies were eaten, and it was agreed that the four children were to return to the farm with us, as we had the largest number of adults who could care for them. As dawn broke, our wonderful committee system unanimously decided that as a teacher, I was the best person to take care of them.

I hate decisions made by majority vote!

As we travelled back to the farm in the early sunrise, I turned around in the passenger seat to look at my new responsibilities. The children were all clearly traumatised and I had no experience in how to deal with that. My own children had been calm and good natured, particularly when they were young. These children were either in a state of high anxiety or in a stupor. Lucy was trying hard to control her tears. Her sister Bianca was silent and moved mechanically. Little Tamsin was sucking her thumb and falling asleep after a long bout of crying, while young Harry had his arm around her, his jaws clamped hard together, his eyes looking at his own knees.

I tried to lift their spirits by telling them that it was going to be like being on school summer camp. I didn't mention that I hated school camp. The whole notion was lost on Harry and Tamsin because neither of them knew what a school camp was, and Lucy informed me that although they were both at a boarding school they'd never gone on a school camp in their lives.

'Well, this is your chance to see what it's like.' After I smiled and deployed my optimistic teacher face, I took a more conciliatory tone. 'None of us are happy with what has happened. But your parents would want to know that someone is caring for you until they come home. I know it's going to be hard, and I want you to know we will all do our best to make you feel happy and comfortable. We all hope it won't be long before they're back and you can go home.' The words sounded so empty and inadequate. They had lost their parents and none of us knew when they would be returning.

Meanwhile, the practicalities of suddenly finding ourselves with children were being put in place. We set up two chalets, boys and girls, with rules. Each chalet had to take care of its cleaning and the sharing of chores, and the arbiter of any argument was going to be me. Oh, how I hate majority vote! Troy moved in with Harry. The boys complained because the girls got first pick of the chores, and the girls complained that the boys had more space. I got to arbitrate on that one!

It took a few days for us to move from that phase to everyone settling into a vague routine. Troy began to enjoy having the very self-confident Harry trotting around in his wake, continuously asking questions. Lucy was warming to suddenly having a little sister to fuss over and did her best to keep Tamsin occupied. Gentle, sweet natured Lucy had the studious look of her father. His grey hair had once been light brown like hers.

The Laughton girls were expert climbers, as their parents were before them. They'd been living in a small hotel when the sickness began. Their parents were jointly writing a book about the most popular climbs in Derbyshire. She took the photographs, and he wrote the text. As the contagion spread, and people died, they found themselves alone in the place, and much like Fay and Inga, they started to treat the hotel as if it was their temporary home. The girls spent their days climbing the crags or rambling across the valley to Carl Wark and Higger Tor for more climbing.

It was Bianca, Lucy's younger sister, who was not warming to anything we organised. She disliked animals, although she could spend hours playing with Gypsy. She had a poor opinion of all the adults, me included, with the exception of William. She even volunteered to share chores with him, which I could see annoyed Peggy. Bianca's whole world view had disappeared with her parents. She'd been the golden-haired baby sister for so long. Now she wasn't. She had become the dreaded and unnoticed middle child. I did my best to make her feel special, but it wasn't enough. She hated everything and wasn't above telling no one in particular that she wished that she had been taken along with her parents. There were times when the adults around her probably wished that too.

Bianca's ability to scale anything with hand and toe holes was her one delight. When I began to seek each of the children out, with the hopes of giving them the very minimal of hastily prepared educational tasks, it was Bianca who was always missing. I'd find her in any number of alarming places, in the beams of the barn, on the house roof, or the even higher stable roof and up any tree that took her fancy.

Bianca had been up a tree near Merton Grange one afternoon, and Giles was certain she was about to fall. She didn't. Instead she took her time climbing down, telling me I was a stupid old cow for worrying so much and that no one trusted her to do anything right. Giles took the opportunity to tell her what an ungrateful wretch she was, and that she should apologise immediately. She told him what he could do with himself and where to go, before stomping off down the path to the stile between the grange and the farm. I followed her, angry at her treatment of Giles. It was time for some home truths, and I was about to give her that piece of my mind that no teacher is ever allowed to do.

She was just ahead on the path when both of us froze. Out of the wood below the farm came the most terrifying, gut-wrenching scream. It wasn't human. It seemed to echo through the trees, unearthly and intense. I had no idea what it was. Then it was suddenly cut short. The creature had been silenced.

We both began to run. I didn't feel safe until we were inside. Bianca, bent over, breathing heavily. Me, coughing, gasping and finding my legs were filled with jelly. All over the farm, they'd heard the sound. It was instinctive to put the livestock inside. Pigs, chickens, even the sheep sought shelter after that noise. William and Troy had difficulty getting the horses into the stables, but Tom said the alpacas made it into their shed before him. In the silence that followed that fearful sound, everyone had raced for safety.

As night fell, we all gathered to eat together. The children and those in the chalets were subdued as we ate. Tom had just complemented Peggy on her excellent curry when even our hushed conversation ceased. Out of the darkness of the night came a new sound, more chilling than even the death cries of a terrified animal.

Ashton whispered, his spoonful of curry halfway to his mouth. 'Was that a lion?'

7. THE BROTHERS GRIMM

No one slept well. Twice in the night we heard that fearful roar again. I found Peggy and Tom sitting by the fire hugging mugs of hot milk at four thirty in the morning. William was snoring loudly in his sleeping bag by the back door.

'We both felt safer in the house,' Peggy poured the remaining milk from the warm saucepan for me. 'Once Will gets to sleep, only an earthquake could shift him!' We sat facing the newly stoked fire.

'It might be miles away. Their roar carries long distances.' Tom tried to reassure us. 'I actually think it could be a tiger.'

Peggy fidgeted. 'What's a tiger doing out here anyway?'

Tom glared at the coals. 'Twycross Zoo.' He poked at the embers, bringing them to life again. 'It's about forty miles away, if you go via Burton on Trent.' He saw Peggy's amazed expression. 'I couldn't sleep, so I looked at some of Arthur's brochures. There was one from the zoo. There could be other places it might have come from, but Twycross Zoo, that's the nearest. If it's from Twycross, it's a tiger. They don't have lions, at least they didn't when the brochure was printed.'

'Damn!' I whispered. Suddenly the situation seemed even worse. I love tigers, always have. As a kid, it was the first cage I'd make for on the very rare trips to any zoo.

Tom talked to his empty cup. 'We're going to have to kill it, if it stays around here. It's a danger to the animals.'

'Of course, we have to kill it. It's a danger to all of us Tom.' Peggy took his cup and her own back to the sink. 'It's not what anyone wants to see happen to a poor animal that's been kept in captivity, but we've got to protect ourselves and our livestock.' She put the cups into the sink and stared out of the window. It was still dark out there. 'Question is, how are we going to kill it? Who wants to risk their life coming face to face with a large carnivore?'

'We could dig a pit and...' Tom's voice faded into silence. 'It's going to be dangerous.'

There were three other weapons at the farm, apart from my crossbow. Arthur owned two rifles, locked away in a cupboard in the office, and William had found a handgun on one of our property searches. It had been sitting on a display cabinet in a sports outfitter's, complete with a neat case and several boxes of ammunition. I wondered if the black hats had overpowered whoever left it there before they could use it. There was also the gun that Giles had taken from the boys, who had taken it from Frank, who had no business having it in the first place. Of course, I knew of another.

Giles arrived for breakfast and the chalet dwellers all hurried to the house to eat. Normally they liked to take it back to their chalets. On this particular morning, being in the company of others seemed sensible. The livestock still needed to be fed. We decided to keep all of them in their sheds until we knew more about the new predator that had arrived in the valley. Teams of two and three went off to feed the animals, always with a backup weapon. I went with Ashton and Troy to check on the alpacas.

The animals were anxious, hungry and spitting at anything that might be a threat. Ashton held the crossbow at the door, while Troy and I took care of the feed.

It seemed like a good time to remind him of the gun. I glanced across at him. 'I wish we had more weapons. If it comes to a hunting party, the better armed we are the better.' Ash agreed from the door, but Troy said nothing. Then he stopped, his face white, and he looked at me.

'Shit!' He dropped the feed and raced out of the barn. I shrugged at Ashton and finished the feed, just in time to collide with Troy on his way back. He had a chip packet in his hand, awkwardly enclosing something heavy. He thrust it towards me. 'Forgot all about this. I buried it when I first got here. Haven't thought about it since. Sorry!'

'Then best you hang on to it. I hope it's wrapped in something inside there. Some time I'll get Giles to teach you how to use it.' As he passed Ash, Troy showed him what was inside the packet and Ash looked up alarmed. Troy left and Ashton addressed me. 'Lucky find, the day we first met you. Troy's been keeping it safe, did he say?'

'Troy was a different person back then.' I explained as we bolted the alpacas inside. 'It was probably a sensible precaution. After all, he didn't know us.' Most of us were wandering back to the house when the Gator Utility, another man-toy of Tom's, came roaring up the paddock with Zoe and William on board. I opened the gate for them and saw the sheep's carcass, or what was left of it, in the back.

'Something bloody big got at this old girl!' William yelled as he drove on towards the house.

The mood was sombre as we clustered around for morning tea. It was usually a time for jokes and interaction between the old and the young. Unless it was cold or raining, we sat outside, gathering around a wooden picnic table. On that morning everyone fed from each other's anxiety and little Tamsin began to cry. I was bending down to hug her when a blood-curdling growl drove her into my arms. It sounded incredibly close and the stable erupted with the stamping and whinnying of terrified horses.

'Everyone get inside! Come along Tamsin, you come with me.' Tom picked up the child and made for the door. Anyone not holding a firearm followed. Troy hovered until I glared at him. He left the chip packet on the table and followed the others.

So, there we were, William and Mac with rifles, Ashton and Giles with handguns and me, with my best William Tell look of determination on my face, while my knees were knocking. In the house behind us, faces were pressed against the windows. We could hear the beast throwing itself at the barn door. It very soon got tired of that, but the anxiety of the horses told us it was still close by.

I've seen tigers on television and in movies. I've seen them prowling in zoos. Safe behind strong transparent barriers, their majesty and elegance have always enthralled me.

When the real thing padded cautiously around the side of the stable, unfettered fear welled up in the back of my throat. It was big. Its powerful limbs seemed to glide rather than slink towards us. It paused. Watchful. Uncertain. I trembled, fumbling to thread the arrow in the bow. How could we be thinking of killing this beautiful creature? Why couldn't it just go away, leave us in peace, and live? It opened its mouth and roared. My face burned. Then it moved forward cautiously, until William took his shot. It stopped again, uninjured. It turned towards William. Giles fired and hit it in the stomach. After a slight stumble, it had Giles in its sights. Blood was spilling from the wound as it moved, still graceful, still unbowed. It had to be badly injured, but it didn't flee. It came for its attackers. Mac fired and the tiger turned in our direction. It was so close now and gaining speed. It would be on Mac before he could take a second shot. It would have to be a gold medal shot. Right between the eyes.

'Mac, duck!' I heard myself yell and let the arrow fly. Mac was quick, dropping low. If I missed, the tiger would have him. The arrow hit above the nose, between the eyes. The eyes focused on me and seemed to ask why. Then it dropped, dead.

No one moved for so, so long. I couldn't breathe and I couldn't stop the tears. My eyes stung with their bitterness. All that was in my blurred vision was the dead creature, its muscles still quivering, the magnificent, beautiful beast that no longer lived, because of me. I was oblivious of the people flooding out of the house, the men rushing towards me. The tiger and I had shared its last moment. Now only I remained. I felt Mac's hands grip my arms, felt him pulling me towards him, and I dissolved into his arms. He held me tightly, both of us shaking. All around us people were moving, milling about, all speaking at once. I didn't hear them.

I have no idea how I got to the house or what happened between then and when I woke, with the morning sun streaming through the window. Mac was asleep in the chair, but my movement stirred him.

'Morning! How are you feeling?' I struggled to sit up. 'You kept on mumbling an apology, even after I'd given you a sedative and you were half asleep. I assume you were apologising to the tiger and not for saving my life.'

He advised me to stay in bed all day, then offered to bring me some breakfast. Keep a low profile, he said. Of course, I ignored the advice and said I'd get my own breakfast. Still trying to show how independent I was, I guess, but jumping out of bed after being given a strong sedative tends to make you a bit wobbly. He steadied me.

'Why don't you ever take anybody's bloody advice?' I even resented him helping me down the corridor to the breakfast kitchen, only to realise why he'd advised me to keep out of people's way for a while. Breakfast for the rest of the farm was just about over and they were all either returning with dishes or making ready to begin their chores. I was surrounded, with everyone having something to say. I appreciated their thanks, but I wasn't in the mood for reliving the event. I still felt bad for the tiger. I wasn't proud of what I had done. I felt somewhat irritated by talk of my crossbow skills, even though they all meant well.

'All right, all right, you can all talk to her later. Give her some space now. Come on. There's jobs to be done and Lexi you take it easy today.' Tom waved his arms like a man scattering crows, shooing them all out.

Bianca ducked under his arm and rushed back to me. She grabbed my hand and said, 'You rock!' before racing out after William.

'Lucky you!' Peggy's eyebrow raised. She put a warm bacon sandwich beside me, as well as all her usual accompaniments for pancake. My two favourite breakfast treats.

Once finished and pleasantly full I helped Peggy prepare lunch and vegetables for our evening meal. When she had no further need of me, I retreated to my room. I tried to rest, but the eyes of that tiger haunted me. I was a killer. I knew all the good reasons why we had to kill it. I just wish it hadn't been me. It was no use trying to reason it out or even rail against the fact that the animal was on the loose. How did it escape? Who let it out? It didn't matter. All that mattered was that I killed it. No matter what I was doing, my mind would stray back to that animal and its death. Mac looked in on me around sunset. I couldn't face eating with everyone. He brought me an apple and painstakingly cut it into slices.

'You're the reason I'm alive,' he told me, when I remarked that he was being kind to me. 'Twice. I need some way to pay you back for that.'

'You don't. I wasn't the only one who rescued you from the black hats and yesterday, well, if the tiger killed you, he'd soon have seen you were too skinny to be anything but a snack. He'd have come for me next.'

He laughed. 'Well, I don't deny I'm slightly on the lean side, but you're hardly a big mouthful.'

He bent over me. 'Rest now!' He got to the door and looked back, grinning. 'You know they're calling me 'Mac-Duck' now, don't you?' He pointed a finger. 'Your fault!'

After he'd gone, I found myself thinking more about him than the tiger. He could be a pompous ass, but there was something about him that part of me was drawn to, while the sensible part was screaming to back away, you've no need for entanglements.

* * *

The tiger was given a royal burial. The children didn't want us to cremate the animal and asked if we could bury it instead.

William did it for them, with the front-loader. Tom's collection of man-toys from the farm store was getting well used. It was a large pit not far from the barn. Troy found one of the tiger's teeth, stuck in the barn door jamb. Lucy Laughton made a necklet of it, using some leather she found in the barn. The two Boyle children picked flowers, and Tom said a prayer for the deceased. William had made a wooden cross and then Lucy hung the tooth around the cross. We all hoped 'Roar', yes that's what the kids called him, would rest in peace.

Tranquillity settled back over the farm very quickly. Days were getting shorter and there was always a full day's work waiting. Ashton had found a book with diagrams of sheep folds with wicker roofing, and that became his project. It probably wasn't going to be big enough to keep all the flock safe, but the ewes and the old ones might benefit from it. Troy organised the children into a working party, and when they were not helping with chores they helped stack rocks or collect twigs for the wicker. Together, Lucy and Zoe were mastering the art of weaving the twigs together. One evening, Peggy showed the children how to make glove puppets from old socks and buttons and William put together a chipboard theatre where they performed their plays.

When he thought I was fully recovered from the tiger kill, Tom asked me to ride over to the fence on the far side of the property to see if it was sound. He thought the tiger might have got into the property that way, and if the fence needed repair, we should do it before the weather got really bad. There was also the matter of the strange light that Zoe had seen a few days after the tiger incident. It reminded me that I'd also seen something in that direction.

The wind was sharp as I rode up the hill to the small rocky outcrop. The fence was somewhere beyond that, somewhere down the hill, beyond the tight copse of ash trees that surrounded a natural pond. The pond was fed by a stream, filtering down through the rocks. Tom once told me that there was a natural spring somewhere up there, but he had forgotten its location. I'd only visited this part of the farm once before, in summer, when the ash trees were in their glory. Now, as I saw them in the distance, they were bare and uninviting.

I left the pony among the trees, grazing lazily. A narrow path, probably made by animals rather than humans wound downhill towards the fence, which looked intact, as far as I could tell. An indistinct mound of fur at the pond's edge caught my eye, something dead. I thought it might be another sheep, killed by the tiger, but as I got nearer I could see it was one of Arthur's deer. I hadn't seen many and it was sad to see this one. Something shiny, a large knife with a distinctive notch in the shaped blade, a Bowie knife, was on the ground beside the deer and whoever owned it had been butchering the carcass. I started to stand up.

Suddenly a strong hand covered my mouth, and an arm began to drag me towards the rocks. I was struggling but it was no use. This man was far stronger than I was, and my crossbow was on the pony's saddle. So, despite of my struggling, I was dragged into the darkness of a cave of some sort. Other hands appeared momentarily as a hessian bag was placed over my head and I found my wrists being roughly brought together and tied behind my back. They pushed my legs from under me and I half rolled, half sat on the dry, cold earth of the cave. The darkness grew and I assumed that wherever I was had a door or something to block out the light. I tried to shake the bag off my head, but it had been somehow fastened to my jacket. Eventually I gave up.

My thoughts turned to the pony. I hoped they wouldn't kill him because they had most certainly been responsible for the deer. To my delight, I heard Bobby galloping past, close to where I was imprisoned. Perhaps they'd tried to catch him. He wasn't easy to catch, particularly when it was to put a saddle on him. Hopefully he'd bolt all the way back to the farm and they'd come looking for me.

I shuffled backwards until I found a wall and used it to push myself to my feet. I tried using the wall to slide my head along, using the roughness of the hessian to gradually work it towards the top of my head, hoping there was enough material to work my head free. There wasn't. I felt my way along the wall until suddenly there was no wall and I fell. I hit my head on the uneven floor and passed out.

When I came around the hessian was gone, and two very concerned male faces were peering closely at me. As I stirred, one stood and moved away slightly.

'She's awake!' The one kneeling beside me said. He shouted, 'Hello, can you hear me?'

'I'm concussed, not deaf.' My head hadn't ached this much since the sickness. An earthy-smelling cushion was put under my head. I was finding it hard to focus on his face. 'You shouldn't have poked your nose into other people's business,' he told me.

'It is my business. I live at the farm and you're trespassing and stealing venison.' At the time I think my dizzy state had dispelled all common sense. I was a prisoner of two very fit, younger men and I was the only witness to their crime.

The standing one came closer and squatted beside me. 'We're hungry and you lot can spare it.' A crack on the head can interfere with your eyesight. I could see more clearly, but I seemed to be seeing double. They were not twins, because one appeared older than the other. They had to be brothers.

'We've worked hard to take good care of our animals. We don't appreciate someone killing them.' I was finding it hard to concentrate.

The younger one, with the finer features, leaned towards me. 'We're just passing through. We saw the big cat yesterday and came in here, but it headed straight for your sheep. I think we scared the deer when we came into the cave, because it bolted out past us and we didn't see it again, until we went to swim in the pond. It was dead already, so we decided not to waste the meat.' He had a vague elfin look about him and in the half light from their weak torch, his eyes sparkled.

'You do know that venison should be hung before its eaten?' I said with such confidence. In reality I had no idea when you should eat venison.

The older one straightened up and sounded weary. 'We don't really care how you're supposed to eat it lady, we're just hungry.'

'You should because if it isn't hung, the meat can sour, and you could be very sick. Look, trussing me up like a turkey isn't helping anyone. Do you think you could untie me? I'm hardly in a position to beat you both up, am I?'

The older one unfastened my wrists. I'd bruised both of my hands when I fell. The younger one said he'd get me some water.

'Why didn't you come over to the farm?' I asked, dabbing the blood from my knuckles and feeling for the dent in the back of my head.

'Because we didn't know you were there, at first.' The older one sat down in front of me. 'We followed the stream and came up the valley that way. It was raining and we found this cave, so we set up here for the night. The next morning, we saw the animals, and we stole some of your eggs. It was all we've had to eat since our rations ran out. We didn't have much to begin with. That's why we didn't come down later. We weren't sure what kind of a welcome we'd get.'

'You're brothers, right? From Sheffield?' I know I should have jumped to my feet and raced away, but you reach a certain maturity when you realise that running away from someone at least ten years younger, and considerably taller, and stronger, was futile. So, I just made myself comfortable.

The younger one came back. 'I got the water from the stream, not the pond. I didn't think you'd want to drink that.' He offered me a plastic mug.

'Yes, we're brothers.' The older one said as I drank. 'I was working away, in Nottingham, when it got bad. My father's been gone for a while, but my mother still lived in the same house we'd grown up in. She died in the epidemic.'

'Were you with her?' It was getting to be the norm that people shared their virus experience as common ground. His hand rubbed the stubble on his chin, and he shook his head as if the events still felt unreal to him.

'We were with her and would have probably stayed there but the round ups were beginning, and we had to escape.' The older brother continued his story as I dabbed the cold water on my head. 'We've seen what they're doing. They've turned the city into a big prison, barbed wire everywhere and have guards pushing people around. We went into the city to get some better travelling gear and watched the trucks arrive. They marched everybody at gun point up the Moor. We saw them separating the men from the women and beating up anyone who got out of line. We hid in a delivery yard until it got dark and then got out of there as fast as we could.' It was a frightening revelation.

A graphic account of what probably happened to the people we knew. My thoughts went back to little Kayla's teddy bear and the scrawled, half written message on the kitchen wall.

'Where are you going to go?' I asked.

'Don't really know.' The younger one shrugged. 'That tiger scared us both. You surprised us. The whole tying up thing was my idea. Mark went crazy when he saw what I'd done.'

The older brother, Mark, nodded. 'Luke sometimes needs to think a bit before he acts. We haven't made real plans, but we'll probably find a vacant place and start from scratch, like you lot. Have to find some chickens and maybe goats. I think we could cope with them. We're pretty handy and up for a challenge.'

I liked his attitude. I noticed they'd set themselves up with a small spirit stove, sleeping bags and a bag that appeared to hold their remaining food. There wasn't much left.

'I didn't know there was a cave here,' I said as Luke and Mark helped me to my feet. It had a flat, dry floor and very straight walls for a cave. The wooden frame supporting the roof gave its true nature away. 'In fact, I don't think it's a cave. It looks more like a mine entrance.'

Mark nodded. 'I think it probably is an old tin mine that ran out before the bigger mines were working. We haven't been further than the entrance. Our torch is pretty useless.'

We could have gone on talking but I could hear voices, quite distant at first, but calling my name. I took a chance and invited the brothers back to the farm. I told them to help me to the mine entrance, and from there I called out to the search party. Mark and Luke looked a bit anxious, not knowing how they'd be treated, and Mark began to pack up their belongings.

Tom was angry that they'd attacked me and gave them both a piece of his mind. 'There's really no excuse for what happened. You should have come down to us. We would have given you eggs. We would have fed you. We're reasonable people.'

'We're very sorry.' Mark said to me. 'We'll get off your property.' He turned to Luke who had shouldered his pack and the pair of them began walking back the way they had come.

We watched for a few moments then Tom yelled out to them to stop.

'Seems silly to send them both packing when they're both strong young men who could contribute to the farm. So long as they don't go hitting anyone else, they could always pay for their food with some labour, couldn't they?' Tom looked to the rest of us briefly for confirmation and then strode off to talk to them.

Mac stood beside me. 'I'm not sure I want to invite them in after the way they treated you. It's a bit risky.'

Ash was more magnanimous. 'We were all strangers at some time. It's Tom's place and he's welcomed all of us. If he thinks they're worth the risk, who are we to question him.' Ash patted Mac on the back and strode off to meet Tom and the returning young men.

'Thanks for the invite,' Luke said when they reached us. 'We're happy to pitch in.'

We hadn't finished the meal before Tom at least was certain we should invite the Thornton brothers to join us. Mark Thornton, the older brother was an electrical engineer who worked under contract, designing lighting for industrial and commercial businesses. He piqued Tom's interest as soon as he mentioned he was also an expert on solar panel installation, batteries and renewable turbines. Shortly after we had finished eating, Tom asked Mark about electrifying fences. Mark went with Tom and Ash to look at the plans of the farm in Arthur's office.

Luke stayed and talked about how they'd travelled on foot from the city, avoiding the vans and using walking tracks when they could. It was hard for Peggy and me to get the children to go to bed, after all these were new people and we didn't see too many new people. Thankfully Troy offered to read bedtime stories to Tamsin and Harry, but I almost had to drag the Laughton girls out of the building. Luke was a mechanic and just like Mark he immediately reminded people of all the things around the place that could keep a good mechanic occupied. It also didn't escape the few women at the farm that Luke was a handsome young man, like his brother. With his elfin looks, wavy hair and pale blue eyes, many were thinking he'd make a very welcome addition to our number.

After Luke retold how his mother had died Zoe asked, 'Do you have any other family?'

'I have three brothers. We're the middle two. We don't know where the others are. Matthew's the oldest, then Mark, then me, and...'

Peggy squealed with laughter, 'Don't tell me the youngest is called John!'

Luke nodded. 'Spot on!' Everyone laughed. 'It's been something we've all had to live with. Our mother, God rest her soul, was a Catholic. Four sons with three fathers. The first two didn't even take her to the altar. My dad did, but as soon as he found out she was pregnant with John, he shot through. Mum raised us all by herself. She cleaned offices, worked on the production line at Bassett's, even ran Tupperware parties to get extra money. She did her very best for us, even if she did drag us to mass every Sunday.'

Zoe shifted her position on the sofa next to Luke. 'She must have been very proud of you all.'

That was a conversation stopper and seeing Luke's discomfort Peggy offered to show him the chalet, where Zoe and I had made the beds before we ate supper. William asked Zoe to help him finish the evening feeds.

That left Mac and me facing each other in the easy chairs. 'Well, good find!' Mac commended me. 'Let's hope they want to stay.'

'Let's hope.'

'I should check that crack on your head.' He came over and waited for me to lower my head. 'It looks worse than it is. The shower you took made it bleed a bit but it's beautifully clean.' His hands were holding either side of my face and I could feel my face starting to blush. He brought his face down to mine, to check my hairline. As he moved the hair, I tried to avoid looking at him, but eventually I did. There was a moment, a split second, before he lifted my chin and kissed me, on the lips. I responded and then both of us drew back. 'Not very professional of me, I'm sorry.'

'Don't be,' I told him. 'Your aim's just not very good. It's the back of my head that needs kissing better.' I told him.

He bent and kissed me a second time. 'Sorry, missed again. I think I'm going to need more practice.'

'I think it could take quite a lot of practice.' I reached up to draw his face to mine, just as someone was stomping up the steps to the door.

8. SCHOOL, MULE AND YULE

It did not take us long after the children came to us before we realised how inadequately prepared we were for them. The Carters, in the company of Inga and Fay, went back to the families' homes and brought clothes and toys, but the arrival of familiar things only intensified the children's sense of loss. Their parents were gone. In many ways, it was worse than if their parents had died, because the children feared what might be happening to them. They all had nightmares, and for a long time we took turns in sleeping in their rooms. After about a month, they asked if they could move into the larger chalet, once used for school camps. It had two bedrooms. The large one was equipped with bunk beds and the smaller room, designed for the teachers, had three single beds. There was also a teachers' sitting room with facilities for tea and coffee making and a microwave. After lengthy discussion, the children requested that we send Mark and William for Tamsin's own tiny bed, which we squashed into the teachers' bedroom. All the girls and Harry shared the room. We would often find Tamsin asleep in her brother's arms in the morning. Troy had a pair of bunkbeds moved to the tiny teachers' sitting room and the rest of the bunks were stacked at the far end of the dormitory. Now there was space for indoor games, their toys and a desk that had been in the teachers' sitting room.

The night duty continued, but I took the majority of nights. It seemed that although I felt totally unskilled to deal with the children's fragile states, I had more understanding, experience and knowledge of how to deal with children, particularly other people's children, than anyone else. It was also apparent that my gradual approach to the education of the four children wasn't working too well. I'd shied away from setting up lessons or making timetables, instead I'd tried to work with each child individually but there was never enough time to fit them all in. Farm chores still had to take priority. Each child found their own way to learning what they wanted. The smallest, Tamsin, was fine and everyone took delight in helping her to learn to count and write her name. At four, she was eager to learn anything from anyone, and our reading sessions were very productive. Harry pretty much taught himself, as I suspected he always had. His enquiring mind had propelled him into the library alcove of Tom's office. In addition to reading he delighted in taking things apart, finding how they worked and putting them back together again. Mark quickly located some unused electrical plugs, screwdrivers and an assortment of discarded equipment for Harry to tinker with. When Luke let him help on vehicle maintenance, he had to keep a watchful eye on the young boy, in case he dismantled anything important.

Since my encounter with the tiger Bianca had become my bosom companion, and while I was in attendance she would study hard. Her maths needed a lot of work, and at first I pressed Ashton into helping, but she rudely ignored his help. Luke got a better reception from her, although I doubted she understood his slightly vague explanations. Like many people who use maths as second nature he'd long forgotten how careful explanations needed to be.

Sadly, Lucy received my least attention. At just fifteen she was in that halfway house between being tween and teen. A private girls' school education had not given her the broader awareness of teenage life as it had for Troy and the children of Wincobank. She was sensible but in many ways innocent. She enjoyed spending time with Peggy in the kitchen and loved wandering over to the grange. Giles had given her free access to his family library, but he noticed that she spent most of her time relishing the quiet atmosphere, taking leather volumes from the shelves and feeling their covers, flipping pages and smelling their age. Sometimes he would find her staring at the many paintings in the long gallery. He encouraged her interest in them by answering her questions about them and if he could, directing her to other images. One afternoon, he showed her his father's collection of historic armour and weapons. It sparked her imagination and I found her telling the children about King Richard the Lionheart and jousting.

I was thumbing through Arthur's brochures one evening, when I suddenly realised that these little pamphlets could be a learning tool in themselves. I handed them all over to Lucy and said we'd be going on excursions together and she could pick. That same evening Lucy presented me with her first list of ten locations. Just the first ten, she cheerfully informed me, because she didn't want to overload me. Apparently further lists were to follow.

'Do you think we'll be safe?' I asked Giles his opinion about going off alone with the threat of black hats, not to mention wild animals and unknown humans. Since coming to the farm most of my journeys had been with others.

'Well, if you need a man to protect you, I could string along.' His reply produced a quick poke in the ribs from me but having Giles beside us along with my crossbow did make me, and importantly Lucy, feel safer.

It amazed me that while the girls' parents had introduced their children to every climbing face in the district, they had never taken them anywhere except Chatsworth House. They'd visited Sheffield, to buy climbing and outdoor equipment, and Chesterfield, to see the remarkable twisted spire and to marvel that someone had actually climbed it.

The three of us covered Lucy's first two destinations in one day. It was one of those clear, bitingly cold, sunny days, when the sky is cornflower blue, and the air is so sharp and crisp it steals your breath. We rode to Bakewell together. She was a far more confident rider than I was, and she would have cantered there much quicker than 'the old grey lady on the grey pit pony', her description of me that she gave Inga and Fay as we walked with them beside the River Wye.

Fay told us about a path that would take us to our second destination without having to use the roads. The two women had never been to the Old House Museum, our Bakewell destination, so we all went together. It was locked but Inga's bolt cutters gave us access to the back door. As we toured the exhibits, Lucy made notes and used her phone to take pictures.

'Where are you going now?' Inga asked as we saddled up.

'Haddon Hall!' Lucy was animated. 'It's really famous and it's been in heaps of films.'

'Must be good!' Inga nodded.

Fay gave her partner's arm a little push with her finger. 'It is famous and rightly so. I think it's one of the most beautiful of all the stately homes.'

'Better than Chatsworth?' Lucy was doubtful. Chatsworth was the only stately home they'd visited, and because the day had been fine during their visit the family had apparently spent most of their time in the gardens.

Giles supported Fay. 'Chatsworth is a stunning place and grand on every scale but wait 'til you've seen Haddon. I think you'll like it.'

The path was narrow at times, but we were in no hurry. It roughly followed the eastern bank of the river and gave us fine glimpses of the valley. Beyond an old bridge, we got our first sight of the house, sitting above the river, with views across the land. The Manners, who owned the house for many years, had certainly been able to say they owned all they surveyed. As soon as she saw it, Lucy quickened her pony's pace.

A small cottage barred our way to the house itself and following Fay's instructions we knocked at the door. In time, an old man peered through at us. I explained that we would like to visit the house, but he told us 'the Trust' wasn't opening it during the 'plague'. We were the first visitors he'd had except for Vince Carter who supplied him with food from time to time.

'It's Errol isn't it?' Giles moved closer to the old man. 'You probably don't remember me, but I remember you. I remember you scoring the winning runs in a game against Baslow when I was ten and you signed the cricket ball for me.' He offered his hand. 'Giles Montgomery.'

Errol peered into Giles' face. 'You look like your Uncle Robert!' He declared and shook his hand. 'So you came back home after all?'

'Bad penny!' Giles laughed and the old man did too. 'This young lady would love to see the Hall because she's only seen Chatsworth and I think she would love to see Haddon. Her parents are away, and this will cheer her up immensely.'

The old man blinked. 'I'll have to come up with you! Can't trust strangers these days.' He turned to Lucy. 'You've seen Chatsworth, you say?' She nodded. 'Then you should see the jewel in the Devonshire Crown. This old lady,' he pointed towards the house, 'has a longer history than Chatsworth and she's still making it.' He gave Lucy a wink. 'Been in more films than Judy Dench!'

So, Errol, eighty-four years old and born not ten miles away, agreed to take us on a short tour. It took two hours, but we didn't mind because what he couldn't tell us about the house wasn't worth knowing. His family had worked there for three generations and he was proud of the place.

Lucy was enthralled. She took more pictures, made endless notes and kept squeezing my arm to show her appreciation. She listened intently to the story of Dorothy Vernon and John Manners, and how she had eloped with him down the famous outdoor steps. Dorothy did actually marry John, bringing the house into the possession of the Manners family, although Errol said that he doubted the secret elopement ever happened. The marriage was probably arranged, and Dorothy didn't escape the house down the famous steps. Lucy insisted she took a photograph with her phone of Giles and me, 'eloping' down the famous steps, complete with exaggerated expressions of fear and passion in our faces. That made the old man laugh. When we got to the chapel, Errol almost brought Lucy to tears when he explained the beautiful white sarcophagus of a nine-year-old boy, Robert Charles Manning, whose mother Violet, mourned him for the rest of her life. As we stepped back into the sunlight of the great courtyard I found Lucy was holding my hand.

Back at the farm, Lucy took no time in converting her new knowledge into stories to tell the younger children and before she went to bed, she asked if she could take one of the hard-backed notebooks I'd taken from the newsagents in Chesterfield. Like Harry, I suspected that Lucy was going to be her own best teacher, seeking out knowledge that was either useful or of interest to her personally.

The weather held up further excursions as we raced through November. Then rain turned the yard into a quagmire, the marsh in the hollow into a pond, and the old, neglected duck pond into a sizeable lake. Lucy did find a new interest. As soon as Mark and Luke joined us the dynamic among the younger people changed. Soon after their arrival, the children had focused on William and Peggy, but now the younger ones and even Troy and Zoe, had the brothers to focus on. Troy and Bianca followed Luke about like puppies. Zoe would take their place when they were not around. She did everything to get Luke to notice her and he was clearly interested. We still had nights filled with tears and regular bedwetting, but the older children were now shouldering the emotional care of the youngest as much as we were. They knew the feeling of loss and they were often better at distracting the little ones' minds. None of us could take their anxiety and sorrow away but we tried.

Mark, the older Thornton brother, had immediately set to work on beefing up our security. With William he searched for the electrical components needed to electrify our perimeter fence and after one of their forays brought back solar power units, generators, a windmill pump and a security camera system. His first job was giving us electric powered gates.

'It's like living in a Hollywood mansion,' Zoe said, when the gates were demonstrated for us.

'Or a prison!' Ashton added. Of course, neither of them had experience of either.

One very sodden morning, when the grass was slippery and the mist soaked through your clothes as you walked, I showed Mac and Tom the mine entrance. Tom had found an old drawing of the mine among Arthur's files with a very rough sketch of the tunnels.

'I must say that I'd forgotten the thing even existed. Of course, we were forbidden to go inside, when we were boys. Our father had the entrance boarded up to stop us. See, here!' He showed us a broken piece of planking that hung limply from a nail on the upright post at the entrance.

The entrance chamber was larger than I remembered it, about the size of a double garage with a higher ceiling than the tunnel beyond. Wooden beams rested on the upright timbers and supported the wooden planks that formed the actual ceiling. With two stronger torches we could see that the single tunnel soon divided into two. Tom thumped every timber support we passed. To see if it was solid and sound, he said. We took the left tunnel which appeared to be going steadily downhill. There were no planks on the ceiling here, just the frames and rough, hewn rock over our heads. Water dripped from above and when we reached a deep pool of water that stretched into the darkness, we turned back. Walking through these eerie passages made me wonder what life had been like for those miners so long ago.

The right tunnel had more twists and turns but was flatter for the most part, until we reached a wider gallery with a timbered roof and what appeared to be wooden bays reminiscent of stables. Tom doubted Mac's suggestion that it could have been for pit ponies but rather a collection point for the tin. Sure enough, further along the right tunnel there was an old trolley, parked across the entrance of one of two new tunnels, and in our torchlight, we could vaguely see a second trolley blocking the access to that new right tunnel further along. The other new tunnel, on the left, stopped our exploration. There had been some sort of cave in. Rocks blocked the way, but the tunnel had clearly gone further before the rock fall. A deep pit had been dug and remnants of an old metal ladder descended into the darkness. None of us felt adventurous enough to clamber down there, so we returned to the entrance.

After dinner that evening, Tom explained what we had found to everyone else. The suggestions for what we should do with the mine varied. Some people wanted to 'board it back up', others suggested it could prove a useful storage area for perishable goods, animals and equipment, while others volunteered it as a bolt hole should the black hats come. No decisions were reached that day.

❊ ❊ ❊

Flour was becoming hard to get for everyone and while Fay and Inga experimented with alternatives Tom thought we should distribute to others some of our own. It wouldn't last forever, and it was better that it was used. Lucy and I set off early, riding towards Bakewell with our precious flour and more vegetables for the Carters. The leaden sky and biting wind threatened rain, but we were well wrapped in our alpaca woollies under heavy anoraks. Once our deliveries were complete Lucy begged me to ride further to Monsal Head. It was on her list. She wanted to see the viaduct. I didn't ask, but I suspected that someone had probably climbed it at some stage. We took the Monsal Trail, deserted now, and easy to ride at our own pace. Lucy used the time to show just how fast she could ride, given the opportunity. She careered through the tunnel sections squealing loudly in the echoing gloom, while I tried to formulate a plan to get her home safely with no broken limbs.

The pub at the head of the dale was silent, although Lucy was sure she'd seen a man at the window. After the black hat raids, it wasn't unusual for people to be cautious. We left whoever it was in peace. Lucy pleaded that we ride further along the trail, but the sky was still glowering, and I wanted to be safely home before dark. We dismounted and began our careful descent into the valley bottom. The ponies slithered on the winding footpaths and I was anxious about what would happen if human or pony had an accident here. All kinds of rescue scenarios went through my head before we reached the relative safety of the valley.

I told Lucy that this was one of my favourite places when I was a child, splashing about in the river and having picnics in the sun. Today was too cold for either activity, however Lucy could see how beautiful the valley was, and we ambled along until we reached the main road to Bakewell. Just past Ashford we took the right turn to Shutts Lane, heading south and home.

'Listen!' Lucy broke into my rambling explanation of Richard Arkwright's contribution to technology. It was going on longer than I'd intended, anyway. I listened and somewhere, there was the distinct sound of braying. 'Donkey!' she yelled and gleefully cantered down the road in the direction of the noise.

Now, I've got a history with donkeys. One tried to take a piece out of my hip when I was a child. It was only later, when I could re-late to the tedious nature of being a seaside ride, that I could forgive the species for their belligerence, but I had spent the greater part of my childhood being afraid of them.

We found the beast easily. It was in a small paddock at the roadside. At first, we couldn't determine why it was making all the noise, until we noticed that in the next field, the bulk of a body was heaving and struggling to rise. The donkey's only companion, an old horse, was in trouble. Lucy was off her pony and into the field before I could stop her. The donkey made a beeline for her, but she was under the wooden fence and into the horse paddock before the alarmed beast could catch her. I skirted the paddocks finding a muddy pathway and reached Lucy as she was kneeling beside the horse. It had been hobbled and had fallen. It was unable to get itself up again. An animal doesn't know that you are there to help, even if you mutter soothing words and pat it gently. The horse was panicking, and I was afraid it would kick one of us as it thrashed about. My brother's trusty Swiss Army knife came out, and I began to cut at the hobbles, at the same time telling Lucy to move back and be safe. That was a complete waste of my breath. She'd dismounted and was fending off the anxious donkey, keeping herself between it and the precarious operation being conducted to remove the hobble. As the tension began to give on the rope the horse increased its efforts, and with a sudden flurry it was free and struggling to its feet. At that moment the horse's head and Lucy's made contact, and she fell backwards, the horse missing her sprawling body by inches.

By this time, I was truly rattled. All day I'd been concerned about our safety. Call it a premonition if you like, but I blame it on my teacher's training to always anticipate the worst-case scenario. The poor girl was dazed, lying on the ground, blood streaming from a wound on her face. I had to half-carried her back to our horses, and I tried to stop the bleeding. The first aid kit that Peggy insisted we always took with us was invaluable. All the saline water balloons and a good deal of sticking plaster around a wound dressing would protect her injury until we got home. I heaved Lucy up into her saddle and reassured her we'd be back in no time.

'But the donkey and the horse!' she wailed. 'We can't just leave them here.'

'The horse was hobbled. It belongs to someone. We can't just steal it.'

'We should. The horse could have died if we hadn't freed it!' She was trembling.

'I have to get you back!'

Lucy was sobbing. 'If their owner cared they'd have come to see what was upsetting the donkey!'

I couldn't tell if she was in shock, but I had to get her back to Mac, quickly. 'Okay, look we have to get back. We'll open both fields and if they want to, they can follow us.' I patted her leg. 'It's the best we can do.'

I opened both gates and mounted up. The donkey took no persuading. It was out of the gate and trotting down to the horse paddock. I'd expected it to go in and stay with its friend. It didn't. As we rode slowly down Shutts Lane, we were followed, at a distance, by a donkey and a horse. The distance between us grew closer as we drew nearer to the farm and further away from the landscape the two animals knew. By the time we reached the turn off to Over Haddon they were right behind us.

Mac did what he could to repair Lucy's cheek. The cut wasn't deep he told her, but he couldn't say if there would be a scar. Her forehead was bruised, and he was concerned, so he suggested she stay in my bed that night and he'd sleep on the living room couch, just to be safe. Bianca insisted that she stay with her sister too, so I spent the night on the other couch.

It didn't rain the following day, but it certainly did for many days afterwards, so it wasn't until December was upon us that we turned our thoughts to Christmas. The Carter's, as usual, were planning a gathering and everyone was drawn into baking, whether it was helping to stir the Christmas pudding or scouring the Derbyshire countryside for stocks of dried fruits, suet, or precious flour. Inga and Fay were busy trialling almond flour and I encountered them several times during my dried fruits search, busy collecting as many almonds, and packets of almond flour that they could find. Fay suggested that Tom should investigate growing almond trees. I passed the idea on to him.

It was going to be a hard time for the children. Their minds were filled with memories of earlier Christmas celebrations, and they shared these experiences mostly with one another. They found that there was common ground. Troy and Zoe became our Christmas organisers, trying to accommodate the wishes of the children as to what they all expected. They were unanimous about who should be Santa, and Tom annoyed everyone while he practised his 'Ho, ho, ho!' A tree, decorations, turkey and crackers were all on the list. Peggy discovered that we had in fact two turkeys hidden away in our freezers. In those early days, we grabbed anything that we thought could be useful. We had no idea how long we would have to manage on frozen food. They were at the bottom of one of our chest freezers. In the spirit of Christmas, we donated one to the Bakewell festivities.

Considering that we were a collection of strangers in a precarious position, with no idea of what the future held for us and struggling to get back to the rural lifestyles of our ancestors, the festive season passed by pleasantly enough. Gifts were homemade and given out on Christmas Eve. Harry had taken great pains to explain that his parents hadn't really encouraged a belief in a real Father Christmas, and they had always received their gifts on Christmas Eve. As they were the youngest two children we all decided that it should be their choice. The children got one gift from everyone, while everyone else got one from the time-honoured Kris Kringle lucky dip. All, that is, except for Peggy. As the farm's own Christmas Eve celebration reached its end, but before the children were escorted to their beds, William produced a small box from his pocket, went down on one knee and offered it to Peggy. He announced that he had still to find a church that was unlocked, but that Tom, who had been a Justice of the Peace, had agreed to marry them. A date was set for Easter. Peggy was speechless. She nodded her acceptance and they kissed. Then she cried.

'I just wish my parents and Will's could be here to see this. They'd planned such a lovely wedding.' She excused herself for a while, and when she returned she was red eyed but smiling. 'I'd hired the dress and everything,' she told me.

'We could always find a dress,' I told her.

'No, it's not necessary. I've got all I need in William.'

At the end of such a special night Mark had an extra gift for us all. He took us to the perimeter fence closest to the house and demonstrated the electrified fence. He threw an apple and the fence sparked into life. We were now protected by an electric fence and a smaller internal fence which protected all of us from accidentally walking into the live wires. Giles decided that he'd stay the night rather than disrupt the fence. I think he was a little alarmed about the fizzle and pop of the demonstration.

Christmas Day was a whirlwind of food, food and more food. Giles, who was our sole invited guest, had surprised us all with a goose! It had been lurking in his freezer. He also produced home-made pâté, cottage cheese and pickled onions. By evening, there was nothing left to do but digest everything and sit around a large fire and talk. Ashton had gained credence with the children through his storytelling skills. Despite his shyness, he had been a keen amateur actor, and with an appreciative audience he was happy to launch into tale telling. Knights and dragons were the favoured topics. So, while we sat, savouring the collection of alcoholic beverages that we'd amassed, Ashton began his tale of Arthur and his knights.

'Arthur was Tom's brother!' Troy piped. 'So, we could say, he was like Tom!' That amused the youngsters.

'So, Lexi could be Guinevere!' Zoe patted my knee eagerly and I smiled down at her as she sprawled on the rug by the fire. From the corner of my eye I could see Tom's face. He looked a little uncomfortable with the analogy.

As Ashton's story continued the knights were introduced. 'Troy should be Galahad!' Mark said, then asked, 'He was young, wasn't he?'

Ashton sighed, people were interrupting his flow. 'Yes, but the most important of Arthur's knights was the one who had travelled a long way to become a member of the Round Table, and that was Lancelot.' Ashton had regained the attention of his audience. 'He was the bravest, the most skilful, and the best looking of all the knights. Everyone loved him.'

The younger female members of the audience began a debate about who Lancelot would be. Bianca was sure Luke was the handsome one. Zoe said William was the bravest and Lucy pointed out that as Mac was a surgeon, he was the most skilful.

'Tell them about the Holy Grail, or Arthur's birth.' Tom interrupted. 'I always liked those stories best.'

'Merlin! Tell them about Merlin!' Mark cried. 'That's full of magic and things.'

'Like your magical fence!' squealed Harry.

'What about the sword in the stone?' Peggy leaned forward.

'Well, that wasn't really in the original legend, but I suppose it's a good start?' Tom stood. 'Carry on Ash, tell us about Excalibur.'

Ash looked pained but felt he should correct any errors in the story before he began. 'I think Excalibur came later. It was a gift from the Lady of the Lake .' He lifted his head, a firm signal that he was about to begin.

He began by telling the story of how the young Arthur grew up in his uncle's castle and was best friends with Kaye, his cousin. Arthur was a wily, skinny kid while Kaye was strong and fit. Arthur was going to be Kaye's squire when he got older. Harry asked for more details about squires before the story could progress and then informed everyone that he was going to be a squire when he was old enough, but he didn't want to clean armour or leather.

Ash told them about the sword in the stone and how all the young knights tried to pull it out. Before he even said it, Ash knew he would have to spend time explaining about tournaments, so once that was done he explained that Kaye sent Arthur to fetch his sword from the tent.

'They were camping?' Troy looked amused and I suddenly had an image of the large caravan parks of my childhood full of people in chainmail, going down to the beach with fold up chairs.

Again Ash explained but he was getting to the climax of his tale and spoke more urgently about how Arthur was rushing through the camp when he saw the stone and the sword. He went up and just took the sword, easy as that, and hurried back to Kaye.

'Didn't people recognise the sword?' Bianca asked.

'Yes, they did, and poor Arthur thought he was in trouble, especially when all the lords and knights told him to put it back in the stone and then take it out again, then put it back again. At this point his uncle tried to take the sword but he couldn't. Only Arthur could do it.'

'Then they made him king!' Harry stood, triumphant.

'Oh, no.' Ash told him. Harry sat down again and folded his arms.

'Arthur was just a boy. He couldn't be king yet. They found him a teacher who could help him to learn about how to be a good king.'

'Lexi!' Harry roared.

Valiantly, Ash pressed on. 'Arthur's teacher was Merlin the wizard who was very wise and taught Arthur all he needed to know. He could also turn Arthur into animals and other things so Arthur would know how it felt to be a fish, or a horse, or a bird.'

Tom stood. 'And I think that's a good place to stop, so you can all turn in, to bed!' There were groans but Tom cheerfully escorted them to the door, still answering Harry's questions as they went down the path.

9. BAKEWELL TARTS AND BARGES

The time between Christmas and New Year was always a holiday time for school children and I thought my school deserved a holiday. The children were doubly rewarded for their hard work by our first snow fall. I've never been much of a snow fan. It's too cold and all the activities that go with it have always struck me as hazardous. Skating, skiing, tobogganing, I've tried them all, as a child and as an adult, and they've never filled me with excitement, only relief when I remain unscathed after doing them. I don't mind walking in snow, or a short cross-country ski, but a full-on snowball fight was something I'd prefer to avoid. While everyone else was out relishing the white stuff, I curled up under a tartan blanket by the fire with a book.

'It's a bit chilly out there,' Tom said, stating the obvious, as he came in rubbing his hands together. 'Young Troy's pelting Bianca for all he's worth. The girl will be an icicle if he doesn't stop.' He stood at the fire warming his hands and his backside. 'Good book?' I showed him the volume. 'Mm 'Wuthering Heights'.' He sniffed. 'Never could get into the Brontë's myself. All a bit gothic!'

I read 'Jane Eyre' at school and hated it, but when I read it again, for my degree, I liked it better. So, I thought I'd try Emily's book.' I made room for him on the couch.

'One of them stayed in Derbyshire I think.' He put his cold hand on my cheek and chuckled as I recoiled at the chill.

'I think Charlotte got a lot of inspiration from her visits to Hathersage. She stayed at the vicarage. The vicar's wife was a friend. Did you know a family called Eyre were the owners of North Lees Hall and she knew them?' I put a bookmark in the page and put it down.

'How did you know that?' Tom gave me one of his cheerful, 'you astound me' looks.

'University degrees sometimes have useful things in them. I enjoyed my literature course. Would you like a cup of tea?'

He followed me into the kitchen. 'I think Peggy left some mince pies around here somewhere. Ah! Here they are.' He put two on a plate and went to sit by the fire. 'You know, I always think this time of the year is for reflecting and planning. You know, looking back on the past and making some sort of plan for the coming year.' He put his feet on one of the stools the children liked to sit on.

'We've accomplished so much haven't we.' He smiled to himself before he went on. 'I was beginning to wonder what I should be doing when you and that dog showed up. Every day was miserable, all alone here, until you came along. I was just going from day to day, fixing things and carrying on as if everything was going to be all right, eventually. You got me out of that stupor. You galvanised me!' I sat down next to him and Tom put his hand on my shoulder. 'I want you to know that I've had Ashton help me write a will and all of this is yours, when I'm gone.'

I was shocked. I'd never even thought about anything like that. 'You don't have to do that Tom, please. I was just grateful you let me stay. I'm still grateful, every day. As for talking about when you're gone, well, I'd rather not dwell on that. Besides, I could easily go before you. And these days, what's a will? Are those kinds of documents going to have quite the same value that they used to?'

He stood and followed me. 'Well, I just want you to know I'm grateful to you and I can't think of anyone else that I'd rather leave it to.' He gave a little laugh. 'Of course, that's not going to be for a long time yet!'

I put my hand on his arm. 'I know that without you I would have struggled. It's been some of the best times of my life helping with the farm.'

He placed his hand over mine. 'I guess we both feel lucky to have the other. Not many people are feeling so positive about their future right now, the ones that are left to have a future. I get out of bed these days and feel as if we have a wonderful future, all of us. Ash has been marvellous creating schedules and I don't think these acres have ever been so productive. I think my brother would have been surprised.'

Tom looked out the window towards the hill. 'I wonder what Arthur would think about all the new livestock we've got. He certainly wouldn't have had pigs and as for alpaca's, well, he didn't think much of them. He wrote to me when they first arrived up the road.' He turned back to me. 'He'd be shocked that we just went in there and got them. Arthur wouldn't have done that. Straight as a die he was, except on his tax returns. But he was a good brother, as I'm sure your brother was too.'

'David struggled for so long with being gay that when he could finally tell people it changed him, for the better, I think. He was more relaxed in the company of new people, but he still loved being very well organised. Lists and fridge calendars were an integral part of his day. When his partner, Lawrence, died it hit him hard, but he was beginning to recover and go out with friends again. He was planning to go to Australia next year to the

Mardi Gras. He'd even suggested I went with him.' We lapsed into silence, each remembering.

A blast of cold air announced Mark's entrance. He busily dusted off the remnants of a snowball. Tom and I automatically went to the kitchen, fussing about warm drinks for everyone as the door opened again.

That night curled around the fire Ashton was urged to continue his storytelling. He had thought to begin the stories of Scheherazade and her one thousand and one nights but then Mark said, 'When we were little our grandmother used to put us to bed because our mother was working. Gran didn't know many stories so sometimes she'd get us to make one up.'

'Were they good stories?' asked Bianca. 'I don't think I could make up one of my own.'

Luke explained encouragingly. 'It was like a game. She'd start the story off and then the next person would take over. You can't change things that have already happened. You just say what happens next.'

'That sounds like fun. Shall we try it?' Tom rubbed his hands. 'Who should start?'

Lucy suggested Tamsin because she was the youngest.

'But she'll say something silly like fairy princesses and unicorns and magic elephants.' Harry folded his arms.

'No I won't!' Tamsin matched his stance, then put her hand to her chin as if she was stroking a beard. With one eye closed, she began, 'Once upon a time, there was a farmer who lived all alone on a beautiful farm with pigs, and goats, and sheep, and alfacas.'

'You mean alpacas!' Harry rolled his eyes and continued the story. 'The farmer was magic and one day he cast a spell and people began to arrive at his gate. They said they wanted to help him with his farm.' Harry tapped Ash beside him. 'Your turn!'

'Some of them were really helpful and the farmer was happy they'd come to help him. There was a beautiful woman who was a witch who had spells to make the most beautiful food.' Ash smiled across at Peggy before turning to Troy.

'And she fell in love with a tall woodcutter, called Will, who could wrestle bulls and fought with the hustlers who came to steal the farmer's sheep.' He threw his arm out towards William, indicating that Will was next.

'Some of the hustlers were just hungry and the kindly farmer gave them some of the witch's cooking and the food turned them back into the handsome princes they really were.'

Mark was next and he pulled a face. 'Right. Well the princes set about building a castle, but the farmer said don't do that because everyone would want to live with us when they see the castle, so the princes hid their castle under the ground.'

Luke gave his brother a sour look. 'What on earth can I say about that?' He looked at his feet for a moment. 'Also in the ground near the castle was a secret dragon's lair. The dragon that lived there was a terrible striped dragon that roared.'

Peggy concentrated and then a smile flitted across her face. 'The farmer also had a friend, a fearsome female warrior. And one day she saved a group of young princes and princesses from the dragon by making it fall asleep.' Peggy looked pleased with herself as she nudged me.

I thought for a moment. 'But the female warrior got injured one day and the farmer had to ask a wizard, who lived by the river, to make her better. The people at the farm were so grateful for the wizard's help that they invited him to stay.'

Mac began. 'The wizard had always lived alone in his cave by the river, but he was happy that he'd become friends with those in the castle. He helped them by giving them magic potions and casting spells.'

It was Bianca's turn. Her expression became serious. 'The farmer was very happy except for one thing. He knew the little princesses and princes missed the kings and queens, so he asked the magician to help him.'

Lucy smiled sadly at her sister. 'Unfortunately, the magician didn't have enough power and the kings and queens had disappeared forever.' Bianca took her hand.

Giles spoke directly to Lucy. 'But the young royals never gave up hope and one day the king, who lived in the beautiful ivy-covered castle on the top of the hill, said he had found them at last.'

Tom ended our little narrative. 'The king brought all the lost kings and queens to the farm and they all lived happily together in the underground castle!'

We all knew that it wouldn't be magic that brought the children's parents back. As they got ready to have their drink before bed I saw Bianca squeeze her sister's hand.

Later Lucy slipped her arm in mine. 'I didn't mean to spoil the story, but I wished we hadn't been part of it.'

'You didn't spoil anything,' I told her. 'We understand it's been hard for you. Just remember whatever is happening in Sheffield, it can't go on forever and then they'll be back. Hang in there!' I put my arm around Lucy and gave her shoulders a squeeze, she smiled tiredly.

Mac was close by and he came and stood beside me as we watched them all head off to bed. 'Looks like she's struggling a bit. It's good she's got you.'

'It's good they've got all of us.' I turned as they disappeared in the dark. 'I never realised that old saying about taking a village to raise a child was so true. Now I do.'

❋ ❋ ❋

The snow didn't stay, but the rain did. It was relentless. Everyone was getting soaked doing the simplest of tasks. The duck pond flooded again and then Claude, the donkey, was frightened by a shaft of lightening and bolted off towards the hills. I'd been out searching for a missing ewe and was on my way back when Claude passed me, so I turned back to make sure he didn't damage himself on the fences. I was relieved to see him sheltering under the ash trees. I was about to start walking back when the thunder got much worse and closer. I headed for the mine shaft entrance only to find Mac there with two piglets that had escaped their pen.

'Pigs!' he said, taking his anorak off and shaking it. The runaways were squealing their displeasure in a cage. A moment later, Claude joined us. Shivering and shaking but glad to be under shelter.

'Donkeys!' I said, and we both laughed.

A bolt of lightning, so close that I swear we could smell the cordite, blasted one of the ash trees. Mac and I went to the entrance instinctively and retreated together at the sight of the tree remnants. I stepped back into Mac and he held me before I could stamp all over his feet. I turned to face him and, well, after that it's a little hazy. We kissed each other. Once, almost by accident, then again, tentatively, a second time. The third kiss was filled with the hunger that had fermented for too long. It was an overpowering sensation. As we parted, he held my face in his hands and we both smiled. We held each other close until the thunder had died down, then we walked back to the barn together, leading a donkey and carrying a crate of piglets.

We went to his chalet. I showered first. There was a nervousness about knowing what you wanted to do, and what the reality might turn into, so we took our time, laughing at our own clumsiness. It was a gentle preparation for something that became passionate and consuming.

✳ ✳ ✳

The daily routine was disturbed again in mid-February, when Inga and Fay announced another party for Valentine's Day. This time it was held in what had once been the cafe above the Original Bakewell Pudding Shop. Bitter memories of the last party fluttered around the room but didn't linger as we celebrated the rebirth of the famous pudding now being recreated by the new proprietors of the renamed 'Bakewell Tarts!' establishment.

Frank and the brothers from the garage were invited by Giles, and to our relief they were on their best behaviour and seemed to genuinely enjoy getting to know others in our little community. Barry was cheerful, while the slightly restrained Liam, his older brother, had scrubbed up so well that he threatened to outshine Luke for the most handsome young man around. The young policeman, whose name I found out was Warren, brought flowers for Zoe and Lucy. We older ladies secretly voted him the most romantic young man of the night. It appeared that the Cliftons, the hobby farmers from Hope, had also been leading lights in the local operatic society and had known Tom's brother. Musicals apparently ran in the blood of the Gresham family. The couple sang a duet, then invited Tom to join them in an item from Trial by Jury. Harry ate so much pudding that he made himself sick, and Tamsin covered herself in jam, but the rest of the guests behaved impeccably. Full of pudding, wine and song, we all meandered back to the Red Lion for a sound sleep.

We lingered in Bakewell longer than we should have done. Animals needed feeding. We'd used a mixture of cars and horses to get home from Bakewell, so the car passengers arrived much earlier than the five riders. Bianca and Lucy rode on either side of Luke, each vying for his attention. He wasn't complaining. Mac and I rode ahead of them, content in our own company. I had moved from the main house to Mac's cabin a week earlier. No one had commented on it to me. It was clearly something everyone else had expected.

Upon our return to the farm that evening Troy met us at the gate and told Mac he had a patient. We left Luke and the girls to take care of the horses as I hurried after Mac. In the house a man was sitting on the sofa, his arm hastily wrapped in tea towels and his face white. Introductions came later as Mac examined the deep gash on the man's arm. He'd been lucky and the cut had missed major blood vessels, but it was clear he'd lost a lot of blood. Mac asked Tom for a bottle of his precious brandy. He needed to put stitches in the arm and it would be painful.

'I'll take the brandy later, if it's all the same to you, Tom. Go on Doc, do your worst!' The man had a rich accent that conjured thoughts of a rolling landscape and apple orchards. A man from the south west, a stranger to these parts. It was hard to tell how old he was. He might have been my age, or much older. He'd spent a lot of time in the sun. His skin had the appearance of dark worn leather and the wrinkles at the corners of his eyes were deep. He was lean and the muscles of his arms hinted at manual labour. Mac used some of our precious antiseptic liquid to sterilize the wound before he began. The man endured the pain of the stitches with only the occasional grimace and beads of sweat at his temples and upper lip. I could only admire his bravery. As I watched Mac sew his skin back together, I wondered how he had found his way to the farm.

'Came by way of Rowsley,' he explained, after downing Tom's brandy in one gulp. 'Met a man setting up to fish. Said his name were Vince Carter. Said that you'd know him. He took one look at me and tells me, you need to go to the farm and see Doc Mac. Said once I got to your road I wouldn't need no address. Said I'd see the gates and the animals.'

'It's a good job you found us.' Mac pointed at the bandaged arm. 'That would have kept on bleeding without stitches. How did you do it?' Mac sat down to give the man a general check-up. It was something he did when he came across patients he didn't know or who he hadn't seen for a while.

'Stupid accident!' the man laughed. 'Coming up from Cromford, I jumped off the deck, onto the bank to moor and didn't notice the mucky iron strut sticking out of the bushes. Scraped my arm down it as I landed. Somebody's old fence, I'm guessing. But sharp it were!'

'You've got a boat!' Tom poured him a second glass of amber liquid.

'Barge, narrow boat, low draft. Thanks.' He knocked the second glass back in one mouthful.

'Where are you coming from?' Mac checked his pulse.

'Based in Birmingham now, but afore that I were in Devises and took boats all over the place. Birmingham's a good base. Things are starting to come together again in Birmingham. Slow, mind you, but there's someone in charge, and they're getting things working again. Only local, mind! Came up the Trent, then the Derwent. You can't go further than Bakewell with anything, on account of the weir, but I'm looking for folk up here for some trading. I reckon you've got things you might trade come the end of winter. I take all sorts. Only restricted to time. If it goes off quick, then it's no good for either of us.'

'Are you the only one doing this?' Tom offered more brandy, but the man declined.

'Not many of us! A couple going north to south, but I like to mix it up a bit. No need to be greedy. Just make enough money to get you by, that's my motto. Earn any more than that and it's the bank that's getting the benefit. Not that there are any of them about, eh?' He stood and took a step back to steady himself. 'Whoa, there, Daisy!' he cried. Mac held him firm.

'I think you'd better rest here for tonight.' Tom patted him on his shoulder. 'We've a spare bed and after breakfast in the morning we'll get you back to your boat.'

The man sat back down. 'Reckon I'll do that. Legs are a bit wobbly like. Reckon Daisy should manage for one night.'

'Your wife?' Peggy asked.

The man beamed at her. 'Bless you love, no, my horse. She pulls the barge when she can. Saves on the fuel.'

Ken had a healthy appetite and had three helpings of Peggy's Yorkshire pudding and two plates of apple pie. He entertained us for a while with tales of his journeys, but Mac insisted that he also got a good night's sleep.

✻ ✻ ✻

There was something about Ken Pocket arriving that left me feeling uneasy and the more I tried to dismiss it, the more I was concerned. I tried to find some explanation for feeling like it and Mac listened before dispelling my anxieties, but I couldn't shake that feeling of something nagging me in the back of my mind.

'You don't suppose he'll wait until we're all asleep and then rob us, do you?' I whispered to Mac when we were in bed. I'd been sitting up reading but couldn't concentrate.

'More than likely! He'll creep into every chalet. He'll take Tom's watch, Peggy's wedding ring and probably young Tamsin's Whinny the Poo doll.' He was grinning. 'Why on earth do you think he's going to rob us? You heard him, he's a trader. He's probably more interested in our jars of jam and preserves than robbing us.'

Looking back over the evening's events, there had been nothing in Ken's behaviour which hinted at anything devious or concerning. I did like him, and yet I couldn't shake the uneasy feeling. Although he'd been friendly and very grateful for Mac's help, there was something about Ken Pocket's appearance that worried me. Mac dismissed my fears and began to stroke the nape of my neck. Then he drew me down to kiss me, and for a while Ken Pocket was forgotten.

I woke with a start. The dream had been so real and now I knew what it was that was worrying me. I dressed quickly. Mac was already gone. I hurried over to the house where William was serving the early breakfast of porridge and toast. Tom and Ken Pocket were sitting together at the table.

'He knows where we are!' I stammered. They all looked up at me as if I was a mad woman, so I repeated myself and still they just gaped. 'He walked to find us. He knows where we are. He could tell the black hats!' All eyes turned to our visitor who seemed stunned by my revelation.

'What is she talking about? Who are the black hats?' Ken looked about him for explanation.

It fell to Tom to explain our fears about the black hats, but the bargee was still mystified. 'That's not what's happening in Birmingham. Seems like a very different setup up here with whoever's in charge'

'We've already lost people that we know. The children's parents were taken and some of us have experienced their brutal collection techniques ourselves.' Mac told him.

Ken stood, clearly troubled by what we had told him. He shook his head. 'I was thinking of going to Sheffield. No reason to go, but thought because I was near, I might.' He looked around at everyone. 'But I won't. I'll head back south. Head down the Derwent and into the Midlands again. Wouldn't tell anyone about this place. You've all been kind to me. Wouldn't do that.'

'They could intercept his boat and force him to tell them!' Ashton's experience of the black hats was still raw in his memory.

'You can trust me!' Ken pleaded.

Tom sighed. 'It's not just you Ken. They're worried that you'll get caught.'

'They're animals.' Zoe suddenly added before rushing outside. Peggy and I both moved to follow her, but Peggy put her hand up to stop me.

'I'll go.' She said and hurried out.

'Or you could tell us you're not going there, and then for some reason you do. How would we know?' Mac voiced the suspicions of everyone. By now the kitchen was crowded. It was everyone's fear, and it was beginning to look like Ken Pocket might have to become our prisoner, if we couldn't risk him being caught.

Tom sighed. 'It's a bit of a problem, you see, Ken. I'd probably trust you but it's not up to me. I'm sure you're telling the truth about keeping away from the city, but we can't risk that. Besides we don't know how far those vans go. They could knab you in Cromford.'

William straightened up. 'Unless we take him back down the canal and out of harm's way. Once he gets to the Trent I think he'll be safe and so will we.' Ken was agreeing enthusiastically. 'So at least two of us should go with him.'

'On the barge?' Troy looked as if he was planning to volunteer.

'On the barge.' Tom also looked like he was considering the trip.

'Well,' William tilted his head. 'That's down to Mac and me.' He could see I was about to speak.

'I know you're handy with the crossbow Lexi, but I doubt if Ken's boat's set up for mixed company. Mac and me, we'll sleep on deck if we have to, besides I'd feel better knowing you're here looking after Peggy and the kids.' Tom was about to interject with his own opinion but William, who usually deferred to Tom, was emphatic. 'Tom, everybody needs you here, you know that, and Ash, sorry old pal, but things could get rough and you're too nice. Besides, you've already taken a bashing.'

'Shame Mark and Luke are over at the tree plantation with Giles!' Peggy glared at William then looked at me and shrugged. Not everyone had our huge stores of fuel, so Giles and Vince Carter had asked for volunteers to help cut and distribute the wood. At the time I'd thought about old Errol at Haddon. He would be grateful for their help.

I might have argued but I could see William's point and Ashton was already asking how they'd get back once they'd left Ken. Tom had a novel answer. In one of the sheds were four bicycles. We'd collected them on our early scavenger hunts through the local homes. William and Mac went off to get two bikes. I helped Peggy to pack food for them all.

'Just typical of him!' Peggy slammed the biscuit barrel down on the kitchen bench. 'Didn't think to ask me before he rushes off on some daft adventure.' She began to make up small parcels of sandwiches and biscuits. It was my job to wrap them and fit them into the haversacks.

I sympathised. 'I didn't want Mac to go either, but we'd all be worrying if we let Ken go alone. The thought of one of those vans coming up the driveway turns my stomach.' I began putting the bread rolls for later days into a bag, while she wrapped cooked meat in greaseproof paper. 'I'm sure those two will be safe.'

'I know,' she reluctantly agreed. 'I just can't bear to think of what I'd do if anything happened to him. Not now!' She looked down at her hand on her belly. 'Something else is turning my stomach.'

That stopped me in my tracks. I turned to her. 'He doesn't know?' Of course, I hadn't known until that moment, and I'm sure that if William had known, he would never have volunteered to go.

'No one knows, except you.' She sighed. 'And it's not the time to tell him, is it? And don't go telling Doc-Duck either because he might let it slip. I want to tell Will myself.'

Tom and Ashton took Ken to our food store-shed and helped him to carry boxes of preserves to the Land Rover. The trade goods were to show Ken our good faith and our willingness to become a regular stop on his route. He said he was just thankful that we had found a solution to the problem he had accidentally caused. Ash would drive them back to Ken's barge, then he would return.

'It won't be long,' Mac said as he kissed me goodbye. 'I'll bring you something back from the voyage!'

'Just bring yourself back. That's enough!' I kissed him back. They climbed into the Rover and we followed them down the driveway. Tom didn't close the gate until the car had disappeared.

10. CAPTURE

Keeping busy helped myself and Peggy from thinking too much about the men and how they were traveling on the barge. I worried about Peggy too. Supposing something did happen to William? Supposing something happened to Mac? Where would Peggy be without her husband and the only doctor for miles?

The weather was cool and dry, and we hoped it would stay that way for them. William was right, the boat was clean but basic. Mac would tell me later that the pair of them slept under a tarpaulin on deck. Toilet facilities were non-existent and washing involved a bowl and kettle water drawn from the river. The three of them chatted idly as the horse pulled them through silent Matlock, southwards. Hire boats were tethered along the riverbank, a sad reminder of busier, more prosperous days, their paint peeling, the wood rotting slowly away. The cafes and souvenir shops slid by, silent and shut, some ransacked, some boarded up, and not a soul to be seen. Thanks to the recent canal restorations, they manoeuvred the boat through Cromford easily, gliding along the canal that had once drawn prosperity to the town during the Industrial Revolution, thanks to Richard Arkwright and his water driven spinning frame. The newer sections enabled the barge to cross to the river where necessary. Cromford itself was deserted, nothing stirred except the trees on the bank side, as the river moved into the rural meadows again.

They travelled at a leisurely pace, with plenty of food for the three days journey. During that time the men had grown to know each other better and William soon ceased to believe that Ken would ever risk the safety of the farm by being caught by the black hats. Ken was exactly what he said he was, a trader, who enjoyed the river life and the contact he had with people. They made several stops along the way, trading some of Peggy's pickles for other goods. Occasionally Ken would reluctantly accept money, or simply a heartfelt thanks, when he knew the customer had nothing else to give. Those transactions showed Mac the kind of man Ken was. It also reminded both Mac and William how fortunate we were, at the farm, living in a cooperative community with land and hands enough to provide for all our needs. They agreed with Ken that they should leave the boat near Belper. All of them promising to see each other again with the kind of masculine bonhomie that comes from sharing a final evening, spent sampling some of the elderflower wine Ken was trading.

When William and Mac left the boat they cycled through the rain, stopping often under shelter. Sometimes the downpour got too heavy to see much further than the front wheels. Neither of them had ridden bikes for some time, and neither of them thought to remember the map and compass we had given them. Both items were continuing south on Ken's boat. So, with dull headaches due to dehydration, or an excess of elderflower wine, they had to rely on William's knowledge of the area, which turned out to be less than he realised. They camped that night in a field near Clay Cross. I have no description of how, or who managed to rig their tarpaulin, but under it, they remained moderately dry until dawn. That was when a thick morning fog rolled over the land and blanketed everything. It planted tear drops on the fence wire and seeped through clothing. The two of them set off, going westward, or so they thought. In fact, they were travelling north, along quiet back roads, and they didn't realise their mistake until they saw a sign for Dronfield, a town south of Sheffield and close to Chesterfield. A sign indicated that Dronfield was on their right, so they figured they should find the next reasonable road to their left and take it. It would lead them westwards and towards Derbyshire. It didn't. They should have taken a second left but didn't. They should have come back to us before sunset. They didn't.

Instead, as the sun went down, they were being jolted about in the back of a van, on their way to Sheffield. Their luck had run out when they reached the next junction after the Dronfield road sign. Turning a blind corner, obscured by a tall barn, they cycled into a group of black hats taking a break before driving their minuscule haul of vagrants back to the city. The mercenaries couldn't believe their luck. Two cyclists easily overpowered without the use of tasers.

Like all those before them Mac and William were questioned when they arrived in Sheffield. In the dark it was hard to tell where they were. Even the interior of the building gave them no clues and the dingy, yellow lighting wasn't comforting. They'd had time to agree their story. Their interrogator was a bored, grey haired man who really didn't care that after fleeing Sheffield during the height of the sickness, they'd been sleeping rough in the south of Derbyshire. He never reacted as they described living off the land and stealing from the dead. Then one day someone had told them that Sheffield was safe, that the city was getting itself organised again, and they would probably stand a better chance of getting work. Mac explained to their captors that rather than being indignant at their apprehension and detention, they assumed this was the beginning of something better for them. The questioning officer blinked and informed them of their error. It wasn't going to be pleasant at all. Separately they were asked what their previous employment had been, and if they had any special skills. At this point the man showed them a handwritten list of the kind of skills that were needed.

'You!' The man pointed at Mac, 'may be called upon later for your medical skills but at the moment you'll be on body collection and burial duties. You'll see the signs at the accommodation where you should assemble in the morning. Here are your food tokens. You don't eat a hot meal if you don't have one. You!' He turned to William. 'Will be on kitchen duties. Look for those signs.' He pointed to a picture of all the duty signs and then repeated the food token spiel. Then they were issued with an empty plastic bowl and mug, but no cutlery.

The official stood and addressed all four of the new arrivals. 'This is not a holiday camp. You will be expected to cooperate and conduct yourselves as directed by the officers in charge. You will be taken to your accommodation and given a room. The cleanliness of that room is your responsibility. Anyone not adhering to expected standards will find themselves in the Winter Gardens pavilion, so I advise you to do your best to comply. Bedding is changed on a strict two-week rotation. You will now be taken to your accommodation.' He nodded to the black hats who outnumbered the civilians, who were beginning to feel like the prisoners they were.

They were both given rooms on one of the upper floors of The Easy Hotel. The rooms had not been cleaned since the start of the pandemic, but the beds were comfortable and equipped with clean towels, if not clean sheets. William went to sleep wondering what Peggy would have said about all the dust. There were no keys, and the doors had no locks, they'd been hastily and clumsily removed.

At dawn, a loud klaxon horn woke the whole building. Mac was tempted to try the shower but the obvious sound of footsteps outside the door suggested that he had better join the exodus. He met William at the top of the stairwell. Below them, men were hurrying. When they arrived in the public rooms of the hotel, they realised why. A breakfast of porridge and bread was being served and both were glad they didn't have to rush back upstairs to get their bowls. Space was limited and the earlier arrivals with rooms on the lower floors of the hotel got seats. Everyone else sat where they could.

'Over here!' It was Nathaniel Boyle, the father of Harry and Tamsin, although it was hard to recognise him. His bearded face was so dirty and swollen and he'd lost a tooth. 'You've got about fifteen minutes to eat before the work teams are called. What duties have you been given?' They told him.

'Lucky for you William, you'll at least be inside and warm and you'll probably get more to eat than we will.' He patted Mac's shoulder. 'Stick with me. It's a bloody awful job and we don't have protective clothing. Clearing buildings is the worst. If you can stomach it, try and get on the cremation and burial detail. It's not quite as bad.' The successful owner of a small hardware empire shook his head. 'I can't tell you the horrific things I've seen and had to do. If it wasn't for my family I'd stick my head in a noose and have done with it.'

'Your children are with us at the farm.' Mac told him. He explained to Nathaniel what had happened, and the relieved father cried.

'Thank you. I don't know what to say. I wish I could let Diane know. Oh, you've made my day. Knowing they're safe and well. It makes all this just a little more bearable.' He was close to tears again, when the front doors of the hotel opened, and black hats began calling for specific work groups. William was one of the first to leave. Mac later recalled that he had the same look on his face as a young child might being taken into a noisy classroom for the first time.

As the body collection group climbed into their bus they were issued with rubber gloves and Nathaniel rolled his eyes. 'Clearance detail!'

The bus stopped beside the canal. Lorries had been parked close to the entrance of a hotel beside the canal and the men who knew the routine were already putting on their gloves. For the next two hours they worked in pairs, and Mac was grateful to have Nathaniel beside him. A black hat in partial protective clothing accompanied a group of six men. It was their task to open each room, so that the body collectors could go in and bring out any bodies. Their task was to carry them out of the building and stack them in the lorries. Two of the stronger men were appointed to arrange the bodies on the lorry. It was clear that the hotel had been quite full at the height of the epidemic. Lunch was a sandwich and a biscuit, washed down with water from a water tank. To his horror Mac noticed that some of the men didn't even remove their gloves before they ate. Mac used some of his drink to wash his hands and encouraged Nathaniel to do the same.

'You must be new!' a burly black hat said to him.

'He's a doctor!' Nathaniel said as if to excuse Mac's unexpected behaviour.

'Doctor or not, he's not getting anything else to drink. Don't waste your water, doctor!' The man pushed Mac over and the rest of his drink spilt over him. That entertained the other black hats.

That was how the whole day went. They were subjected to the humour of the guards and Mac's actions had obviously singled him out for special treatment. He might have gotten into more trouble if Nathaniel hadn't continued to remind him not to retaliate.

'I've seen them beat people for the slightest reason. You don't mess with them.' Nathaniel said as they were driven to the Moor

Market Hall where the main meal of the day was being cooked. It had been a shopping hall, now cleared of its booths and kiosks and with only the minimum of lighting working.

In the centre, a rudimentary kitchen had been organised. This installation fed the whole of the Sheffield population. They served one hot meal per day, prepared the porridge for breakfast and made the lunches. William had quickly impressed the other kitchen staff with his experience as a sous chef and was already trying to make improvements to a kitchen with no trained staff and limited supplies. Tables were reserved for families of which there were a few, including the Nevins. Black hat surveillance was more relaxed here and William was able to talk to the Nevins about their own abduction experience. William recounted the story to Mac and Nathaniel as they walked back to their own hotel.

The black hats had placed the Nevins' family in a double room in The Ibis Hotel, but Kayla had her own cot. While Mr Nevins worked as a dishwasher and general cleaner, his wife was in the laundry and their daughter was in the children's creche. William said the man in charge of the kitchens was an idiot but was at least smart enough to see that William knew what he was doing. He was moved from dishwashing to meal preparation.

'They've no idea really!' William shook his head. 'They're relying on scavenger raids into the market gardens and allotments. No wonder everybody's half starved.'

It was a mild night, but the ever-present black hats carrying guns made it feel oppressive. Some of the younger men and women had organised a fitness circuit around the city centre and provided they kept within the sight of their guards they were allowed to exercise. Some of the guards were also sauntering along with some of the younger women.

'Diane says those gorillas are always bothering the nurses. They've been told not to fraternise, but they ignore it.' Nathaniel said. Mac noticed that Nathaniel tried to avoid eye contact with the black hats, and he wondered how many times the poor man had been knocked about. 'Diane was working at the dispensary in the Town Hall, but they moved her. No one will tell me where she's gone.'

Just as they reached the end of Fargate, a young jogger passed them but instead of continuing past their hotel, the young man ducked down the narrow street between Telegraph House and the Lloyds building. As soon as they saw him, two black hats were in pursuit.

'People still try to escape.' Nathaniel kept walking, while his companions remained staring down the lane to where the sound of gun fire could be heard. 'Don't worry. They're using rubber bullets, but they still hurt. He'll get a bashing for that. Crazy really because the whole place is ringed with razor wire.'

'Have you been hit with a rubber bullet?' Mac turned his attention to Nathaniel.

He shrugged. 'Couple of times, when I first got here. Wouldn't do it now.' The two black hats could be seen coming back up the street dragging the young man by his upper arms. He was bleeding from the head. Mac instinctively rushed towards them and one of the black hats raised his weapon. Mac informed him he was a doctor.

'Don't care if you're the Prince of Wales! Step back!' The black hat snarled.

Nathaniel tugged at Mac's arm. 'Leave it alone Mac! You can't help him.'

On their third day, two guards came for Mac during the clearance detail. They wouldn't speak to him as he was escorted to the Town Hall and manhandled him up the staircase to the mayoral offices. He was left sitting on a wooden chair in a long, ornately decorated corridor. It seemed oddly surreal to him, all that opulence and him in filthy clothes, smelling of other men's piss and decomposing bodies.

Further down the corridor, a ginger haired man came out of a room, marched towards Mac, scowled at him, and entered another office nearby. Mac could hear raised voices but not what they said. A short time later the same man came out again, looked Mac up and down then stormed back to the door he had originally come from. He slammed the door behind him. Then there was quiet again.

Eventually, the nearest door opened and a thin, rather pallid man with rimless spectacles peered out. 'Doctor?' He looked down at the folder he was holding. 'Macintyre? Good! Come in, come in.' He gave Mac a quick look over. 'So sorry for the way you've been treated. Sugden and his men are a little heavy handed, but their job is extraordinarily difficult. Conditions will get better, I'm sure, but at the moment everything is so chaotic. I'm sure you can appreciate that. Do sit down.'

Mac couldn't determine if this man was a delusional fool, out of touch with reality, or some Machiavellian mastermind trying to trick Mac into expressing his own disgust with the whole place. Mac said nothing.

'My name is Ambrose Pelham, the current administrator here. It's been quite a terrible time, I can tell you. Riots, disruption, mass hysteria and unspeakable looting going on. Impossible for me to deal with alone. I mean, I was in Treasury, just a senior clerk, in the Treasury Department! I had very little chance of establishing any kind of order. The surviving councillors gave advice, but I had no idea how I was going to handle everything. I mean, it wasn't ever supposed to be me. I was only put on the list to make up the numbers. I was floundering, I can tell you. Our councillors engaged a private militia one of them knew. It's been efficient but incredibly heavy-handed. When Sugden and his team arrived things got a little better but they're only a small proportion of our protective force so I'm afraid most of the guards can be more aggressive than I'd like them to be. No doubt, when the proper peace-keeping force arrives they'll be replaced. My orders were to bring people into the city for their own safety and I've done that.' He put his hands together like a bank clerk announcing a loan approval. Ambrose Pelham was a delusional fool, and it had been his misfortune to be the only one left to accept the role of temporary administrator.

Mac wasn't sure if he was expected to comment on the administrator's remarks, so he said nothing. Pelham didn't notice. He was already looking at the folder in front of him.

'Doctors of any kind are in very short supply, and although it would have benefitted us all for you to remain here, in fact, that was my request last evening, when I first saw your file and contacted Birmingham, but...' he sighed, and returned his hands to the loan position. 'One of my colleagues is still arguing for you to remain. However, apparently Birmingham's need is greater than ours and I am to take you there, myself, tomorrow. I shall make arrangements for you to shower and have a clean bed and clothing tonight. Is there anything you'd like?'

'Yes,' Mac answered. He was angry, hungry and suddenly aware of his own importance. 'Your thugs apprehended a young man who was with me. I'd like him released. There's also a very capable businessman, who could be better employed, rather than clearing dead bodies from buildings. I'd like him and his wife to be set free too.'

Ambrose Pelham laughed. 'I'm afraid I can't do that.'

Mac folded his arms. 'Then I'm afraid I won't be going anywhere.'

Pelham's eyes narrowed. He could look quite threatening when he tried hard. 'You don't understand doctor, you have no choice in the matter.'

'Oh, I think I have every choice, administrator.' Mac kept his arms folded. 'You can take me to Birmingham, but when I get there, no one can make me cooperate. As you've already said, doctors are in short supply and I doubt Birmingham would understand your reluctance to release a few inconsequential men and a woman, in return for the cooperation of one of Britain's leading surgeons.'

Pelham pushed his spectacles back up his nose. 'I'm not sure Sugden or the councillors are going to like it.'

Mac stood and approached Pelham's desk. 'You're in charge aren't you, and this Sugden should be doing what you say. As for the councillors, aren't they answerable to Birmingham?' Pelham's cheeks paled. The man was clearly afraid of anyone who appeared to be more forceful than himself, and that appeared to include this Sugden person.

'Alright, let's make it easier for you.' Mac smiled at the cringing fool behind the desk. 'You can tell them that Birmingham has already agreed to the release of my friends. It's out of your hands. Blame me. I just want to see them on their way, safely, before I agree to any trip to the Midlands.'

Pelham's face brightened. 'I suppose I could do that couldn't I? Just tell them the order comes from Birmingham. Excellent! I'll do that.'

Mac hadn't finished. 'I want to see them safely out of your hands before we head south. Perhaps they could leave this afternoon?' Mac could tell the man was under a great deal of pressure, trying to keep his own little fiefdom under control while pleasing his superiors in Birmingham. Pelham was already bending under the weight of his many responsibilities.

Pelham was almost as good as his word. William and Nathaniel were released and given the bicycles that Mac and William had ridden before their capture, along with two pouches full of food. According to Pelham releasing Diane Boyle was a little more complicated. Apparently she'd volunteered to nurse some of the very old people at a facility out of the city. She was too valuable. Pelham assured Nathaniel Boyle that Diane would be sent home as soon as they could spare her. Mac had trouble convincing Nathaniel to leave without his wife but promised he would do all he could for her, once he got to Birmingham. Mac handed William a quickly composed letter for me and asked him to tell me how much he loved me. He waved them off and then followed Pelham to the Leopold Hotel, which had solar hot water and a bed waiting for him.

Only half believing their good luck, William and Nathaniel headed south out of the city. They stopped once to check the bikes and their food parcels to see if any tracking devices had been planted on them. They couldn't quite shake the idea that the authorities were eager to keep tabs on the population and to round up and control rogue elements. Just to be certain, William suggested that they didn't come directly to the farm but to head for Hathersage instead. They spent a night in the Millstone pub, overlooking the town of Hathersage, their bikes hidden in one of the bedrooms.

Still convinced that someone might be following them, the following day they rode along the Hope Valley turning left at Brough, and on to Bradwell. Nathaniel knew a vacant house there, where they could rest for a few days. Unable to dispel their anxiety, they decided to ditch the bikes at Tideswell and walk. From there they left the roads, crossing fields but sticking to woodland and thickets whenever they could. They staggered down the road to the farm in the late afternoon. Mark was manning the gate and he hardly recognised them, bearded, their clothes filthy and smelling of sweat.

As soon as he saw the two men Tom insisted that they have a shave and shower before they met everyone else. As luck would have it, Peggy and I were in the children's cabin, supervising their favourite and very boisterous game of pirates' gold. It was a gleaming William and a tidy Nathaniel who walked in as the game reached its climax. Instantly, the gold was forgotten as the two children screamed their father's name and rushed to his side. Peggy was only slightly slower to embrace William. Both of them in tears.

'Daddy!' Tamsin poked a finger at Nathaniel's mouth. 'The tooth fairy will give you a wish tonight!'

'The fairy already gave me my wish, both of you.' Nathaniel was close to tears as he held them tightly in his arms. The emotion in his face so raw I had to stare at the carpet to stop myself from crying.

I waited for a few moments before asking the inevitable question about Mac's whereabouts, simultaneously with Harry who asked where his mother was, and the girls asking about their own parents. The men looked unsure of how to begin. Nathaniel explained to Harry that his mother was safe but had to wait for Mac's help to bring her home. He also said he was certain he'd seen the girls' father, but he wasn't sure where he was now. He felt sure that Mac would help the Laughtons, when he could.

'And Mac?' Tom had put his arm around my shoulders.

'He's the one who got us released.' Nathaniel's eyes were apologising before he even explained. 'He agreed to go to Birmingham because they need him there. He made a bargain with the administrator. He'd go, if they set us free.' I felt as if a huge hole had just appeared in the floor and it was dragging me down into it. I wanted it to succeed. I couldn't stay in the room. All those reunions, it was too painful. I nodded my thanks to Nathaniel and started for the door, but William intercepted me.

'He told me to make sure you got this.' He handed me a grubby piece of paper. 'And he said I had to tell you he loves you, a lot.' I muttered my thanks and walked out, my pace increasing as I moved away from the children's chalet. I had to escape, run, because I couldn't bear the misery that was choking me. I couldn't swallow. Tears blinded me as I stumbled down from the stile that led to the mine. I ran and ran, until I could see the mouth of the mine. I wanted to hide. I didn't want their pity. The mine only served to remind me of the day Mac and I were here with the piglets and a donkey. I slithered down the wall and allowed my misery it's full fury.

By the time I returned to the house the mood of celebration had passed. It was agreed that until he felt able to return home, Nathaniel and the children would have a chalet at the farm. There were plenty left. Arthur had built two dozen, plus the school dormitory, and a very large dining hall that had never been fitted out. It had gone on Mark's list as something he wanted to complete. With Tamsin and Harry gone, the sisters and Zoe also moved to a cabin and Troy joined Mark and Luke in their bachelor pad. Ashton was relishing his own private space.

Tom was sitting at the table, alone, playing Patience when I walked in. He looked up but said nothing. I went to sit opposite him.

'So, Mac's gone to Birmingham?' He didn't look up but kept placing his cards.

'Apparently so, rescuing fathers into the bargain!' I'd said it without thinking, but luckily Tom didn't pick up on the plural.

'It was a very thoughtful act.' He considered the card in his hand and then chose a different one.

'Very!' I rested my elbow on the table and cupped my chin in my hand. There was silence for a while as he played, and I watched. It was a silence waiting to be filled but it wasn't uncomfortable.

At last he said, 'You must feel very proud of him.'

I sat up. 'I'm not proud, I'm furious with him. He left me behind.'

He stopped looking at the cards and looked at me. 'He'd want you safe. He'd want you here.'

'I'd be safe with him.'

'How could he be sure of that? He's no idea what's waiting for him in Birmingham.'

I looked down at the table. The polish had worn clean away from some places. 'We could have faced it together.'

Tom put down the cards and reached for my hand. 'Look at it this way. He's just doing what he told us he was planning to do in the first place, before he met us. He's gone to Birmingham. And if Ken was telling the truth, Birmingham is better organised, and it sounds to me, a lot more civilised than Sheffield. Who knows, once he's established, he'll probably send for you.' He pressed his lips tightly together. 'Then I'll be the one crying.'

I squeezed his hand. 'The plan was for Mac to return home Tom, and William has returned. I guess I just felt a bit miserable after seeing everyone else reunite.' I sat back in the chair. 'It is good to see Nathaniel with his children again though.'

He stood. 'Yes, it was nice. The children have their father and Peggy has her William.' I couldn't help wishing Mac had come back for Peggy's sake. No one except Mac knew how to deliver a baby. I'd had three of my own, but I wasn't taking notes and I was yowling like a banshee.

That evening, Mark, that surprising Thornton brother, had volunteered to make a curry and had ordered everyone out of the kitchen while he performed his miracle. It was indeed a marvel, complete with papadums, and it was consumed with relish. He had even made a small, less spiced version for the younger children. Peggy was complementary and said that he could repeat the performance any time he wished.

'I spent some time in India, after high school, doing voluntary service.' Mark explained. 'It got me interested in local food and curries are so good when you're living on your own, a batch can last a week.' He leaned towards Peggy, 'but I'd love to try some French recipes.'

As we were tucking into Peggy's ice cream William stood and made his announcement that he was going to be a father, slightly spoiling it by joking that the wedding was more urgent than ever. Peggy rolled her eyes but squeezed his hand tenderly.

Later when Peggy, William, Tom and I were all sitting by the fire, as we had often done when they first arrived, Peggy voiced her slight fear about giving birth. Since she'd known she was pregnant she'd been looking through Tom's library but the nearest volume that had any mention of births was a horse manual, and she was pretty sure that wasn't going to be of very much use.

'Well, Lexi's had three children so,' Tom smiled contentedly, 'she's going to be a good help.'

'Me?' I shook my head. 'Just a passenger, I'm afraid, Tom. You might as well ask Nathaniel. He's got two children and he was there at their births. He said so, tonight. He, at least, could see what was happening at that end. I was too busy at my end.'

Peggy leaned towards me and put her head on my shoulder. 'You will be there though, won't you? I'm not sure what a midwife actually does, but I think I'll need one?' She reminded us about how we'd gained enough knowledge to manage the farm and now we needed to get more knowledge about childbirth. 'Just in case,' she assured us, 'We need to have another library visit!'

Another visit to the library was agreed upon. Tom commented that in times past, it was the midwives who delivered the babies themselves. I pointed out that these days midwives were a specialised health professional and unless parents specifically asked for a trained birthing midwife, it was always a doctor who delivered children. There was less risk. I didn't want Peggy expecting me to deliver her baby. The mere thought of being responsible for that, well, I couldn't even imagine how I'd cope.

* * *

Meanwhile Mac was settling in rather comfortably, in the five-star apartment he'd been given in the city centre. When Pelham's car arrived in the city Mac was met by the Head of Medical Research, Rowland Grenville, and driven to the apartment in a luxury car. Definitely an improvement on his reception in Sheffield. Grenville did point out that this was just temporary as some more convenient accommodation, though not as palatial, would be provided on the University campus, where the research group was currently setting up laboratories. As for the administrator, he had been met by two uniformed soldiers, who briskly escorted him to a waiting vehicle that Mac couldn't see, but Pelham was looking nervous.

The following morning, Grenville gave Mac a tour of their facility. It was certainly impressive. The university was just south of the city and while most of it was now unoccupied, the medical team was given access to all areas and could call upon additional support from what remained of the two nearby hospitals. The greatest problem appeared to be staffing the facility, as most doctors, in fact most medical staff of any kind, had been on the front line during the battle against the virus. The vast majority of them had not survived. So far, the group had only managed to locate ten general practitioners, two of them well above retirement age but eager to help, three anaesthetists, two biomedical researchers, one highly respected tropical medicine specialist, an infectious disease physician, two clinical immunologists, three final year students, one surgeon, a dentist and a vet.

'We would be grateful for the partridge in a pear tree at this stage.' Grenville joked after reciting his list. 'I'm afraid apart from our two immunologists and the infectious disease specialist, we're like astronomers looking at the sky without a telescope. We're waiting for some unknown Galileo figure to burst onto the scene and lead the way. Contact with the outside world is sporadic, mainly because it's left to ham radio buffs. There was a group in the USA who managed to contact us through the internet but once that went down, we knew we were on our own.'

'So, the medics and researchers here are the only medical professionals to survive in Britain?' Mac was grateful for his first cup of coffee in a long time.

'Not necessarily,' Grenville stirred his drink, 'there could be other medical people out there. There is a chap in Scotland somewhere that we've been trying to locate, but no one's seen him in months, so it could be that he's dead. Trouble is, we can only access those people that gravitate to the cities, and the authorities there let us know who they've got. The major cities all had that directive from the powers that be, but there are a lot of rogue administrations and some appear to have totally ineffective leadership right now.'

'The thugs managing Sheffield are pretty terrifying.' Mac wasn't sure the people in Birmingham had any idea of how bad it was in that particular city.

'That's being taken care of.' Grenville gave the impression of a man that was always relaxed, no matter what the emergency. 'There should have been protocols in place, an anticipated chain of command. We apparently lost so many people up there that there was no one left to reboot government other than that buffoon you met.'

'Where is Pelham? I haven't seen him since we arrived. Is he staying at the hotel?'

Grenville's face broke into a sly smile. 'Pelham is not going to be returning north doctor. He was court-martialled last night and faced a firing squad this morning.' He saw the look of horror on Mac's face. Grenville burst into laughter. 'Seriously, that was a joke!'

Grenville took a drink. 'Pelham will have to face some form of inquiry at some time in the future when we can afford time for such luxuries. Right now, he's languishing in a one-star hotel with locks on the doors to keep him there.' He settled back into the modern black leather couch. 'Rest assured that the new administrator heading for Sheffield is a man who's well-equipped to deal with the situation. He's also got armed soldiers to help him. You'll probably get to meet him before he leaves.'

Mac had to wait for his new accommodation to be prepared. More pressing tasks took precedence, such as the moving of equipment to the laboratories. Mac was obliged to walk back to his palatial apartment near the Bull Ring. He went to explore the deserted city centre, trying to get the image of Ambrose Pelham standing before a firing squad out of his mind.

11. A LITTLE LEARNING IS A DANGEROUS THING

Spring is one of my favourite times, no matter where I am. That year it was threatening to come early, and by the end of February the forsythia bushes in the sheltered hollows were budding and the first spring bulbs were in flower. Beneath the silver birch copse between the farm and Merton Grange there were signs of the blanket of bluebells that would appear in April and everywhere, deciduous tree buds were swelling and bursting into lime green splendour. Even the sheep looked ready to drop their lambs, an event that Tom wasn't expecting until late March. He set about getting the barn ready and began to instruct Troy and Nathaniel, his hand-picked volunteers, on what would happen when lambing started

Peggy was nauseous almost every morning, so I undertook breakfast duty. The Laughton sisters helped and would often ask if they could add pancakes to the menu. This had been their speciality at home. It was a difficult time for the girls, seeing Nathaniel and his children constantly reminded them that their own parents were still missing. Nathaniel had wanted to tell us about his experiences in Sheffield, partly to reassure me that Mac had been a hero, and partly because talking about it seemed to make it easier for him. Of course, he only talked about it in the evenings, when the children had gone to their cabins.

After his time in Sheffield William was anxious that he and

Peggy should be married soon. They both agreed on a quiet, farm only affair, which eventually grew to include Giles and most of our local friends. Inga and Fay offered to do the catering, which was much appreciated as Peggy couldn't always face the kitchen, and no one seemed too enthusiastic about my cooking. None of the men even volunteered, except for Mark who was given a try-out, guest spot. Zoe, Troy and the children decorated the half-finished dining hall for the occasion. Dressed in our 'come-as-you-are' daily clothes, we watched them say their vows before Tom, who pronounced them married. Peggy threw her bunch of daffodils in the air and Gypsy, who had been learning to catch balls thrown by the children leapt into the air and caught it.

I hadn't left the farm for a while, so when Tom suggested that I accompany him to Bakewell to visit the Carters, and Inga and Fay, I was looking forward to the outing. We swapped vegetables with the Carters and gave eggs and milk to Inga and Fay. William had also butchered two pigs, so we packed some pork and bacon. Vince Carter was delighted to see us. Donna had been suffering from bronchitis for some time and although she was recovering, she was still in bed but was eager to hear all the news, so I popped upstairs to say hello but didn't stay long as she was easily tired.

Vince was happy for the company and we shared a cup of tea in the sunny weather. As he poured the strong brew he looked across the tiny round table to me. 'No news from the Midlands then Lexi?'

'No news is sometimes good news!' Tom put in, making us both look his way, to avoid any misunderstanding of what he meant, he added, 'I mean, he must be getting involved with the work he's doing and anyway, it would be hard for him to drop us a line, wouldn't it.'

'No news Vince. How about you? Seen any black hat vans recently?' I took one of his offered biscuits.

'Not so much. I reckon they think they've cleared the place. But I'll tell you what I did see this morning.' He leaned in towards us. 'Signs of a fire. I'd gone to the Millstone to take some of their cellar stock and spotted it from the hill. Must be somebody out near The Plough pub. Funny how everyone gravitates to a pub?' He chuckled.

Tom looked at me. 'Worth investigating?'

I wasn't very enthusiastic, but Tom seemed eager, so we went.

We found him easily, still stacking his fire with tree branches and old wooden crates. He looked up and smiled. The sign said it was a trout farm and there were certainly fishponds. He beckoned us to join him. He was a short man, probably younger than his looks, because his receding hairline was hurrying to evolve into a bald head and his short beard reminded me of an ageing biker. His smile was genuine and his eyes bright.

'Sorry, can't leave this fire. Been tidying around a bit, though heaven knows why. No idea when this place will be up and running again, but I'm trying to keep it neat, as best I can. Fished those branches out of the ponds. Can't have the little 'uns hurt themselves on stuff like that.' Just as he spoke, a fish broke the surface of the nearest pond. I saw the flash of scales in the sunlight.

'Is this your place?' Tom asked as he helped carry another branch to the fire.

'Nope! The manager was overseas when this all started. If I know him, he'll search heaven and earth to find a way back. If he's still alive.' He offered his hand to Tom. 'Keith Bradshaw. I used to help out sometimes. I live over at Pilsley. Right now, it's my village. Nobody else is left. I did a deal of grave digging for a while. Thankfully I can use a forklift. Before you, I haven't seen a soul since the last bloke in the village gave up the ghost. Where are you from?'

Tom told him the vague vicinity, Over Haddon way, then asked him about the black hats. Keith hadn't seen anything. He'd never been to any of the local towns or villages. He had no need. He'd lived alone for a long time and was pretty much self-sufficient being a vegetarian.

'Just me, now!' he said. 'Miss my girls, though. Some dickheads from the city killed them off early on in the piece. Haven't had the heart to replace them.'

To a casual listener his words might have sounded callous, but I'd heard someone else talk about 'their girls' like this before. 'You're a beekeeper?'

'Apiarist!' he corrected me with a grin. 'Among other things, yes! My paid job was working for the Chatsworth Estates but the job that I enjoyed most was looking after my bees. The Estate used to sell my honey at the shop there. It earned me a fair bit in the tourist season.'

'I expect you're quite happy to be on your own,' Tom said cautiously and of course I knew what he was thinking. None of us had been very successful with the bees, so we'd just left them to their own devises, still in Doctor Grint's garden.

'Don't have much choice.' Keith wiped his hands and opened a cool box beside the pond. Inside were two fine trout.

'Well...,' Tom began. He explained about the farm. Then he mentioned Doctor Grint's bees and Keith's face lit up, so Tom pressed on. 'Of course, if you like your own company sometimes, the doctor's house is empty. We could even provide you with some chickens of your own, and it goes without saying that you're welcome to dinner any time.'

Keith came to dinner and stayed, not in one of the chalets, but as Doctor Grint's new tenant. His trout went into Peggy's freezer and he promised her that he could get more, if we were not too greedy. It made Peggy smile. He seemed overjoyed when he found out that we had horses. He didn't have a car and had been walking everywhere. Borrowing a horse meant he could keep both sets of hives going and provide good honey for barter. All he had to do was wait for a swarm building in the Grint hives. We were all asked to keep a look out for a swarm, when a new young queen would be on the lookout for a new home. As he drank some of Giles' wine, he told us that he had known the good doctor through their shared bee keeping activities and he had liked him.

Tom gave him Doctor Grint's instructions. He laughed. 'Wasn't always easy to get along with, but once you started to talk bees, his eyes'd light up and he'd talk the hind leg off a donkey.' The following day, he'd already made the acquaintance of Grint's girls and both parties seemed to like each other.

Peggy's morning sickness began to fade, but in its place the anxiety about the coming birth began to grow. She tried hard not to show it in front of the others, but sometimes I would find her sitting quietly alone in the pantry. She excused it as pregnancy blues but when we began to talk, her fears came bubbling up to the surface. She made me promise to help her and begged me to find more information about midwifery. Tom and I decided to make an excursion to get books on the subject.

The Chesterfield library was almost unchanged since our last visit, except for more spiders and graffiti. We couldn't find any medical books, except for the St John's Ambulance first aid manual, which doesn't really cater for childbirth.

'We might have to go into Sheffield.' Tom said as we sat in the deserted square in Chesterfield.

'What about the black hats?'

He shrugged. 'We'll use the side streets and keep a careful look out.' It didn't seem like a great plan. 'They won't hear the Rover, those vans make too much noise.' I was about to offer him all kinds of reasons why we shouldn't head on to Sheffield, but Tom countered, 'We have to help Peggy. Where would you look for a book on midwifery? You're a teacher. Where would you go?'

I told him I'd probably try the medical department library at the university. He'd found a rather antiquated telephone directory from the library and began flicking through the pages.

'Royal Hallamshire Hospital!' he cried triumphantly. 'University of Sheffield Medical School.' He handed me the directory. I had no idea if the university still occupied the same buildings. The directory was probably out of date. Tom thought we should check it out anyway. 'Can you get us to that address via the back streets?'

'Let's look at the old street map in the car. What I wouldn't give for a proper navigation system sometimes!'

'Trouble is a guidance system might tell you the fastest route, but it wouldn't factor in a collection van.' Tom mused.

'True!' I stuffed the directory under my arm, and we headed for the Rover.

It wasn't so hard to get to the Hallamshire. At least it was on the southern side of the city, meaning there was no need to be close to the centre. We only had a couple of major roads to cross to get us to the hospital's location in Broomhill. Before we hit the city limits we did use the main roads, driving through Dronfield, until we reached Greenhill. Then we ducked through the deserted streets of Beauchief, around the edge of Millhouses Park, through the Knab Farm estate to avoid Carter Knowle Road, took a torturous weaving path around the cemetery and finally reached Broomhill. We crossed the main road and parked in the empty 'Staff Only' car park. Through our whole journey we had not seen a single living soul. William might be right, that the existing few survivors were all crammed into converted shopping malls in the city.

It hadn't occurred to us that the whole building might be locked. I was considering alternative ways into the building when Tom broke a window by smashing it with a wing mirror that he'd broken off a nearby car. If it was alarmed, the building didn't have an emergency backup. There had been no grid electricity for months. I climbed through the window and found a door that I could open to let him in.

The library was amazing, a palace for study, with rows of books on subjects I didn't even know existed. I would have loved to spend more time in there, but it would soon be dusk, and we had a long way to go home. Tom found a midwifery section and we came out with a dozen books, including 'Skills for Midwifery Practice', which the blurb assured me was invaluable for all students. We were so pleased with ourselves. I was thumbing through the list of chapters as Tom turned left instead of right, heading straight for the city. I yelled at him and he apologised, saying he'd turn around at the traffic island ahead. He did, putting us on the dual carriageway. At least we were now heading out of the city and I began to feel better.

'That was a close one!' he laughed nervously.

'Take the next right towards the cemetery.' I told him, as some strong headlights half blinded him, and he automatically slowed. There was a loud pop and suddenly the Rover became a wild thing, swerving and skipping. It was all Tom could do, to steer it towards a concrete barrier, which we slammed into, shaking every bone in our bodies. Before we could recover our senses, both front doors were opened, and angry voices were telling us to get out. We obeyed, too shaken up to argue. They hoisted us up into the back of the van and slammed the tail gate shut behind us.

'I'm so sorry. I'm sorry!' Tom was muttering over and over again. I saw a cut on his forehead and tried to dab it, while telling him that everything was okay.

Of course, it was very far from okay. We were in a black van and heading towards the city. I didn't even look at the other occupants of the van until we were unceremoniously yanked out, into what appeared to be a delivery bay. The halogen lights made me blink and I followed everyone to stand in a line. It wasn't a long line, five or six people, it's too hazy to remember. There was one other woman, a young one, with a bleeding lip. She glared at everyone, including me when I was told to stand next to her. The black hats told us that we'd be asked a few questions before we were given a bed for the night. The men were taken away first. I watched poor Tom still mouthing that he was sorry, still pale from his accident.

The angry girl and I were told to sit on the floor. We sat there for a long time. Another van arrived with a handful of people, including a middle-aged woman and a young one, perhaps in her twenties. When the men were taken away, the women came to join us. The middle-aged woman started to talk to the girl and was pushed by the guard who told her to, 'Shut it!'

'I was just going to ask…' The woman said.

He grabbed her arm. 'You'll learn pretty quick you don't just ask, anything.' He gave her another shove. 'Sit down with them.' He pointed to us. There might have been a time when I would have defended the woman, but I was still in shock and feeling colder by the minute. My sense of injustice was purely centred around me at that moment. My backside was getting numb from the cold and even the angry girl was fidgeting. It was pathetic to feel so relieved when another van arrived. The guard told us to stand. This was the last van. It contained an old man and an old woman. They held each other close but were manhandled apart, and the old fellow was dragged off yelling to his wife that he loved her.

'Right ladies! Time to go!' The black hat pushed us in front of him. 'To the left, through the door!'

The room was wonderfully warm after the chill of the delivery bay. There were no windows but another door on the opposite wall. In the centre was a small table, neatly organised with a pile of paper sheets and a plastic folder. A woman in black pants and shirt was scowling at us. 'We'll be taking you to your temporary accommodation in a moment.' She sat at the table. 'Line up in order of arrival.' We did and she began to ask the same questions as Mac and William had been asked.

'What did you teach?' She asked me when it was my turn. She looked tired. She'd probably been doing this all day.

'Subjects or age groups?' I asked.

'God love us!' Her eyes widened. 'Love, I just want to know if you taught basketwork to disabled blind people or just your common class of school kids.' She sighed.

I told her my experience. She wrote things on my sheet of paper, put it in the folder and asked me to sit on one of the chairs at the back of the room. I listened as she repeated the process for the other people. The young girl with the split lip was told she'd be on cleaning duties and after the usual information about food tokens she was sent to sit on the side chairs to the left of me. The twenty-something woman was told she'd be working in the laundry and was sent to sit with the girl. I don't know what the middle-aged woman did for a living, but she was told she'd be in the kitchens. She began to argue, at which point the woman in black stood and slammed her fist on the table.

'I don't make these rules, and you don't get to argue. We've no need for an accountant. I don't care how bloody good you were or how many corporate high-flyers you helped to fiddle their taxes. Right here, right now, we need you to be in the kitchens.'

'And if I object?' The woman stood her ground.

The woman in black pants came around the table. 'You don't want to know. Troublemakers are sent to the Winter Gardens. It's a mixed internment area. The inmates get fed once a day and have sleeping bags. They're guarded and they don't get to come out.' She faced the middle-aged woman. 'Annette, you don't want that. Take the kitchen duty. Here's your food tokens. Kitchen staff are encouraged to eat any surplus food if they wish. Bonus for you!'

Annette, chastened, nodded and went to the chairs on the right of me. The black-pants woman went back to her seat, composed herself and went through the same routine with the old lady, who smiled as she came to sit with me.

'And now, ladies, you all have a short trip to your accommodation. You'll be supplied with a bed and something to eat. The duties begin tomorrow, and I advise you to respond quickly and obediently to any instructions. This place relies on the cooperation of everyone.' She opened the other door on the opposite wall. It let in the cold of the night. She waved to the pair sitting on the left as a black hat came in. 'Prem!' she told the guard, who ushered them out. When someone came to collect Annette, he was told 'Easy!' to which Annette looked alarmed.

'The Easy Hotel, Annette! All kitchen staff stay there.' As Annette and her guard left the woman in the black pants beckoned to myself and the older woman next to me. We were the only two left. 'Sheila, meet Lexi!' We gave each other a brief nervous smile. 'You'll be staying in rather more comfortable accommodation. It's where I stay too.' She picked up the plastic folder with both our sheets inside. 'Follow me!' Outside, a small electric car was waiting.

'Please get into the car.' We did and she went to the driver's seat. 'Not long now! Then you'll be able to have a nice rest.' Sheila and I looked anxiously at each other.

The car stopped at the Surrey Street entrance of the Town Hall. We both recognised it. She told us to wait for her, then turned back. 'You're both sensible ladies but just in case either of you were planning an escape, the whole of the city is guarded at night and they do tend to shoot first and ask questions later. I shan't be long.' She locked us in the car.

We were silent for a moment. Sheila was looking out of the window. 'I don't fancy trying to climb out of the window anyway. Too old for that!' She turned to me. 'I hope my husband's all right.

He'll be worrying about me.'

'Perhaps you can find out where he is tomorrow.' I was worrying about Tom. What kind of job would they be giving him? 'I know someone who's been in here and he said there are times in the day when you can walk up and down Fargate and even meet and talk to each other.'

'How did your friend get out?' Sheila asked.

'It's a bit of a story, but they were really only released because a mutual friend asked for their release and he was important enough to make it happen. But if what I was told is true it means you will probably get a chance to try to find your husband.'

'I hope you're right.' She continued looking out of the window. It was very dark, and I couldn't see much other than the building. 'So you're a teacher? I'm an educational psychologist, well I was before I retired. Before that I worked as a forensic psychologist in the prison service.' She and I both saw a pair of black hats coming along the street, both carrying modern infantry rifles. 'Not very friendly, are they?' The men peered into the car and we both felt grateful that our driver returned at that moment.

'Sorry to keep you both waiting.' She parked the car on Leopold Street and took us into the hotel of the same name. I had never been inside any Sheffield hotels before, but the Leopold was certainly not the cheap budget kind. 'I'll take you to your rooms, and we can talk about your jobs a little.'

We were in adjacent rooms on the first floor and there were no locks on the doors. It all felt rather strange and lonely. She sat us both down on Sheila's bed, introducing herself as Clare. 'I don't want to be unkind to the other women you came in with. They'll be doing valuable work supporting our efforts to bring a little order to the chaos, but you two have some skills we desperately need.'

She was pacing. 'When people started dying in such large numbers, the very support systems we'd all relied upon just collapsed. People have been struggling to cope with not only their loss of friends and family but with what to do now.' She looked down at us. 'Imagine how that is for the children who witnessed the sickness, death and crime that accompanied the virus. The most traumatised and vulnerable members of our society have been through hell. We know we've already lost some of them to unspeakable violence and others are suffering from mental health problems. The body recovery teams have uncovered some horrendous things. Some children, who are now orphaned, are here, in the city, and sadly some are incarcerated for their own protection. That's where you come in Sheila. We'd like you to try and help them if you can.'

Sheila sat back on the bed. 'That's quite a challenge!'

'One that needs your expertise, I think. Up to now, those children have been locked in a secure environment for their own, and our, protection, but reading your CV, I'm hoping you'll at least try to help them.' She looked down at her hands. 'That's why I went to speak to one of the councillors working here, to ask his permission for you to get involved.' She gave a little smile. 'Brian is the most supportive member of our surviving council and I thought he might agree. That's why you're being treated like a VIP. Please give it a try. If it doesn't work out, you'll be transferred to laundry duty. I just think we need to help these kids.'

Sheila nodded acquiescence. 'Then we'll give it a chance. I assume from what you've been telling me that the children can be a bit physical? If that is the case I'm going to need someone with me, to help me.'

'Of course, I'll get on to that tomorrow.' Clare turned to me. 'Alexandra, we desperately need someone to spend time with our other orphans. Some of them can be a bit naughty and some are withdrawn, but I'm sure their behaviour is nothing different to what you will have come across in your normal teaching experience.' Most of my teaching life had actually been at elite schools, normally for above average students, where problems usually arose from the self-opinionated or over-anxious parents rather than their children. By the sounds of it, Clare wanted me to handle some deeply disturbed children.

'I assume you would like me to try to teach them something while spending time with them?' I replied rather lamely.

Clare's expressions changed. 'I would love that to be the case, but the education of children around here has not been a top priority. We don't have many children here at all. I think many of the local kids seem to have died from the virus. I don't know the numbers, but it would seem that certain parts of the population were hit worse than others. Of the few children here in the city most of them are with their families. They're all housed in the Ibis Hotel. When the parents have their duties, the children go to a childcare area. No one there has any qualifications. We asked for volunteers. Children that are twelve years or older work, just like the adults.'

'I had no idea!' Sheila gasped. 'We've gone back to Victorian times!'

'Earlier in history than that, I'm afraid.' Clare contended. 'The Victorians at least had a liveable city, employment of some sort and education.'

She stood, wished us a good night and left.

Sitting on the bed in my hotel room, looking at my comfortable surroundings, I reflected on everything I'd seen in this place of incarceration, and what William and Nathaniel had told us, and I decided that Sheila and I were lucky. I just hoped that poor Tom had been equally fortunate.

* * *

By the time Clare collected us the rest of the city had been working for at least an hour. We had been delivered our breakfast and even taken a shower because the hotel had solar heating. I got to meet my children first. Fifteen of them, all sitting on the floor trying to look interested in the few toys that had been given to them. They spent their days in a large conference room on the first floor of the Town Hall, now bare of everything except chairs and a few toys. Their only human contact were the corridor guards who were instructed to look in on them and to settle squabbles if necessary. They slept, Clare informed me, in a dormitory one floor above. The room was locked at night and two buckets were provided in case they needed the toilet. Three women supervised them in exchange for extra food tokens for their families. At the door, she handed me a class roll and left me to it. I looked down at the list. Most of the children had both their first and family names recorded but four of them only had their first names.

My first mistake was to expect them to behave as if they were in school. I rang the bell that someone had kindly left on the only standard sized chair in the room. A couple of them gave me a brief glance and then went on with what they were doing. I called them all to come and sit in front of me. A few actually came and sat down. The rest ignored the call.

I decided they probably needed time to get to know me. Unlike regular school where children arrive with certain expectations and unwritten rules of behaviour, transmitted to them by siblings and parents, these children were far removed from all that kind of normality. I decided to divide and conquer.

'Hello, what's your name?' I asked a little girl in a dirty pink dress rolling a ball to a second child who wore jeans, a striped T shirt and hair long enough to be of either sex.

'Isabelle.' She looked at me, reached up to my face, which I thought was rather sweet, grabbed my hair and pulled. The reaction she got was more than enough reward for her and made her companion roar with laughter. My hand shot to the side of my head where the hair had been tugged.

'Silly old cow!' The long haired something shouted at me.

'Are you going to cry?' Asked a thin girl with mousy curls. 'Don't cry in here. They don't like it.'

'Who doesn't like it?' I asked standing quickly so that Isabelle couldn't reach my hair a second time.

The thin girl pointed towards the wall.

'Do some people cry in here?' I asked her.

'Course they do!' the thin girl looked at me as if I was stupid. 'We've got no mums or dads. Nobody wants us. You'd cry if no one wanted you!' Her voice had gotten progressively louder and when she'd spoken, she turned her face to the wall.

I was stunned. Looking around the room, I noted how dirty the children looked, and some had sores of one kind or another. They really were the forgotten children. I suddenly felt overwhelmed. I couldn't do this. None of my years in a classroom had really prepared me for this. The child with long hair was looking intently up at my face and it suddenly occurred to me they were all watching my reaction. People cry in here and then someone shouts at them.

I patted the long-haired child on the head before putting my arm around Isabelle and telling her that I didn't like having my hair pulled. I asked her if she liked it. She shook her head.

'Good. Then let's not do it to each other shall we?' The little girl looked confused. 'There's such a lot of fun we can have in this room.' I said to them all.

'No there's not!' the thin girl said. 'There's nothing to do and we have to stay here every day.'

'Well let's see if we can have some fun anyway.' I crossed the room to where a basket contained a collection of plastic balls, like the ones you find covering the children's creche in certain furniture stores. I picked some of them up and threw them up in the air. Thinking they'd all come and join me I was astonished to see them all freeze in horror.

'What's wrong?' I asked. All the children looked at each other but said nothing.

'We're not allowed to play with the balls.' The thin girl finally replied, getting to her feet.

'Why not? They're in the room. Why can't you play with them?'

She pointed to the wall again. 'Because we left them in a mess, and someone slipped on them.' I looked at the two balls in my hands. 'So, you're telling me that these balls are dangerous balls and if they're left lying around someone could get hurt.

Well? You'll just have to get them back in the basket before I can empty it!' With glee, I began throwing the balls out into all parts of the room. For a few seconds the children stared uncertainly at this strange mad woman in their midst.

Then the thin girl yelled, 'I get it! It's a game!' and she rushed forward to pick up balls and put them back in the basket. She was joined pretty quickly by an overweight boy who began laughing as soon as he'd picked up the first ball. Eventually most of the children were involved, racing about trying to get the balls back before I could scatter them again. I was laughing and some of them were too. I had played this game before with children, and I knew that it naturally gains momentum. Pretty soon the children were screaming with laughter.

Suddenly, the door banged open. 'How many times? Keep it quiet in here!' The man boomed. He was livid as he looked around at the petrified children who'd been stopped in their tracks. Then he saw me. 'Crossbow woman!'

12. UNEXPECTED GIFTS

The children looked terrified and none of us moved for what seemed a long time. He was solidly built and to someone Isabelle's size, he must have seemed like a giant. I knew who he was, even though the last time we'd faced each other he had worn a black facemask. He lowered his voice and remained standing in the doorway. 'What the hell are you doing here?'

'I'm taking care of the children.' I sounded slightly defensive. Isabelle slowly crept to me and put her arms around my leg. 'What are you doing here?'

He pointed to the wall, his voice calmer now. 'My office.'

'Oh,' was all I could think of to say. A couple more of the other children drew closer to me. 'We were just playing a game.'

'Bloody loud one.' His eyes moved around the room. Fifteen pairs of eyes looked back at him with apprehension and fear. 'Try and keep the noise down.' He closed the door and left.

Still holding my leg Isabelle looked up. 'Bad man!' I put my arm around her.

'Let's try not to make him angry again today,' I said to them all and then smiled. 'But I think we might get noisy again tomorrow!' The older ones grinned at each other. 'Now can you all just come and sit around me so I can find out your names.' Most of them came. Two sat further away than the others and one boy remained where he had been the whole time, sitting in the corner of the room, his face turned to the window.

'I'm Lexi,' I began. 'I was a teacher.' I looked down at the list. Fifteen names. Fifteen lives that had been devastated by the chaos, loss and uncertainty caused by the virus. 'Now, I already know Isabelle. Thank you for telling me your name. Daniel! Which one of you is Daniel?' And so I uncovered the names of my little flock. Sasha was the overweight boy, Megan, the thin girl. Her brother in the striped T shirt and long hair was Ewan. Rowan was the boy looking out of the window. Megan told me no one knew his name and I'd found it only by identifying all the other children.

'He doesn't talk to anyone. He's sad.' Megan dismissed him and looked around the room. 'These toys are boring. No one wants to play with Barbie dolls. We've been here for weeks and there's nothing to do!'

'Well, I'll see what I can do about that.' I slowly peeled Isabelle off my knee and took a quick inventory of the room's toys. Plastic rubbish most of it with limited appeal, the kind of toys that arrived on Christmas morning and went in the bin sometime in the new year. Some even required batteries. The children went back to what they were doing before the game, all except Sasha who was still collecting the balls to put them away.

'All tidy now!' Sasha beamed triumphantly. He was perhaps nine years old, but I suspected his physical and mental capabilities placed him much younger. I thanked him and then asked Megan what usually happened at lunchtime. I had no watch and no idea of the time.

'They leave sandwiches and some water. They'll knock on the door.' She was making patterns in the small, long pile rug in the very centre of the room. 'The food's crap. We only eat it because we're hungry,' she didn't look up as she made her patterns.

'Does anyone come in and talk to you?' I was beginning to get a picture of their bleak situation.

'Only him, when we make noise.' She pointed to the wall without looking at me.

My only equipment was the pen and the list of children's names. I had no idea how I was going to entertain them throughout the rest of the day, so I could do little but watch their play. They appeared to have evolved their own routines. Most of the little ones played alone or with a partner. Isabelle, when not attached to my leg preferred Ewan. Two of the older four children, Daniel and Sasha, were never involved with anything for long but occasionally helped the little ones or organised a game. Megan drifted, sometimes interfering in the younger children's games, rarely amusing herself and doing everything in a bored, distracted way. Sasha also enjoyed interaction with the younger ones, and at one point he gave a ride to Noah on his back, crouching down onto his hands and knees. Rowan didn't interact with anyone. He stared out of the window.

Lunch arrived in a plastic crate. We all ate in silence. It was unnerving. In a standard school situation I was used to a lunchtime full of noise. The only one to leave any food was Rowan. He opened the bread roll, took out the filling, which he ate, and then gave the bread back to me. I had no idea if any of the children had allergies, but I suspected that children with allergies wouldn't have survived for so long. In the afternoon, the younger ones just lolled about on the floor, some falling asleep and the teacher in me was tempted to tell them a story, but I didn't. Instead, I went and sat close to Rowan who was still silently looking out of the window.

'What do you see Rowan?' I asked. He didn't reply. I sat there with him until the others began to resume their play. That's when I asked if anyone would like to hear a story. I sat on the floor because Ewan had occupied my chair and began to tell them the story of Theseus. I was still telling the tale, when the evening child minders arrived. It was five o'clock. The three women explained that for extra food credits, once they had finished work in the laundry, they would come, collect and supervise the children's evening meal and put them to bed. The children had a roster for showers twice each week. One, sometimes two, of the minders would remain the whole night. They took it in turns. They didn't know all of the children's names.

I followed them to the dining hall, the old Moor market. There were tables reserved for families but everyone else sat on the floor. I sat on the floor with the children until I noticed Sheila beckoning me. Her day had been somewhat more fraught than mine. She had been spending time getting to know her patients and had doubts about how well some of them would respond to therapy. 'The first thing I need to do is get their basic needs taken care of. They need more freedom. They are locked in the old police cells, all day, it's criminal.' Her face creased at her unintended pun. 'Seriously, I have to get someone in authority to do something for them.'

'Who exactly is in authority?' I asked her. 'There must be someone telling the black hats what to do.'

Sheila rested her chin on her cupped hand. 'Strikes me that the ones you call black hats, the so-called community surveillance force, or CSF, are pretty much a law unto themselves. According to Clare there are two distinct groups. The first group were brought in by the local councillors. Don't ask me who they are because no one seems to know. They were advisors to the first administrator, a man called Ambrose Pelham, who isn't around anymore.' While she was explaining, I noticed her eyes searching for someone.

She apologised. 'I'm looking for my husband, Norman. They said everyone comes here to eat but I haven't seen him, yet. Sorry, where was I?' She explained that the first black hats to arrive in Sheffield were mercenaries, hired by one of the local councillors, supposedly to maintain order. They were poorly trained, and they seemed to have adopted a culture of forceful coercion and violence when dealing with ordinary civilians. They remained under the direct control of the council. A second, small group of men arrived more recently, brought in by Pelham.

'The second group of men I've been told were better equipped and trained than the first group, and while the administrator was around they kept things under control. Since Pelham left, the councillors have allowed things to slide, and things are getting bad again. There's a thriving illegal drug market, mostly using food credits, a couple of illegal gambling haunts and prostitutes doing a roaring trade down by the canal. I heard from one of the guards at the police headquarters that his boss, a man called Sugden, had tried to stop the rackets but that the council were taking backhanders and even running some of the scams.' Sheila apologised and said she really needed to find her husband. I went back to the children, who were also preparing to leave the dining hall.

'Will you come again tomorrow?' Megan asked. I told her wild horses wouldn't keep me away. Then, like everyone else who could, I took my permitted walk down Fargate, taking in the work being done to board up buildings and keep the streets tidy. Joggers passed and families walked with their children. If you tried really hard you could almost imagine it was somewhere close to normal, but the ever-present men with guns wouldn't let you think that for long. I kept an eye out for Tom, walking up and down twice, but I never saw him.

* * *

The next day was a turning point. While I couldn't make any headway with Rowan, the other children were eagerly awaiting my arrival. I'd spent breakfast wondering how we could make use of the minimal equipment we had. I was almost tempted to walk down the corridor to where I thought the councillors might be and try to plead with them for more toys or equipment, but the two brutes with weapons standing in the corridor put me off that idea.

Instead, we used what toys we had to play new games. The box of second-hand toy cars became the focus of a game about colours with the younger children. The four plastic action figures, and the Barbies became part of a role play. The children acted out stories they knew for everyone. We had ball rolling games, and even some Maths using the cars. What wouldn't I have done for a set of paints and an easel?

When I heard the sound of metal filing cabinet draws moving, I put the basket of balls in the middle of the room. 'This time I'm going to let two other people be the throwers. Daniel and Ella go to the basket. Remember only one ball at a time in each hand. Go!'

The noise was appreciatively louder than yesterday and everyone except Rowan took part. It took no time at all for the door to bang open and our neighbour to appear. The children froze and looked at him. He pointed a finger at me. 'You're doing this on purpose?'

'Who us?' I straightened up. 'We're just having our morning tidy up. That's all.' He didn't move. 'Show him Ella and Daniel, go on!'

Although they looked a little doubtful, expecting him to yell at them again, the pair began to throw the balls and the rest of the children started their chasing and giggling again. Our visitor straightened up and put his hands on his hips. In a short time all the balls were back in the basket and they turned to face him. His expression had not changed. He gave the room a quick survey, 'Right!' he said and left.

'He didn't shout!' Daniel pointed out.

'No, he didn't.' I agreed.

In the afternoon it rained and most of the children slept, except for Rowan. We played more games and had story telling time, where I retold a second Greek myth. Shortly before the end of my day Clare popped her head around the door. She watched the children doing their tidy up. It was a new concept to some of the children, or perhaps something that they had forgotten they used to do at school. Their tidying wasn't perfect, but I let them decide how to organise it.

'So you think you can handle them?' She asked, sitting on the one chair.

'It would be a lot easier if we had more equipment, books, paints, more educational toys, and could I take them outside some-times?' I knew that Megan and Daniel would be listening. I hoped it would show them that I genuinely wanted to improve their lives, that I was on their side.

'Not my decision, but I'll ask. The equipment is a bit difficult.' She stood again. The night carers, the name I'd given the overnight child minders, were arriving. 'There's no way they'd let you leave, and they'd say they couldn't spare any CSF, the community surveillance force, to do it.' She patted my shoulder. 'I'll do what

I can. In the meantime,' she handed me a spiral bound note pad and a pen, 'I thought these might come in useful.'

I looked upon the pad and pen like precious tools. I could use it myself to make notes, but I could also hand it out as a reward for the students to use. I noticed that Megan had already noticed it in my hand before we left the room for the night.

I didn't see Sheila in the dining hall. I wondered if she had managed to find her husband Norman. I did notice Annette, the middle-aged female accountant that I had met the first night in captivity, serving the potatoes. I thanked her when she served me, but she didn't respond. I checked the hall when I arrived for any sign of Tom. I imagined him waving at me or calling to me across the busy room. I didn't see him, even when I walked through most of the dining room when I left.

My mind was bouncing between thoughts of Tom and how I could find out where he was and what equipment I would put on a list for the children, if I was asked for one. I decided to return to the makeshift classroom in the Town Hall to write my list. The men at the front door recognised me and one even nodded as I went up the grand staircase. The door beyond was closed, so I assumed our neighbour had gone wherever black hats went after work. It was still light, so I began my list. I was writing my tenth or eleventh item when I heard the filing cabinet again. It was only then that I wondered if I should have asked someone's permission to come back to the room.

There was a toilet at the far end of the corridor. Through the day I'd become quite familiar with it, escorting the children. Before I'd arrived they'd used similar buckets to the ones in their bedroom. It was beginning to get dark, and I had no idea if the building was locked up at night, so I decided that I'd make a trip to the bathroom and then leave.

Our bad-tempered neighbour's office door was open. He was standing at the window, his back to me, a shirt was on his desk, the standard black shirt they all wore. He was taking off the one he was wearing exposing his back to me. I was transfixed. His back was covered in an intricate and colourful tattoo. Koi fish in a swirling river, clouds above chrysanthemums, twinning dragons, demons and a black and white pagoda covered his skin. He must have sensed me because he turned quickly. The tattoo covered his chest too.

'Irezumi!' he said. 'Japanese traditional tattoo. Got it in Tokyo.'

I turned to hurry down the corridor.

'You're here late!' he said, drawing me back to the door. He reached for the new shirt.

'I was making a list of things I'd like to get that could help the children. It's no life for them being cooped up in that room every day. I'd like to get them outside if I could and get them more toys. There's a toy shop down the Moor. Do you think that I'd be allowed to raid it for things like Lego, puzzles, that kind of stuff?'

'Maybe.'

'I don't expect we'll get them but ...' I stopped myself blathering on. I didn't want him to detect how nervous I was. He held the shirt in his hand and moved towards me.

'Want to see the mark your crossbow left?' He pointed to his left upper arm. There was a deep circular dent and untidy stitch marks. It was an ugly disfigurement on an otherwise impressive physique. He was close to me now. 'Any idea how painful it is to have an arrowhead removed without anaesthetic?'

I took a step away. 'I had to do it. I thought you were going to shoot someone. You were holding a gun.'

'I'd just shot it into the air to get everyone's attention. I wasn't going to kill anybody.'

'I didn't know that!'

He stepped towards me. 'Well, now you do.'

'We were scared. You can't blame anyone for trying to defend themselves. Your thugs manhandled a young girl and beat someone up when he went to help someone else. We didn't want to be pushed into those vans and taken away.'

He spread his arms out. 'And yet here you are!'

'Not by choice.'

'No one comes here by choice.'

'You did.'

He came even closer. I could feel my heart pounding in my ears. 'You think?'

I stood my ground. 'So if it wasn't your choice, who sent you?'

He stopped, gave me a strange quizzical look and grinned, shaking his head. 'No one sent me. I came because that weak bastard Pelham asked me to come. That's all. It's what we do. We get paid to bring order.' He'd finished buttoning his shirt but glanced out of the window. 'Let me take you back to the Leopold. It's dark and women out there alone aren't safe.'

'You're saying I'd be safe with you?' I was still clutching my notebook.

'Absolutely.' He took me firmly by the arm. 'Believe me, there are some very scary people out on the streets after dark and not all of them are CSF.'

He kept a firm hold on me until we got out of the Town Hall. Then he let go of my arm. He was right, without streetlights the city did feel more threatening. He nodded to the black hat who guarded the entrance to the hotel. 'Looks like rain later.' He said to the man.

'Just my bloody luck.' The man replied.

He escorted me to my room. At first, I was surprised that he knew which room I was in, but then I realised that as he was effectively in charge, he could probably locate anyone. I felt quite vulnerable in that moment, knowing that I had no lock on the door.

'Thanks for that.' I faced him. 'You were right. It was a bit dark and scary out there. I'll try to finish in daylight in the future.' He just grunted acknowledgement and went further up the corridor, to the room on the end, and slipped inside. I was about to open my own door when Sheila opened hers.

'I heard a man's voice and I just wondered...'

'I had an escort from the Town Hall. How was your day?'

'Better' she told me, 'but I still haven't found Norman. Have you seen your friend Tom?'

I told her that I hadn't been able to find my friend either. 'Perhaps there are some people that don't eat at the same time as the rest of us. Can you find out what duty Norman's on?'

'Who should I ask? All I see at the police station are CSF men and they won't provide information about other people.'

I suggested she speak to Clare if she saw her at breakfast. She patted my arm and wished me goodnight. It wasn't all good. I found it hard to sleep. When I eventually did wake up I had a weird feeling that the door had just closed. The lighting in the rooms worked but it was minimal, just a small bedside light, which I switched on. There was no one there. I fell asleep soon after and didn't wake until the klaxon went.

❋ ❋ ❋

The first person I met in the dining hall was Marie, the woman who had been taking care of the boys at the Meadowhall Mall. She told me what they had seen from the back of the van, including my shot that hit the black hat. I told her that Troy was with us at the farm. She nodded with a relieved smile. He was the only one of her boys that she hadn't accounted for since her arrival. She worked in the kitchens, which as she said was nothing new to her. The supervisor was friendly, and she always had extra to eat.

I was issued with a new grey tracksuit at breakfast, so my own clothes could be laundered. Clothes washing was done on a weekly basis. Everyone had been given spare clothes, except for the children in my care, which was an oversight that I was determined to raise with Clare.

When I arrived in the classroom that morning I was met with quite a surprising scene. The children were all sitting on the floor, facing my chair. On the chair was a large whiteboard with whiteboard markers, a pile of jigsaws of different levels of difficulty, some puzzles, and several boxes of Lego.

'We were waiting for you to get here. We didn't touch them.' Megan stood stiffly as if she was speaking at an assembly.

I couldn't help smiling to myself when I realised I'd left the note pad in the room and the page with the list of equipment was gone. I put some of the items around the room, puzzles, two person games, Lego kits, a fit together ball bearing game, a card game, a skittle set and dominoes. I told them they could try what they wanted but to take turns if more than one person wanted to use it. I was relieved when there weren't any arguments about who played with what first. I put a box of Lego beside Rowan. I asked him if he liked Lego. He continued to look out of the window.

Later in the morning, Megan came and told me she could hear the man next door using his filing cabinet. The new gifts were carefully put on one side and the basket of balls came out. The screaming and giggles began. I think they had as much fun standing around the room pretending they were playing as they would actually playing the game.

On cue the door opened. He was leaning on the door jamb. He looked around at the children who yelled in unison, 'Thank you very much!' His face never changed from vaguely bemused. I had to laugh. Isabella, who had promised me that she would not pull or bite anything, was given the job of taking two balls to him.

'Do you want to throw them today?' She asked him, as if butter wouldn't melt in her dear little mouth. When he looked towards me I pointed to the basket. Without any expression he swaggered to the basket and squatted behind it. He observed his adversaries, his eyes moving slowly from left to right. They waited with great intensity for the battle to begin. Suddenly he began to throw the balls in all directions across the room, far and wide. I walked across the room and closed the door because the squeals were even louder than on the first day. Looking back on that moment I couldn't tell you who was having the most fun. When the children decided to cheat and stack a heap of balls in the front of Isabelle's dress, he picked the little giggling girl up and carried her to the far end of the room, away from the basket. Sooner or later, both sides began to flag, and he sat down and told them they'd won. There were loud cheers, and a few tired arms were thrown up in the air to signify the victory. They were all breathless.

He stood, straightened his clothes and walked to the door. 'Don't let it happen again!' he said as he closed the door. Some of the children laughed and then erupted into excited conversations. They liked the man. He must like children after all. Will he come and play again? What's his name? I told them I didn't know.

'It's on his door.' Daniel announced with a cheeky grin. 'I saw it yesterday when I went to the toilet. It said, Lord Mayor's Secretary.'

'That's a funny name,' Ewan laughed. I explained why I thought that wasn't his name, but until they were told otherwise they decided they'd call him Mr Secretary.

The day went well. Just before the night carers arrived Rowan stood up. Everyone else was tidying their things. He came over to me and handed me the unopened box of Lego.

'Would you like me to give you this one tomorrow?' I asked him. He shook his head. I was feeling disheartened but then he went to the pile and pointed at one of the advanced sets, a spaceship from a movie. 'You want to do that one?' He nodded. I felt so elated I could have opened a bottle of bubbly right there and then.

After they had all gone I knocked on the door marked 'Lord Mayor's Secretary'. His voice was sharp as he called me to come in. He was looking out of the window, like Rowan, only standing. 'Did you want something?'

I just stepped over the threshold. 'Only to thank you for getting the things for the children. You're now their hero.' He nodded but didn't turn to face me. 'Well, really, that was all.' I turned to go but stopped. 'I was thinking of coming back later to do some work on the whiteboard and make some notes. Can I get you anything from the dining hall?'

'Don't come back here tonight.' He instructed me turning around. 'There's a councillors' meeting. No one's allowed up here.' I nodded and turned back to the door. 'But, if you're not busy when I get back to the Leopold, they have a small bar, if you'd like to have a drink?'

❋ ❋ ❋

He knocked on my door and we went down to the bar together. It was a long narrow room with great arching windows that looked out into the courtyard. It would have been a beautiful sight if the courtyard lights had been working. There were only three other people there and no one serving at the bar. It was a self-service setup. We each served ourselves and went to sit in the corner by the window. The three black hats clustered around the bar paid us little attention, except to greet him.

'So you're a teacher?' He said resting his hands on either side of his whisky.

'Seems a long while ago, but yes. I'm Lexi, by the way.'

'People round here just call me Sugden.'

I nodded. I'd heard that name mentioned before, and not always in a positive light. 'Nice to meet you Mr Sugden. And what about you, what were you before all this started?'

'Soldier.' There was a short pause. 'Did you know the guy you thought I was going to kill?'

'Not then, but we got to know each other later.' I leaned back into my chair to study his face. 'Why was there so much violence? Why collect people anyway? The trucks even came into the countryside and took people who were quite happily surviving without any help from Sheffield.'

'Our orders were to bring everybody in. Sometimes it got ugly. I don't deny that some of our guys get too physical. I had to split my team up and put them in charge of a van each, but even then, some of those jokers like to give their fists some exercise.' He took a drink. 'So, were you out there with your family? Got children or a husband?'

'Yes. Three children and an ex-husband. You?'

'Not in my job. It's not easy for a woman to cope with somebody who comes and goes so often. Didn't want to give anyone that bother.' He regarded his glass. 'It's not always easy to leave the job behind.'

'Any other family?' I asked.

'Dead.' He looked up at me. I apologised.

'Don't apologise. I don't grieve. They died a long while ago. I've an aunt somewhere but we haven't seen each other for a long while.'

So we talked. I told him about my family. He asked about why I'd left Belgium. I just said I'd wanted to come home to see my brother. I never mentioned Anton or anything about how depressed I'd been when all my ideas of what my future would look like disappeared into thin air. I didn't want to sound needy. I wanted to sound independent, capable, so I was pleased by what he said next.

'You handle those kids well.' He smiled at his drink. 'You handled me pretty successfully too. Never thought I'd be playing ball games with kids on this job.'

I laughed. 'I really just thought your manly indifference needed a kick in the guts. Those kids were scared of you, and they needed to know you weren't the ugly ogre from next door that you pretended to be. You impressed them so much, don't be surprised if they come knocking at your door, hounding you to play with them, and then you'll be cursing me.'

'Too right!' He finished his drink. 'Want another?' Of course I did. He got them both. I noticed one of the men talking to him and looking over at me.

'So, what did he have to say?' I inquired once he had sat down again.

'He wanted to know if you were one of the canal alley girls. They're, umm…'

'What did you say?' I cut in.

'I said it was none of his business. He's not one of my team. They know me better than to ask.'

'Your team keeps your private life, private.' I nodded.

'I have no private life.' He drank. 'It keeps things simple. I'm here to do a job.'

'Surely there's someone in your life, someone you care about.' I felt suddenly sad for this incredibly handsome man who was saying he never allowed anyone into his life.

'Not so far.' He said it slowly and looked me in the eyes. His glare was steady and self-assured, set into an attractive but serious face. It sent goose bumps down my spine. I reached for my drink, and my face felt flushed. What exactly did he mean by those words, and was he suggesting something by that look he gave me? I focused on my drink and curled my toes inside my shoes to calm my rising nervousness.

He put his elbows on the table and cupped his right fist in his left hand. 'You and those goddam kids.' He shook his head while smiling. 'It took me ages to settle down to some work after that.'

It was the kids he was thinking about. I wrestled with my disappointment. Strange how one's expectations can be dashed even before you are fully aware of their existence. For a moment there I had felt the thrill of feeling special to him, and now it was gone. I reasoned with myself that at least the children had been able to work their magic on him.

I asked Sugden where he'd travelled and where he dreamed of going. We just talked and it was relaxing, pleasant. I got the impression he had few opportunities to talk as we were doing.

'I think you should come and visit us more often. We could be your daily entertainment.' I suggested. Our glasses were empty, and we stood. 'Frankly, I think you were the highlight of their day.'

'You were the highlight of mine.' He was smiling. It suited him.

We went up to the corridor together. He waited for me to open my door. I turned to him. 'I've really enjoyed tonight. Thank you.'

He leaned against the door. 'We should do this again sometime.'

'I'd like that.' I said, and the smile he gave me had me rushing inside my door before he could see me beaming like an idiot.

* * *

In the dining hall the following morning, Sheila stirred a dollop of jam into her porridge. 'So, not all the CSF are morons.' She gave me a quick smile. 'Sorry but the corridor walls in the Leopold are very thin.'

'Oh, we just went for a drink, but yes, not all CSF are morons. I like him.'

She spoke to her spoon. 'I heard the voice, but he didn't stay long.'

I put down my spoon. 'I'm sorry if we disturbed you.'

'Rubbish! You didn't.' She waved the spoon at me. 'I just hope he lives up to your expectations, whoever he is.'

We separated at the door and went to our respective charges. I considered mine were by far the more rewarding. We'd expected to hear 'Mr Secretary' sometime, but the corridor was quiet, so we got on with our new activities and hoped he might show up later. He didn't. On her way back from the toilet Isabella, the Braveheart, knocked on his door but no one answered. By the time the night carers arrived I was getting curious and made excuses for myself to stay longer in the room.

Eventually, I had to give up and head to the dining hall, where I was cornered by Clare. She told me that I had been given permission to take the children for a daily walk but if anything happened I would be held responsible. Looking back, I was never told what the consequences would be if something did happen.

People were beginning to have their evening walks and runs when I got back to the Town Hall. I promised myself that I would leave before it was dark and that I'd actually gone there to get my notebook. At first, I couldn't believe what I saw. The room had changed. There were several desks, two painting easels, a bookcase with a few books, clean butcher's paper, exercise books, pencils and coloured felt-tip pens. I checked the sign on the door. Most magical of all, in the centre of the room was a beautiful wooden rocking horse. I was speechless. It was a different colour, but it reminded me of the one Derek and I had bought for our children. When I'd composed myself, I went and knocked on Sugden's door. It was locked.

I was about to leave when I saw him coming up the corridor.

'You've seen the room then. I hope it looks more user friendly now.' He said pleasantly.

We admired the toys together. 'There's a shop up at the Botanic Gardens. I remembered seeing it. The stuff wasn't doing much good there, so I went back with one of the vans.' He explained.

'They're gorgeous, and the rocking horse is stunning. Every child should have a rocking horse like this, they're such beautiful toys.' I patted the horse's mane.

'Nice toys don't guarantee a happy childhood.' His hand was on the horse's head. There was a hint of sadness in his voice. 'Lucky for these kids, they have you to brighten their days.'

'I'm a poor substitute for their parents.' I didn't look at him. I was wishing I had my time again when my children were small. 'The time when a child is enthralled by a rocking horse is so fleeting you never appreciate it enough until it's gone.'

'Their parents would be grateful that they've at least got you.' He'd slid his hand down the mane and it rested above mine. We looked at each other for a moment.

Then he took his hand away and said, 'I need a drink, want to join me?'

We picked the same table, and he went to the bar. We were the only people there. He came back to the table grinning, with two glasses of the amber liquid. 'Glen Dronach is a fine malt, see what you think.' I had never been a whisky drinker, but I was willing to join him.

'It's quite nice.' I said after tasting it, I put the glass down.

'It's a lot more than nice!' he protested. 'This is one of Scotland's finest. Whoever the bartender was here he knew his whisky. This would have set you back a few pounds. It wouldn't be the usual whisky price.'

'You're a whisky connoisseur?' I tried a second sip.

'The Scots have the best, although the Irish stuff isn't bad. I've been offered some real horse-piss stuff in bars. This is like finding white truffles on the menu. This drop has a richer taste, aged in old wine casks from Spain.' He held up the glass and smiled at it.

'Do you drink a lot of whisky?' I was still trying hard to taste the value of this elixir.

'You thinking I'm an alcoholic?' He put his glass down but looked amused. 'I drink it for the taste, not to get drunk. Whisky was about the one thing my father taught me that we agreed on.'

'If the drink is so special, you should take the bottle with you. After all, most people, including me wouldn't know the difference.'

'Maybe, this is one thing I could teach you about.' He folded his arms and rested them on the table. He didn't know that was how Anton and I first met, at a wine tasting, and he had volunteered to teach me how to spot a good wine. My expression must have given something away. 'Or not.' He added. 'Not everyone likes to drink whisky anyway.'

'Oh, I'm willing to get lessons on whisky!' I brightened. 'All the more reason to hide the bottle. Hiding's not stealing. Let's find a place.' Like a pair of kids, we stooped around the bar area looking for a satisfactory hiding place and finally decided to hide the whisky behind a very large bottle of Drambuie.

'Who drinks Drambuie, after all!' I joked as we left the bar.

We laughed most of the way to my room. When we got to my door he told me that he had things still to do and left to head back to his office. The following morning, he was waiting at the playroom door, ready to see the children's reactions. It was worth it.

'It's like all my birthdays, all at once!' Daniel marvelled. Rowan never got to his corner. He walked slowly to the horse and stroked it as if it was real. Then he sat on it and began to ride. He didn't speak or smile but he was with us, among us, for the first time. He still looked out of the window.

'Worth it!' Sugden said quietly, smiled at me and left.

After lunch we had our first walk. They reminded me of the Von Trappe children when Maria first arrives at the house. Anyone seeing us would have believed I'd been drilling them for weeks. They didn't even need a pep talk. They all knew that this was a privilege that had not been granted to them before. They walked in pairs, more or less, and behaved impeccably. By mid-afternoon, I was thinking that this was going to be one of my best days for a very long time. I hadn't found Tom, but otherwise life was beginning to make sense again. When we met Sugden outside his office on our way back, he drew me to one side.

'Tonight, stay here. Don't go back to the hotel. When it gets dark, bring the children down to the playroom. Let them sleep there. You'll need to stay with them.'

'Why? What's happening? What's going...'

'I can't talk right now. Just do what I'm asking, for their sake.' He squeezed my arm gently. The tenderness of his gesture stuck with me. Whatever was going on, he had thought of us. I went early for dinner at the dining hall hoping to see Tom or Sheila, but I saw neither. As dusk fell, I sat beside the rocking horse and waited for whatever was about to happen.

13. SEPARATION AND REUNION

I decided that whatever was about to happen, the women caring for the children should be with their own families. It took a bit of persuading but when I told the children to get their sleeping bags and come downstairs to the playroom, the poor women knew they were beaten. One reminded me that I'd get punished for disobeying the rules and I told her I took full responsibility. The other two were already out of the door and hurrying back to their accommodation. After a short playtime the children settled down. Isabelle was hugging her Barbie telling her not to be afraid and Ewan twitched in his sleep. I wondered what the children were like in the night. Perhaps I saw them at their best during the day. When they were first brought to the city it's possible the early weeks consisted of tears and wet beds.

It was twilight when the whole building echoed to the vibrations of approaching helicopter engines. Megan rushed to the window and we followed just in time to see two helicopters landing, one outside in the Peace Gardens and another up the road at Barker's Pool. There must have been more of them because we could still hear the sound of others approaching.

'More guards.' Daniel groaned.

'No!' Megan sounded very certain. 'They're real soldiers I think. They're wearing a combat uniform.' We all looked at her in amazement. She was insistent. 'My grandad was a soldier, he had to wear one.'

'Let's all stay safe. Come away from the windows and let's sit together on the floor.' I had to physically urge Rowan away but at least he came with me. Then we heard shots being fired and Ella began sobbing. I pulled her to me and tucked her under my arm.

Daniel rushed to the window. 'They're everywhere!' A loud explosion brought him scurrying back to our huddle. We could hear the heavy footsteps of men running down the corridor and some of the children began to cry.

'They're not coming here. They're going outside.' I tried to keep them as quiet as I could, and I was grateful to Megan and Daniel for hugging the other younger ones. Someone was sitting with their back to mine. It was Rowan. I was facing the door, he was still facing the window, which was lit up with some sort of lighting, as well as with the flashes of weapons.

We heard men shouting below and in the street, but we had no idea who it was or what was going on. It was in that moment my mind was a blur. Why were the CSF and the military firing at each other? Had Sugden known this was going to happen and that was why he had instructed me to stay with the children? Only later did I find out that Megan had been right. The men arriving in the helicopters were members of the army. The black hats had taken hostages and the army had attacked their accommodation block. In the hotels, the soldiers had used loudspeakers to instruct everyone to remain where they were. In the Easy Hotel, which was mostly men, those instructions were only partially obeyed. After being the victims of the CSF, the men were eager to go out and help rout their oppressors. A group of them managed to overpower their own guards. Tom was among them.

The children counted four helicopters. Military personnel had been decimated, just like the general population. The combined forces were tiny compared to their pre-virus days and relied mainly on the fact they were up against inferior opposition. In Sheffield's case that was true. London had not been so easily subdued and neither would some other cities be in the future.

Some of the black hats were making a last stand in the Town Hall. Sugden must have suspected that, and it was why he'd asked me to stay. He knew that without me the children would have been terrified. We remained sitting on the floor until the firing subsided, at least in our local vicinity. We heard sporadic fighting long into the night. Some of those unfortunate to be used as human shields by the cowardly black hats had been injured and two were dead. Now, the black hat resistance firing appeared to be coming from the entrance of the building. I suppose it was obvious what the next step for the army would be. Cannisters of tear gas were fired into the lobby. We heard the men downstairs begin coughing, and yelling, so I risked going out to see what was happening. The gas was already working its way up the staircase. I called the children to me and told them to follow me. I know very little about tear gas, but even I know you have to get away from it or your eyes sting and you start coughing.

Together, we stacked the Lego boxes against the bottom of the door and then I used the old iron doorstop used to prop open the conference room door to break the window. I tried to break the window by just hitting it with the doorstop, with no impact. Sasha picked up the doorstop and lobbed it at the window. That worked. I hoped there was no one down below in the street. Then we clustered around the window, avoiding the fragments of glass. The gas began to seep through the gaps between the door and its surrounds and in between the Lego boxes. We covered our faces and eyes as best we could. It was a terrible time and all of us were frightened.

Eyes were stinging and Ewan began coughing. Then the door was pushed open and two soldiers with face masks came in. I told them who we were while the men very quickly picked the two smallest children and gave them their face masks. They led us down the grand staircase coughing and blinking, everyone holding hands. Then we were out into the fresh air. Some of the children were crying. Some still suffering from the tear gas. All of us were stunned by what was happening around us. There were noises all around us, the clamour of movement, shouting, weapons being discharged, which all melded into a cacophony of sound. A soldier instructed me to take the children into the Peace Gardens for safety.

It was a chaotic sight. The army clearly knew what they were doing, but we and the few other civilians who had been in the vicinity were ignored. There were injured people, mostly soldiers being attended to by a medic and another soldier. A group of black hats were being guarded. I searched their faces to see if Sugden was there, but he wasn't. There were bodies too, lying where they'd fallen. I guided the children past several. Other soldiers were still inside the Town Hall, probably searching for people. Occasionally we heard firing from inside. A few people were beginning to come out of hiding and like us were being told to stay in the Peace Gardens.

I took the children to the fountain, which wasn't working but there was water, and got them to wash their faces and hands. Some were still coughing so I helped them to take a drink. I would never have encouraged anyone to take a drink from a fountain, but then I'd never experienced tear gas before either. The night was very dark, beyond the temporary lights set up by the army. Sitting beside the fountain on the floodlit grass reminded me of attending a football match, years ago. The children were huddling together because the night was becoming cold, and I was growing more concerned about finding somewhere warm for them when a young soldier with a clip board came over to me.

'Excuse me ma'am,' he gave a slight bow. 'Are you the lady looking after the children in the Town Hall?' I told him that I was, and these were the children. He told me we were being given temporary accommodation for the night in the Novotel hotel on Arundel Gate. We had one king suite and four queen suites. When he asked if we had sleeping bags I told him they were back in the Town Hall. The young man was saying he'd try to find us something when a tall officer strode over.

'Are these all yours?' he asked, smiling at the children. The young soldier explained. 'That's a bother for tonight, isn't it, Briggson. Where else do we have that has bedding?'

'Well, sir, there are spare rooms at the Leopold,' Briggson looked a little unsure. He knew that the hotel had been earmarked for senior personnel during the Pelham administration and he'd assumed his own senior officials would stay there. Hence his reluctance to house the children there. 'There are rooms available now the CSF are gone, and it's heated.'

'Excellent. Can you fit them in?' Briggson nodded. The officer turned to me. 'Marvellous job you did of getting them out safely. I'm Commander Stanforth, by the way.' I told him my name. 'Carry on Briggson, get them there quickly, this dear little girl is shivering badly.' He looked down at Isabelle who gave him her sweetest smile.

So it was that one teacher, and fifteen children spent their first night of freedom in the rather luxurious comforts of the Leopold Hotel. When we got there Briggson, and I organised the rooms. The king size beds were going to help. Everyone shared a bed, and I had my original room, which I shared with Ella and Isabelle, but I felt I should call on Sheila and find out how she was and if she'd located Norman.

'I was lucky,' she told me. 'I was on my way back here when it all started, so I just hurried inside. I did think about going back to the police station, but I thought that was going to be a dangerous place. My young people would be safe locked up in their cells. I can't imagine the CSF gave in without a fight.' She looked at the back of her hands. 'I didn't try to find Norman, it was too dangerous in the night. Hopefully I might find him in the morning. How about you?' I told her.

'So further up the hotel it's wall to wall children!' She laughed. 'Bless 'em. I'll come with you all for breakfast tomorrow, wherever that might be happening, if it's happening.'

When I got back to my room, the two young girls had spread themselves across the bed. Sleeping, Isabelle, with her knotted curly brown hair and angelic face was the epitome of innocence. I took the blanket from the cupboard and tried to make myself comfortable in the chair.

* * *

Sheila and I escorted the children to breakfast after being told that food would be available in the usual place. The mood in the hall was subdued. Despite the events of the night before and obvious absence of the black hats, people were worried about what was going to happen now. Was there going to be a new administrator? What about the councillors? Most people were certain they were behind some of the scams going on, including the disappearance of food and essential items supplied by Birmingham. We caught snippets of the gossip as we ate our food. The battalion kitchen was already serving a variety of meals and that was a change for the better.

'Sasha! Sasha!' Suddenly a woman was yelling from the other side of the hall and people quickly moved aside to let her through. 'Sasha!' She threw her arms around him. She was almost the same size as him, small, round and beaming with delight. 'I thought you were dead, they told me you were dead. My baby! My boy!' She hugged and kissed him.

Sasha peered over the top of his mother's arms at me, grinning. 'My mum!'

His mother sat with us at the table. She kept one protective arm around her son while he ate, and kept looking down on his head, smiling to herself. Sasha kept stopping to tell his mother little details about his time in the playroom and how he'd had to break a window to let us breathe fresh air. His mother told us that she'd been taken to hospital with the virus and when she was released, there was no one at home. Her husband had died on his way home from a business trip. She searched the streets for days but couldn't find him and there was no one she could tell or even ask for their help. It was a tale that repeated itself later that day. The two cousins, Ali and Etiram, had lost all of their parents but their uncle and aunt were still alive. Later that day, Clare made it possible for the children to return to their families. Sadly, it wasn't the same for the rest of the children.

'Good morning ladies and children. How are you this morning?' The Commander greeted us. Tall, medium build, but with a slight stoop, perhaps the sign of his recent past behind a desk, he looked tired, having been up all the night organising accommodation and incarceration. He had a weathered face, one that had seen many warm climates, and his sparse greying beard mirrored his hair. Andrew Stanforth was a seasoned veteran but one who managed to maintain a cheerful disposition. I was later to find out that he loved being around children. He came and sat among us. He was on his fifth coffee, he told us. 'We'll take the injured back to Birmingham today. There's doctors there.'

'Her husband's a doctor and he's there!' Sheila told him.

'We're not married,' I said, 'but yes, my partner is a doctor and he's there.'

'Oh really? There aren't many of them.' When I told him Mac's name he smiled, 'I've met him. So you are the famous lady with the crossbow!' He smiled broadly. 'He's very proud of you, you know. Told everybody the story of how you saved him with your crossbow!'

Before he could say more, I heard a familiar voice was shouting, 'Lexi! Let me pass! Excuse me! Lexi! Lexi!'

'Tom!' The scruffy old tramp was covered in dirt and smelt like a pigsty, but it was Tom and I hugged him tightly.

He was in tears. 'I searched for you last night, but I couldn't find you. I was so worried. The guards at the Moor told me you'd be at the Town Hall and when I heard that I thought, my god, I hope she's safe.'

He turned and beckoned a man who had been slowly following him. 'Look,' Tom grinned. 'I found Matthew, the oldest Thornton. He's been here all the time.'

I didn't need Tom to tell me who he was. He had fairer hair and skin colour than his brothers, and he was a few years older I guessed. His features were broader, but there was certainly a family resemblance in the hooded eyes and the chiselled cheek bones. We shook hands before I introduced them both to Sheila and the children. Tom and Matthew left to collect their own breakfast. Tom's arrival prompted Sheila to ask Commander Stanforth if everyone was having breakfast in the same place. When she knew that, she finished her bacon sandwich quickly and hurried off to search for Norman. The Commander offered to escort us back to the Town Hall, as he was on his way there. He hoisted little Ella onto his shoulders and held Isabelle's hands. He didn't have to tell me he had his own children, who he hoped were well and happy on their grandparents' farm. As we were about to leave, the sound system that had blurted out the klaxon each morning announced that the new administrator was going to address everyone from the balcony in half an hour. The Commander took us all the way back to our room. He stood with me at the door watching the children retrieve their toys.

'It must have been quite horrendous for you all last night.' He folded his arms. 'These little ones have been through a lot.' I agreed. When Commander Stanforth was told it was time for the announcement we followed him into the Town Hall foyer. Before he left us, he bent down to Isabelle. 'Don't forget to wave to me when you see me on the balcony.' Then he ran back up the steps.

Tom and Matthew Thornton worked their way through the crowd to join me and the children. Tom immediately began talking to the children and asking their names. 'I was in the Town Hall looking after them.' I told him. Then I said, 'Remember the black hat I shot with my crossbow?' Tom nodded. 'He remembered me.'

Tom's eyes grew wide. 'Oh God! What did he do?'

'We sorted a few things out between us. Sugden managed to get the children toys and things to keep them entertained.' The memory was tinged with sadness. 'I wonder where he is now. He's possibly dead.'

'Sugden's not dead.' It was Matthew Thornton. 'I heard the soldiers talking about it. He's on the run with a few others. They haven't been located yet.'

I wasn't sure how I should have reacted, but I was glad he was free. I didn't say anything because at that moment the loudspeaker crackled into life. Above us, The Commander and another man were standing on the balcony, preparing to address the people. They waited until everyone in the gardens and along the road came together in front of the Town Hall.

It was a fairly short speech by the new administrator Graham Caxton, introducing himself and The Commander, and hoping that everyone had managed to get some sleep. Caxton was slightly shorter than Andrew Stanforth. Nevertheless he was a rather imposing figure, in a pale blue sweater which complimented his dark skin tones. He was fashionably bald, clean shaven and had the assured bearing of a man who was accustomed to leadership.

Caxton gave us all the bad news that until further notice, we would be asked to remain within the city cordons, for our own safety. People were allowed to exchange accommodation and generally move about freely, but until all of those involved in the Pelham administration of the past months were dealt with, the people were asked to remain within the city. Food and other necessities would be provided and there were plans being made to give everyone more freedom of movement. The speech seemed to satisfy most people. That is, except Tom and me. We wanted to get back to the farm.

When I took the children back upstairs to the playroom to collect some toys I saw Tom and Matthew Thornton speaking with The Commander in the foyer. The Commander looked up at me.

Whatever Tom had said The Commander nodded. Tom and Matthew left, and I was eager to devote the rest of my day to the children.

Later that afternoon, when the window in the playroom had been boarded up and the broken glass removed, we returned to the room. We had another visit from The Commander and this time he brought a friend, Graham Caxton. While Stanforth went straight to the Lego corner, The Administrator spoke to me. Close up, his face was pleasant, his skin smooth, and the creases at the corners of his dark brown eyes seemed to indicate a face that smiled readily, as he was doing now as he spoke. 'Andrew tells me you're the one who took on the day care of the orphaned children and also that you're a close friend of Professor Macintyre. We met briefly before I left Birmingham. He's a good man.' He looked around the room. 'So what was your psychology field?'

I laughed. 'I'm just a teacher. Clare, the woman who designated what duties new arrivals were given asked me to work with the children. I've no special qualifications to really help the children through their anxieties and loss.' I pointed to Rowan who was back sitting against the window. A different window because his old one had been hurriedly boarded up. 'I have no idea what that boy needs. All I can do is be kind to him.'

Caxton folded his arms. 'Sometimes that's enough. My first priority in Sheffield is to restore kindness and the best way to do that is restore people's confidence in a future for themselves and their families.' He leaned towards me. 'I don't have any qualifications for this job either! I asked to meet you Lexi, not because of what you've done here, which must have been a tough job, but I've been talking to Tom Gresham.' Caxton explained. 'Your friend was telling me about your farm.' He stooped to stop a ball and rolled it back to Noah. 'It sounds amazing, what you've accomplished.'

I didn't say anything at first. I was guarded about anything I said about the farm and feared that in his present excitable state, relieved at finally being free of the black hats, Tom might have given its location away. 'It's his farm really.'

Caxton faced me. 'Yes, that's true, but he says you were the driving force during its early development.' He smiled at Isabelle when she offered him her Barbie and then she asked him to put her jacket on which he obliged with. 'I'd like to see it for myself.'

'Why?' I knew my reply was guarded, but I didn't know this man. He could be as ruthless as the nameless Sheffield councillors. I realised that in his position he could do virtually anything he wanted and if he was in the mould of the previous administrator, he could torture us to reveal its whereabouts. 'I'm sorry but you can't.'

'Tom has already invited me.' He looked disappointed with my reaction. 'I understand if you're concerned about the farm's security. I'm willing to abide by your blindfold rules, all the way from the city, from the Town Hall, if it makes you happy.' He straightened up. 'Tom and I agreed to leave in two days' time, if that suits you?'

'And what about the children? I can't just leave them, abandon them like everyone else. I can't.'

He straightened up and smiled. 'All taken care of. There's a child psychologist driving up from Birmingham as we speak. She should be here by morning. She's very good. I know because she's my sister and she's been working with children suffering from trauma and loss for UNESCO. She has agreed to set up an orphanage here. There are very few children who have survived the virus, but some of them are orphans. I'll introduce you at breakfast and you can spend the next two days giving her a trial. I promise you if you're not happy, then I'll go to the farm with Tom, and you can stay with the children. Does that sound like a fair suggestion?'

'You managed to get that organised very quickly.' I was still suspicious.

'I spoke to her husband.' He nodded at Stanforth, who had reluctantly prised himself away from playing with the children in the Lego corner.

'My wife is a workaholic and a glutton for punishment.' Stanforth assured me. 'She's a very experienced psychologist. I mean she manages me well and she often says I'm a kid in big boy trousers!' He became serious. 'If she can find a suitable building, I can promise you these children will have a new beginning.'

* * *

That night sleep didn't come quickly. I was hoping I'd like Mrs Stanforth. I wanted to get back to the farm, but I'd made a commitment to the children and I wouldn't leave them unless I was satisfied. My dream had me wandering back to the farm, back to the past. I was trudging up the farm's driveway with a puppy and a broken pull-along. A tiger leaped across the flesh of a man, covered with a Japanese tattoo, the man who had been pierced with an arrow. The man who brought a rocking horse for a group of noisy children. Everything came back to him, and he would haunt the edges of my dreams for months to come.

14. CAXTON

There was no denying that Caxton had brought hope and enthusiasm back into the lives of the two hundred and sixty something survivors. He was not someone who locked himself away in an office. From the very beginning he was out and about, speaking to people, listening to their concerns and supporting those who needed help. On the second day of his time as administrator, civilian volunteers were assisting and preparing to take over the kitchen set up by the battalion. The army had cleared an even larger area in the Moor market hall, and thanks to their engineers had made use of the existing food preparation facilities. For the foreseeable future this was where the population would eat.

On my way to breakfast I caught up with Sheila. She was still on the lookout for Norman. Apparently, one of the other old men had said Norman was taken to the 'infirmary'. That confused Sheila, as the hospital of that name had been closed for years. The man didn't know anything else, so Sheila was on her way to ask Caxton where on earth her husband was being kept. Caxton was in discussion with The Commander and a woman who I assumed was his wife and Caxton's sister. She shared her brother's fine features and his posture. As soon as Caxton saw us approaching he broke off his conversation, perhaps because of the grim look of determination on Sheila's face. I noticed he hadn't shaved, and I wondered if he had been up all night too. He listened as Sheila explained, gently holding her hand and eventually putting a protective arm around her as she became too emotional to speak further.

'I'll get on to it right now Mrs Burrows. Get some breakfast with

Alexandra and I'll find you when I know more.' He joined Commander Stanforth and his wife, and all three of them went back up into the Town Hall. After breakfast, Sheila went to the police station and I found Mrs Stanforth waiting for me at the end of the first-floor corridor in the Town Hall.

Karen Stanforth was everything I'd hoped she would be for the children's sake. I introduced her to the children as a friend who was taking over because I had to visit the farm, and then she spent time moving around the room watching and interacting with them all. She finished the session by suggesting that she learnt the ball game. Karen really got into the spirit of things, rolling around on the floor as the game ended and insisting she was exhausted.

'You've done a great job!' she said as we walked back to the Leopold. 'The little fellow, Rowan, I noticed he isn't willing to be part of the group. What can you tell me about him?' The answer was very little. I'd hoped to uncover more but all Clare could find out was that he'd been found wandering the streets. The only way they knew his name was he had a single word name tag on the back of his shirt. It wasn't certain that Rowan was even his first name, it could be his family's name.

Before the evening meal, I found Tom and Matthew Thornton enjoying the weak sunlight in the Peace Gardens. They'd both volunteered for a clearance detail, trying to tidy up the gardens after the battle. In the daylight, I could see that a large part of the Winter Gardens had been spared but glass and debris were scattered everywhere. As we sat, watching people gradually head towards the Moor, I tried to make conversation with Matthew, explaining how his brothers were much appreciated. He was polite but guarded. He set off alone to get his meal. Tom and I followed behind him at a distance. I still needed to talk to Tom about Caxton coming to the farm. I reasoned with Tom that we didn't know the man enough to trust him with all the lives of our own farm family.

'It can't harm anything,' Tom argued cheerfully. 'He's agreed to a blindfold.' He added quickly, 'and so has Matthew.' His voice dropped slightly. 'I have to confess, Lexi, I like the man and he wants to see what non-farmers can do with just a little help. He's explained that he wants to implement self-sustainable farms for the city, and that sounded a sensible idea to me.'

Tom changed the subject, telling me that the oldest Thornton had started to explain why he wasn't with his brothers and his dying mother. Matthew had been on his way to find his family when he was intercepted by the black hats. He hadn't seen his family or Sheffield for a long time. Before I could ask him where he had been I heard someone calling my name.

'Alexandra, I'm so glad I found you. I've been looking for you everywhere.' It was Administrator Caxton. 'I was wondering if you'd come with me. I've found Sheila's husband.' Caxton began to move away, so I tapped Tom's shoulder and followed him. He was walking briskly with his hands behind his back. 'I hate this part of the job!' Caxton said under his breath and I wondered if he was actually talking to me until he stopped and faced me. 'It isn't good news.'

We found Sheila reading the proposals for courses that had been posted in the Town Hall entrance. When he spoke her name, she turned expectantly. Caxton reached for her hand, but it flew to her mouth. No one spoke, until Sheila asked if she could see Norman. She gripped my hand as we followed Caxton towards the Fargate shopping area. A mortuary had been set up in the chemists. The ground floor was half full of neatly arranged body bags. Caxton led us up the stairs to where several other body bags were set out on trestle tables.

'The medic says it appears to have been a heart attack, shortly after you arrived here. Would you like to see him?' Caxton waited for Sheila's nod, then led me away while she spent time alone with her husband. He bent towards me as he spoke. 'I worry about her now. She's on her own and although I know she's tenacious, they were married for over fifty years. She told me so. It's a long time to be together.'

I watched as she wiped her eyes and wrapped her arms as far around Norman's upper body as she could. She had made very few friends since her arrival. Like me, she had been detached from duty groups, focused on the young people in her care. Now, her group of disturbed and struggling young people were also being handed over to others and she was alone for the first time in half a century. I hesitated before I spoke my thoughts to Caxton. 'I could ask her to come to the farm. She might refuse and I can't make her, but she'd be safe there and she could come back here if she wanted, couldn't she?

He looked down at me. 'I was hoping you'd say that. Clare has offered to keep a friendly eye on her if she decides to remain here.'

I looked back at her, sobbing silently beside the body of the man she'd shared her life with. 'Sheila's alone now. She doesn't even know if her children are alive. They were both living overseas with their own families.'

Caxton took a deep breath. 'They were lucky to have each other for so long.' He was watching Sheila intently.

'Did you lose someone in the sickness?' I asked.

He turned back to me. 'Fortunately, I haven't had someone to lose for quite some time. I envy the longevity of their relationship.' He paused as if he was unsure what to say. 'At least you know your partner is safe in Birmingham.'

I didn't respond. Instead I moved towards Sheila, who had zipped up her husband's body bag and was coming back to us. I would ask her about her future plans later. Right now, her eyes were puffy from tears and she looked lost in a trance. She was struggling to keep in control.

'Thank you for finding Norman. Is it going to be possible for me to bury him?' Sheila asked quietly.

'Yes.' Caxton reassured her. 'I'll have Sorenson get back to you on that.'

Sheila thanked him again and then asked to be alone for a while. Caxton and I watched as Sheila headed back to the Leopold Hotel on her own.

'Poor woman!' Caxton watched her go. 'Would you mind checking in on her later? Perhaps, we could catch up this evening as well? I wanted to ask you more about the farm, and about what you thought of Karen.'

I agreed and told him that I liked his sister. Then I went in search of Clare, to let her know about Sheila. She'd been supportive of us both during our time with the children and I hoped she might at least keep an eye on her when I left.

'I'll certainly do that.' Clare was quick to say. She was pinning up some more information about the quick courses in the entrance hall. 'Ask Sheila if you like, but if she wants to stay here, I'll look after her. I'll be able to keep an eye on her because we're moving to the Leopold Hotel.' Clare's face brightened. 'I found my husband this morning and we'll be staying to get things organised here.'

She looked at the boards. 'Mr Caxton certainly hit the ground running! He'd had all these suggestions for useful courses, like the horticulture, handyman skills and crafts, basic cooking and first aid before he came. This morning I saw him talking with the facilitators, the people who are going to be teaching the courses. I've got a very good feeling about him.' She turned to face me. 'You're leaving us soon, but will you come back? Maybe even teach something?'

'I want to return, if only to visit the children but anyone missing from the farm makes more work for the others so I might not be able to return often.'

When I looked in on Sheila later in the day, she'd been crying but was making herself a strong cup of tea. 'I'm not sure what I want to do. It's a kind thought, and I'm very grateful but I don't know any of your friends. I know a few people here and I'm going to sign up for some of the courses. Keep myself busy.'

I was willing to accept her decision but couldn't resist introducing her to Tom. We'd arranged to meet after he and Matthew had finished their clean-up work in the Peace Gardens. As luck would have it, Marie was on her way to the Moor at the same time. She hugged Tom and I as if we were her long-lost family.

'Now I'm trying to find all my boys again. I plan to move us all into a hotel together, so I can keep an eye on the little perishers. Can't wait to get back to the mall.' She set about telling Sheila and Matthew about her last encounter with us. I could tell that Matthew Thornton was surprised when she mentioned the crossbow, but Tom reassured him that I was perfectly safe to be around.

'Sure' he said, 'I'm just interested to know why you're so good with such a fancy weapon.' One of his eyebrows raised a little.

I shrugged. 'My husband was a competitive archer. He introduced me to bows and arrows when we were engaged.' So, I'd put a lid on that topic. Tom, Sheila and Marie took over the conversation. I stood listening but spent the time wondering why Matthew seemed rather unfriendly, a man who kept to himself. Even now while watching him out of the corner of my eye I noticed he was someone who kept to the side of events. I had hoped that meeting Tom and hearing from Marie might have changed Sheila's mind, but it hadn't. She would stay within the city, make new friends and attend the courses that interested her.

❋ ❋ ❋

Caxton, Tom, Matthew and I, left Sheffield after breakfast, in Caxton's brand-new Range Rover. I'd opted to sit in front so that I wouldn't have to make an effort to talk to the taciturn Matthew. Our first stop was the roundabout where we'd been picked up by the black hats. Thankfully our Rover was still there, dinted but drivable once we changed the wheel, and so was its precious cargo of books. Tom and Thornton changed vehicles leaving me with Caxton. I couldn't wait to get back and show Peggy all the books we'd found on childbirth. Caxton's pristine Range Rover had similar controls to our old one, so when we changed drivers at Bakewell, and Caxton put on his blindfold, I enjoyed my first drive in a top of the range vehicle.

Giles was at the petrol station, helping Frank and the boys build a chicken coop. At the gate, our convoy was met with cheers as the children ran up the drive beside us on the way to the house. Arrivals were rare enough for them to be excited, particularly when there was more than one vehicle. Halfway up the drive I told Caxton that he could remove his blindfold. His first moments at the farm were seeing the farmhouse emerge from the trees and a group of excited people hugging us and all talking at once. The Thornton boys were overjoyed to see their brother and were full of questions.

'Let's get inside to make introductions and explanations, my old bones are aching, and my backside needs that fireplace. Any chance of a cuppa?' Tom drew the excitement indoors, where we could all sit, even if it was only on the threadbare rug. There were never enough chairs. Tom introduced Caxton and Matthew, for anyone who had been half asleep or oblivious to Luke shouting to everyone that it was his brother. I let Tom take the lead in explaining where we had been and what had happened before we left. Peggy had automatically moved to the kitchen, getting tea and coffee ready to celebrate. I followed her. As the kitchen was on the other side of the kitchen bench and still part of the large living and dining room, we could still listen to Tom's account. William came up to collect a tray of biscuits and milk. We had all forsaken sugar long ago, conserving it for baking.

William looked a little concerned. 'Tom says you met the black hat that you shot.'

I smiled and patted his arm. 'Yes, I did, and he even helped me get equipment for the children.'

Then I remembered Marie and told them about our meeting. Troy, who's ears could always pick up on any private conversations, looked up. 'She's well and when she can, she'll be going back to Meadowhall.' He smiled, but secretly I was hoping he wouldn't want to go back and join her. It was still going to be a difficult life for Marie and her boys.

Peggy excused me from kitchen duties so that I could show

Caxton the farm. Tom had already taken off with the Thornton boys, eager to see what they'd started at the mine entrance. I was interested in their construction work too but decided to keep Caxton away from our escape bunker. We visited the gardens, already planted for summer crops, the stables and the pens of our other animals. I pointed through the trees towards Doctor Grint's house and explained about the bees. Just as I was showing him the unfinished mess hall I saw Giles heading down the hill towards us.

'Darling woman, I was so worried. Where were you? What happened?' He threw his arms around me and kissed me on both cheeks. After further chastisement, I introduced Caxton. Giles was polite but uninterested in the administrator. Whatever was happening in Sheffield was of little significance to him. He told Caxton that as far as he was concerned, every survivor should be moved out of unhealthy urban environments and be forced to live a rural, healthy lifestyle.

'I totally agree!' Caxton surprised us both. 'But training and relocating three hundred people isn't going to be easy. Some will object and try to live as they did before. They'll find that impossible without supermarkets, public transport, power and every other modern convenience. Money has no value, at least for the time being. Trading in goods and services must replace currency. If people don't make that adjustment soon the concern is they'll struggle and possibly resort to crime. There are also those we need to take care of, such as the very old, the disabled and the very young. I have to make sure that we create a system that can include everyone. Eventually, when the system is up and running with elected representatives to drive it forward, in a direction that suits the people it serves, I will move on. My job, if you like, is to make my job obsolete.'

He explained that back in Birmingham, when Caxton knew he was coming to Sheffield, he'd had a chance conversation with

Mac, who had described the farm. Four other regional cities had suffered the same fate as Sheffield. The sickness had been sudden and virulent, destroying all normality in a few weeks. Hospitals, transport, schools, emergency services, the police and fire services were decimated and unable to function. Medical staff dropped dead attending the sick. Police stations were left unattended, and in some cases, prisoners died in their cells. Public transport ran short of drivers after three days. As he talked, my thoughts went back to the days I spent searching for my brother, the streets littered with debris, dead bodies and even a burnt-out school bus.

'Whatever Sheffield was like at that time, London and its satellite towns were worse.' He rubbed his hand across his forehead, as if trying to erase the memory. 'When I left Birmingham, half the city was burning, and no one checked the bodies anymore. People died on the street without help, and their bodies robbed, even of clothes. Crime was rife. So was opportunism. I saw one woman exchange her wedding ring for a bag of carrots. It was bad.' We started to walk back to the house. Caxton had agreed to stay the night, so that he could talk to us in more detail about how we had organised ourselves.

'Isn't there some sort of pandemic response plan?' Giles dug his fists into his pockets.

'There was and it was totally ineffectual!' Caxton stood and looked around, taking a deep breath. 'Past outbreaks have been more like a wave, starting in one location and spreading out, giving countries time to put plans in place and at the same time collect data to share. This time, as far as I know, it happened everywhere at the same time. Three days after the first cases were reported in over forty-five countries, it had already killed more people than any other pandemic event at a similar stage. After a week, it passed the American death toll of 2020. There was no time to gather data on the likely incubation period, early symptoms, or which sections of the population were the most vulnerable. It seemed like it hit everyone. Some people got a mild attack. I was lucky enough to be over it in a few days, but there was no one collecting data at the time. The best that the few surviving statisticians in Birmingham could extrapolate from data gathered later in the Birmingham area was a mortality rate of larger than seventy percent! God only knows what the figures are now. We will be collecting data on the Sheffield population while we are here.'

We'd reached the house and Giles took the first step up to the door then turned around. 'Do we know what happened in other countries? Are we still in touch with anyone outside our island?'

'Since those early weeks there's been very little communication.' Caxton sighed. 'About a month or so after it began, a group of French people appeared at the entrance of the Channel tunnel. They seemed healthy and were taken to London. On the way there, they began to show signs of illness, but not the virus. They had typhoid. They all died. The tunnel entrance was sealed. Since then, there's been no contact with anyone. Amateur radio buffs have been in touch with Ireland, the USA and Canada but not for long. It would seem radio operators have become as rare as doctors.'

✻ ✻ ✻

'How long will Mac be in Birmingham?' Peggy asked Caxton after our meal. She'd been impressed by our haul of medical books but was still hoping Mac would be back to deliver her baby. His reply was vague. He didn't really know. It wasn't his department. He knew the medical group were working hard but he had no idea of any timeframe.

When most of the others were watching a tense chess match between Nat and Luke, Caxton drew me aside with Tom. 'I hate to ask,' he kept his voice low, 'but is there any chance of you both returning with me. I'd really appreciate any help you could give in setting up farms for Sheffield. If you are there in person to explain what you did and to answer questions it might help to convince others that they could do the same. Many of the people we are dealing with have had no experience of rural life before and early indications are that they are a little hesitant about giving it a go. Time is not on our side. We need to start these farm projects soon.'

Caxton went on. 'I'm asking now because I know you can't agree just like that and I know you'll want to talk it over with everyone here. I want to be up front about this. We need your help. So far, army recognisance teams have been scouting likely sites, mostly municipal parks and gardens, but you have experience of community farming, as opposed to family farming. You have a better idea of what is required to maintain a small community of people, all formerly strangers to one another, and make it sustainable. You see it isn't just the farming practices we need to worry about, we have to try to support people in building a resilient community.'

When the time came for the others at the farm to share their views with Caxton it was clear there was some anxiety about taking the time away from our farm roles. We had all navigated a steep learning curve with the farm and were proud of our new skills, and the teamwork that we now had in place. We had found a system and ways of doing things that had improved our efficiency at our jobs and made things flow smoothly. We had brought order to chaos and were apprehensive about how new demands on our time might disrupt our daily patterns. We also knew there was a lot more work to do around the farm.

'We've got enough on with this place,' William said, 'besides I can't leave Peggy again.'

'We've got half-finished jobs here,' Mark chimed in, but then qualified it with, 'but once that's done we could give a hand, couldn't we?'

'In the meantime,' Tom cut across them all, 'Lexi and I should go back. I made a bit of a name for myself with the older chaps in the Moor and Lexi, well, she's well known too.' Tom turned to Caxton. 'I might also suggest that any people you pick to live in these new farms should, perhaps, come here for a couple of days and see how it works.' He saw Ashton's concerned expression. 'With all the usual security measures in place to protect us of course.'

Caxton returned to the city with Tom and me. This time I drove the old Land Rover while Tom went with The Administrator. Luke had promised to work on the Range Rover while we were gone.

* * *

'As you can see,' Commander Stanforth, now in shirt sleeves and no tie, was justifiably proud. 'While you were away visiting friends in the country, we were getting to work here.' He pointed to the portable display panels arranged around the long gallery in the Town Hall. 'We've drawn up a list of trades and professions important for re-establishing some form of civil society and stabilisation of the situation, and we have already got a list of qualified people signed up. We also had separate sign-up sheets for volunteers eager to learn those roles.' He shrugged. 'Long term plans of course.'

He escorted us to the next set of boards. 'Possible and probable farm sites. We've got at least four that we could get started on pretty soon, depending on what you think.' At the next boards, he sighed before he explained. 'This board has only been up for two days and it's full of volunteers to get involved in more urban renewal projects. It would seem that there's a wealth of amateur carpenters, weavers, dressmakers and cooks just itching to get started with some help from us. One of the new projects, 'The Twilight Weavers', have already found premises and just need the equipment and raw materials to get started. We think we've got enough teachers, mostly retired, to set up a small primary school, but secondary teachers are a bit hard to come by. I take it you're not available?' He looked hopeful, then resigned, as I shook my head.

'Four retired nurses have set up a temporary clinic and dispensary, with the medic's help, and we've got a team of researchers finding accommodation for housing and commercial endeavours. Now that people are beginning to look to the future again, and understanding they will receive help, it seems that Sheffield folk were only too happy to grasp opportunities.'

'Except perhaps where farming is concerned.' Caxton noted. 'Any chance you've drawn up a list of volunteers for the farms?'

Stanforth looked concerned. 'Oh, er?' He moved to the next set of boards. 'You mean something like this?' We laughed.

They had decided on groups of twelve to begin with. If families were involved, one parent would be initially involved while the other parent remained in the city with the children. It shocked me to see how few families had survived intact. We agreed to go out and view the first four sites that afternoon.

The army had done well. Each of the sites had access to water and plenty of room to keep some animals and grow their own food. If there was no accommodation on the land, there was always plenty on the doorstep. The army, together with volunteers, were already clearing buildings of the dead and filling mass graves. Tom was particularly impressed with the Crookesmoor Parks plan. The Ponderosa events ground was large enough to grow grain crops, enough for bartering purposes. That evening we celebrated with Caxton, his sister and The Commander in the Leopold Hotel bar, now open to all. The following day, we were going to meet the first three new farmers who would be returning with us.

* * *

It took a further day before the final farm lists were posted and meetings with each group were arranged. Tom and I attended most of them and I was glad to see Clare there too. She talked enthusiastically about her new coordinator's role. She had taken a leaf from our book and raided the Central and University libraries for appropriate books. What had started out as part of the new farms plan, soon became a wider search for reference books to help blossoming infant industries. She and her husband Leonard were setting up home in a rather fine Victorian house near the university. Late in the afternoon, Tom and I were guests at a chilly outdoor barbecue where the new farmers got to know each other.

After breakfast the following day we went to collect our guests. Caxton came to make the introductions and then left, after telling me that he was going to ask Birmingham to send Mac back, if not for good, then at least for Peggy and her baby. I was grateful for that.

As we drove south, we tried to get to know our new recruits. They were hesitant, wary of us, I suspect. Who wouldn't be after what had happened to them in the city? The young woman, Heather, who had short frizzy hair, large expressive black eyes and blue-black skin, began to talk first. She was asking questions about what livestock we had, and would someone be able to tell her about chickens? Her eyes were bright and enthusiastic, and she struck me as someone with determination and a clarity of thinking. I hoped we could answer all of her questions and that she would enjoy her stay. Roger, the older man was about my age, with thick grey hair and rimless glasses. He was taking more notice of where we were going than the others. He said little but looked out of the window. I was glad we had warned them about wearing the blindfolds from Bakewell onwards. Lastly, Eric, who was late twenty something or perhaps early thirty something else, didn't speak for a long while, but when he did, we couldn't stop him talking. He felt the need to tell us about his life before the sickness. He'd been an apprentice welder, something we all thought would be useful in his new life, and a guitarist in a rock band. He'd travelled overseas a lot and even reached the Everest base camp. He was good at taking the rough with the smooth, he said, and couldn't wait for this new challenge to begin. By the time we reached Bakewell, we'd all got a good idea about Eric.

These three people were the first visitor group, but three more groups came later. They all followed similar patterns, and each lasted a week. We'd share our experiences with them, show them around the farm, and try to help them decide what areas of the farm most interested them. Some came with a clear idea of what they expected and what they saw as their role. Sometimes they left with their ideas strengthened. Sometimes they needed a major rethink. Horse enthusiasts whose experience had been limited to trail riding suddenly found caring for horses a whole new, and not always enjoyable, experience. Eager souls ready to pat and play with baby piglets found the boar tusk extraction too much to take. The girl who just loved baby lambs didn't find the older sheep quite so cuddly, but she at least found her true calling in the kitchen with Peggy. By the time she left, we knew for certain that the crews moving to the Hillsborough Park farm would be well fed.

It wasn't always left to me and Tom to ferry our students. Our second run was made by Nathaniel and his children. Caxton had found their mother and they went to collect her. She had been sick during her time in Sheffield and before they felt safe to go back to their Cheshire Cheese home, they decided to spend longer with us. No one seemed to know what had happened to the Laughtons. Caxton suspected they were dead. A mass grave was found in a traffic island near the canal. Interrogations of the surviving black hats brought to light that some of their prisoners had tried to escape and were shot before they even reached the city. The truth behind that was hard to verify. The administration had too few resources to pursue it. The only thing for certain was that neither Laughton was in Sheffield. The girls were inconsolable. We all tried to help them but only time would lessen their sorrow, or the unlikely sudden appearance of one or both of their parents. The Thorntons, followed by William and Zoe, made the last two runs. On that very last run, returning the would-be farmers, there was an additional guest, Sheila.

'Thought I'd pop over and see how you're going and take a look at this amazing place myself.' She was sharing my chalet, which had two bedrooms. I gave her the double and spent the night on the bunks. She gave me a wry smile. 'The Administrator talks about this place all the time. He nearly convinced me to give farming a try, but you know, I love the new adventure I'm on.' She told me about her courses, from carding to dying spun wool, all connected to the new enterprise she was helping to steer, 'The Twilight Weavers'.

'Not all of us are over fifty but the start-up crew were, so that's where the name came from. Someone suggested 'The Silly Old Buggers' but we canned that!'

'I'm not just here for a sticky beak, you know.' As we continued our tour she followed me back into the small sitting room. 'We want to barter some of your wool and alpaca fleece. We've started producing yarn for local spinners, if you know any, let them know. We're starting to make garments.' I told her that I knew of a spinner who would love more wool and that we'd be happy to trade. Ashton was our barter expert and I introduced her to him.

She creased her nose. 'Oh dear, that young man! He's going to drive a hard bargain and I shan't be able to resist such a good-looking chap.'

'Oh Sheila!' I gave her a hug. 'I've missed you.'

'Have you heard from your man in Birmingham yet?' I said no.

When the new farmers were finally ready to move Mark and Luke went back with Matthew to help where they could. I might have gone with them, but I was busy reading up about midwifery and getting more anxious with every page turn. I even wrote a letter to Mac and asked the Thornton boys to pass it on to Caxton, who had earlier offered to pass on any mail to Birmingham.

Peggy was getting larger, and I had no idea what to do if something unexpected happened. With the help of Zoe and the Laughton sisters, I'd managed to convince Peg that we could cope with the meals, but she insisted on sitting at the table, directing us. Her disapproving sniff could send Zoe into heated bouts of kicking the wall in the corridor. On one occasion I did have to march upstairs to the library to calm down after she'd given me a lecture on making gravy. After all, as far as I was concerned gravy came out of a packet from the supermarket. You just added water and heated it!

Matthew returned with several skeins of wool for us and the Carters, letters from Clare, Sheila and Karen, and one precious one from Birmingham. In the letter, Mac confessed to being a poor writer of letters, and this was confirmed by the hastily scribbled note itself. It was longer than I expected and full of chatty details about his accommodation, his work and the state of the city. Sadly, more of Birmingham's overall population had died than Sheffield's. Mac confirmed some information I had heard in Sheffield, that the army had been deployed as soon as it became obvious that London was becoming dangerously lawless, and that water and power services, and the sanitation system had all been affected.

Like many other professions the army's numbers had been decimated, and only three command units remained consisting of a hotchpotch of individuals. Sheffield's unlawful administration had necessitated the deployment of one of those units, but they had now moved on to Manchester, leaving Caxton in charge. Karen's recent letter also informed me about the withdrawal of the army unit. Karen was in the midst of finding a home for herself and the twelve orphans. In my reply, I wished her luck and promised to visit as soon as Peggy's baby was born.

Mac also wrote about his colleagues and how they were all trying to respond to their new situations. Those with experience in viral infection were taking the lead, concentrating on developing their understanding of the virus in order to determine the appropriate vaccine development. The remaining medical group helped where they could as lab technicians to the researchers. Mac also found himself being called upon for his surgical skills at the hospital, which was the only facility known to be performing surgery in the country. Then his letter told me that he'd met a friend of mine from Brussels, Ansgar Falk. Falk had hardly been a friend, and just the mention of his name conjured memories of a time I wanted to forget. He'd been some sort of official, possibly at NATO or the EU, but I don't remember. He was a friend of Anton's, not mine. I had found him cold, aloof and hard to talk to when we socialised, but I doubt he would have told Mac that. More likely Falk would have given him the unflattering details of my last relationship. If Falk had mentioned any of that to him Mac did not mention it, but he did take a whole three lines to tell me how much he missed me, and that he would try and return for Peggy's baby. That piece of news was a comfort to all concerned.

15. SEASON OF FRUITFULNESS

Summer stretched out, and it was good to be close to the land, to watch things grow and relish the sounds and smells around us. For a time, we could forget everything beyond our electrified borders. With the exception of visits to Bakewell and helping Nathaniel and his small children return to their home, we were content to work the land, and attend to our animals. We shared the evenings, sometimes with Giles, often out of doors, except when the midges were collecting in columns above our heads and nipping our ears. Even on those occasions, the midges usually brought bats skittering overhead, and without streetlights the Milky Way spread above us in all of its brilliance.

When we could Giles and I would ride or follow some hiking trail that he knew. He was a wonderful guide. Since some of us would be required to travel to and from the Sheffield farms, Caxton had issued the garage with a fresh supply of petrol. The fuel allowed us to drive further than our bikes or the horses could take us. Frequently both the Laughton girls came along too. Giles seemed to enjoy having the girls along. Bianca wasn't confident on a horse, but she was in her element scrambling up Grinsbrook Clough, then shepherding me through the peat on the Kinder Plateau. 'Come on Granny,' she'd shout into the wind, 'you can make it!', her eyes bright, her face wind-beaten but smiling.

Late in August we had a surprise visit from Caxton. He brought news of the other farms set up around Sheffield and promised to return the Thornton brothers for harvest time. He said each of the four farms had chosen to specialise in particular types of farming, according to their location, while all of them would endeavour to produce their own vegetables and keep small animals such as chickens and goats. The Crookesmoor team had taken Tom's advice and were experimenting with grain crops on the Ponderosa show ground. Along with their vegetable and small farm animals, the Hillsborough crowd had contacted Keith, our experienced trout person and Doctor Grint's tenant, who had put trout in their lake, not to mention honey on their toast. Graves Park had a small herd of cows and some goats, as well as a vegetable garden. While egg production took centre stage at Endcliffe, they were experimenting with watercress and mushrooms.

Caxton also brought another letter for me from Birmingham. It was just as chatty as the first with mention of Mac's work and the team that he was a part of. He had been called upon to use his surgical skills on a few occasions and was now involved in a number of research projects with the infectious disease physician. Apparently my clever Scotsman had done some postgraduate work in the field before choosing to be a surgeon. He apologised for not writing more. He said he was missing me.

'They're keeping him busy,' Caxton confided in between throwing sticks for Gypsy as we walked through the alpaca field.

'Seems so. You saw him?' The animals came to inspect Caxton, but when they saw me they melted away. He was obviously harmless and not worth their spit. They're still my favourite animals, next to the crazy sheepdog that is. Gypsy offered me the stick, so I threw it.

'Had lunch with the whole crowd.' Caxton continued. 'But I almost missed him. He was caught up in some tests with Anna Grant and came late.' He bent down to take the stick offered by

Gypsy.

'Anna Grant?'

'The senior virologist!' The stick twisted through the air, and Gypsy barked cheerfully in hot pursuit. Caxton watched her antics before he went on. 'They're working to try and identify the characteristics of the virus, and its response to antiviral drugs.' He rubbed his hands together to get rid of the bark remnants and probably dog saliva too. 'Or something like that. She did explain it, but she lost me after two sentences, and one of those was telling me it was going to be a very complex and a slow process.'

We began to walk back as I asked for more news from Sheffield. Caxton was happy to comply. 'The Twilight Weavers', Sheila's spinning and weaving group, was fast becoming an outstanding success, with interest from other reviving cities and even a couple of canal boats coming regularly down the canal to trade. This was mostly thanks to Clare, who requested a car, then drove north as far as Leeds to seek out survivors with sheep and show them samples of what the mill could do. The foundry had started up, thanks to Thornton expertise and would soon be producing scythes, saws and knives. The conversion team had transformed some of the shopping areas to provide administrative spaces, workspaces and hubs for information. The dressmakers had been thrilled to receive a shipment of denim and cotton from Birmingham. On a sombre note, the mass grave site on the traffic island had been excavated, and the bodies given a better burial after efforts were made to identify the individuals. The plan was to try and identify all of the deceased.

'I'm glad to hear that Clare is trying a few new employment positions!' I broke the stick in half to signal to Gypsy that the game was over. She never objected but ran off to find something new to do. 'How is Karen coping without her husband Andrew?'

We stopped at the gate. 'She's used to him not being there. Karen was handling life when she was six. My sister got lost in Brighton one summer, and according to my mother she took herself to the St John's first aid caravan and told them she was lost and could they use their megaphone to find her mother.' He leaned against the stone gatepost. 'Everybody, including Karen, keeps asking when you might be coming back for a visit? We've got the green light for the next four farms. That would mean most people have either taken up farming or they're working in the city. We've made good use of the Thornton boys and they're promising ongoing visits to the farms, if I give them petrol. The restoration teams are a lot more organised now, still clearing buildings and also helping to refit or clear sites for the use of the farms or our city enterprises. The Thornton's, along with the two other electricians we've discovered, have been training the farmers and the city crew in electrics and plumbing. They actually found someone who can jury-rig the city drainage and sewage system, enough for our needs anyway.'

'I would love to see all of these changes some time.'

'Return whenever you want to.'

'I can't leave right now. Peggy's due in September and I'm the only thing she's got vaguely resembling a midwife!' I confessed that the whole thing scared me, but I couldn't let her know that. 'She needs my help.'

He opened the gate. 'I understand. We've asked for more people with medical experience. So far we've got four amazing nurses and a retired St John's Ambulance couple.' He stuffed his hands into the pockets of his jacket. 'It's just good to see you. You've a lot of friends in Sheffield, you know. Maybe once the baby's here you could come back for a visit, maybe even take one of our courses?' He closed the gate behind us.

His visit unsettled me. I knew I wanted to go back to Sheffield. I'd become more attached to those children than I had ever expected and although I knew Karen Stanforth would probably do a better job than I could, I missed being with them. For a short while, Caxton had thrown me off my contentment cloud. A part of me wanted to see the amazing strides they were all making, both in the city and with the children. Perhaps sometimes I craved more of a challenge than the farm was giving me, but I thought I was still needed, and that Peggy's baby was challenge enough. After that, the Thornton boys' plans for the mine were bubbling in my head.

September was racing towards us far too quickly. Having a better grasp of our storage needs and capabilities we were determined to reap better rewards from our labour. There was pickling to begin, the freezers to fill, and the firm fruit to be stored in Arthur's old apple loft. Peggy was consigned to being the armchair expert. Everyone else took part. Bianca made a very runny strawberry jam and Lucy threatened to put anything that stood still long enough in vinegar. William and I had lots of fun making sausages and almost perfected the art of curing meat. The others complained about our smoky aroma for days. We had made a good start when the Thornton brothers returned from the other farms to pitch in. The autumn would see us well prepared for winter.

Matthew Thornton, during this time began to show his very diverse skill set, acquired from holding down an amazing array of jobs. He took one look at Arthur's very old smithy and began to restore it. He had trained for a whole year as a farrier and had been part of the team to plan the metal foundry in Sheffield. He was also a plumber and seemed to know almost as much as his brother about technology. Luke told me he had been in the army too. The man was a cornucopia of talents, but casual banter still seemed to allude him. Unlike Luke and Mark, who were very open, relaxed and straightforward, Matthew was not forthcoming about himself and the concealment seemed to be deliberate. That autumn, I never felt totally comfortable in his company, although I could not explain why.

* * *

One fine September morning while I was manning the gates, two bicycles came into view. I kept out of sight, which was the usual rule, expecting them to go past, but instead they slowed to a stop and came towards the gate.

A deep Somerset voice yelled, 'Anybody here? C'mon open up. It's Ken and I've got a present for you all!'

'Ken!' I was already operating the gate. 'It's good to see you!' Ken and his companion pushed their bikes through and then rode ahead of me towards the house.

'C'mon Gel! Keep up!' Ken yelled back to me without introducing the other man. By the time I got to the house the pair were already seated. Lucy was making a pot of tea and everyone in the room was smiling.

'Ken's brought me a wonderful present,' Peggy rushed to my side. 'Well, for you too, I think.' She turned to the stranger who was looking slightly bemused. 'This is John Shawcross, Doctor John Shawcross.' At first I just nodded until the full importance of what she'd said hit me.

'A medical doctor?' I turned to him and he grinned. He told me later that I looked as if I'd just won the lottery. For me, it was just as wonderful. He'd been a chief resident in a London hospital for two years and might well have died had he not been on a hiking holiday with his cousin when the world went pear shaped. His last patient was his cousin, who had been hospitalised in Merthyr Tydfil in Wales, but died shortly after. After heading back towards London, only to hear so many fearful accounts of what was happening there, he headed north trying to follow the A49, making for Stoke-on-Trent where his parents lived. They were dead by the time he got there, but that's where he met Ken. After a good meal and a new pair of shoes, he had agreed to travel north with Ken, although his eventual destination was Birmingham. During their uneventful canal journey, Ken told him about the little Peak District community. John decided to accompany Ken to the farm, having heard so much about us. He had no relatives or friends in Birmingham anyway. Peggy had already coaxed the doctor into staying with us for a while. Doctor Shawcross was happy to oblige once he knew about Peggy's pregnancy.

Tom took no time in welcoming him, offering him the largest double chalet as consulting rooms and generally going over the top in trying to accommodate him. His welcome overwhelmed John. He'd been close to despair many times during his long and lonely trek. His family were gone, his career was in tatters, and the prospect of ever finding a secure place in the world seemed remote. Yet, here was a little group of individuals surviving, even flourishing in an idyllic setting. By nightfall, Ken was tucking into a Peggy-special pie and John had been shown his rather spacious accommodation. The following day he went on a trip with Tom and Ashton to the deserted medical centres scattered in our local towns. They had lunch with Inga and Fay, shared a beverage or two with the Carters, and returned mid-afternoon with a furniture van full of medical equipment. They had loaded a hospital bed and boxes of personal protection equipment, sterilising equipment, lighting, and assorted medical supplies. I suspect many of us slept more peacefully that night in the knowledge that there was a doctor around again, I know that I did.

'So,' Zoe stopped peeling potatoes and put down her knife. 'If we're going to have a doctor here, shouldn't we be setting up a proper surgery, with seats and everything, and have visiting times?' Since Luke and Mark had returned to Sheffield to help the second group of farms get organised before the winter, Zoe had been mooching about, grumbling at her routine chores and generally annoying everyone. It was clear she was missing Luke, and perhaps she was also restless. She had been annoyed to find out that Luke would be spending some time at the Crookesmoor Farm where Heather, the Sheffield farm recruit he'd met when she had visited us, was specialising in keeping poultry and training to be a mechanic.

'I'm not sure that an actual surgery is necessary yet,' Peggy told Zoe, while she completed pummelling bread dough. Since John arrived, Peggy had reclaimed her kitchen and we, her pot stirrers, dish washers and general factotums were put back in our place. I didn't mind. I spent more time with my alpacas who had replicated themselves while I was away on the Sheffield farms. The chocolate infant had been christened Toffee, which was quite out of order as her parents bore the elevated titles of Inti, the Inca sun god and Pachamama, the goddess of fertility. Actually, Pachamama's name had been shortened to Patch long ago by everyone, including me. There wasn't much you could do with Inti. Our herd also increased through new additions from further afield. We now had two wethers, found grazing near Castleton, named Capac and Yupanqui. We also acquired a male and female pair, Pachacuti, a wonderful black male, sadly nicknamed 'Cutee', and Coya, his mate. I could see that Toffee's name was probably the future trend, because sooner or later I'd run out of kings and deities. It had been impossible to get anyone to learn the correct words for an alpaca male, female or offspring. They were known as male alpaca, female alpaca and baby.

'Well,' Zoe pouted. 'I think we should at least let everyone in the area know there's a doctor here again!'

Peggy stopped pounding and looked at her. 'That's probably a good idea! Why don't you find Tom and suggest you both drop around the neighbours and tell them?' Zoe was out of the door in seconds, grabbing her anorak as she went. About five minutes later we saw the Rover heading down the drive.

Peggy and I exchanged a look of returning calm with each other and she went back to pounding the dough. I went back to Sheila's list of shearers with experience cutting alpaca fleece. We had both types of animals, the normal Huacaya and the silkier Suri. I wanted to make sure anyone we hired would be capable of leaving them looking less like army recruits with short back and shingle-style sides. Tom and I had tried to do the best we could, but the aftermath was animals that looked like they'd been sent to a penal colony. I could feel Pachacuti's embarrassment. Clare had located four men with shearing experience from around Derbyshire, Yorkshire and Lancashire who would be willing to stay at the farm and shear sheep and alpacas in exchange for lodgings, food and bartered goods. I had to get that organised for spring, before the winter set in.

'Is John about?' Matthew Thornton arrived at the door, his face was white. He'd sliced into his finger with a knife while he was helping William to shore up the mine roof. We'd decided to use the mine entrance for extra storage until we agreed on a better plan for its use.

'He's in our makeshift hospital.' Peggy told him, and on seeing Matthew's face, she quickly added. 'Lexi, could you help Matt?' The rag they'd quickly bound around Matthew's hand was covered in patches of blood. I hurried to the door.

'I can manage.' His voice had an edge to it, and I might have been tempted to take him at his word, but his face told a different story.

'I'm sure, you can! But I'd like to make sure you get there in one piece. You're looking a bit pale.'

'Just the blood. I hate the sight of my own.' His tone had become more amenable.

John sat Matthew down in his cabin and began removing the blood-soaked rag. Holding the hand aloft John cleaned carefully around the wound, revealing a jagged and deep cut, still spurting blood as John continued to clean it. Even my legs felt a little weak looking at it.

'I think you'd better sit down.' John muttered to me.

'You can go.' Matthew added without taking his eyes off the doctor's work.

A deep breath. 'I'm fine,' I said. 'What can I help you with John?'

It wasn't as traumatic as I thought being John's assistant. He examined the cut carefully before giving Matthew the bad news. There was no nerve damage and he'd been lucky, but it definitely needed stitches, and we had no anaesthetic. The eldest Thornton endured seven stitches. The beads of sweat on his forehead and the occasional grimace were the only outward signs of the pain of his ordeal. I caught the doctor glancing up at his patient's face from time to time, checking on his condition as we proceeded. Although I never asked, I was fairly certain John had never performed this kind of procedure without local anaesthesia before. Just another new experience made necessary by the pandemic.

'I've had worse.' Matthew told no one in particular.

'I don't doubt that.' John replied. I began to wonder what Matthew could have been through that would have been worse.

John was putting a dressing on the finger. 'It was lucky the knife was clean and not something that had been used in the garden. I've put antiseptic on it, and I'll check it again tomorrow. You need to keep the area clean and avoid damaging the stitches.'

Matt stood. 'Thanks Doc.' He turned to me. 'And you Lexi for coming down here and helping the doctor out.' He gave me a friendly smile.

'Well,' I shrugged, caught off guard by his disarming manner. 'The cinema's closed and there's nothing on TV so I had to find my excitement for today somehow.' The two men laughed.

'You could always come up to the mine and learn how to use a hammer.' Matthew offered with a grin.

'I know how to use a hammer!' I protested.

'Not today you won't,' interceded John, 'at least not with Matt. He's got to rest that hand.'

Outside the doctor's cabin Matt repeated his suggestion, 'I meant it about coming up to the mine and getting involved. There's always room for another worker.'

I told him I'd think about it.

❈ ❈ ❈

'So, I was thinking we should try and make mincemeat for Christmas mince pies,' Peggy said one morning as the persistent rain ran down the windows. She was reaching up for the old, large stoneware mixing bowl she loved. It had been in Tom's family for three generations and Peggy adored it. Holding it with one hand, she suddenly let out an ear-splitting scream and bent double. I rushed into the kitchen. 'Get the bloody bowl before I drop it!' she hissed. The bowl rescued, I helped her to the sofas and tried to get her feet up, but she winced again. 'Get John!' She cried. I didn't wait for further instructions.

John was making a list of medications he wanted Tom to try and get when he next went to Sheffield. Simple stuff that was probably in everyone's home medicine cabinet before the sickness. He came at once. William was in the barn and saw us both rushing back to the house. He dropped his screwdriver and followed. Between us, amid contractions, we managed to get Peggy over to a bed.

With the knowledge that there would be no chance of drugs to ease her pain, Peggy had also been studying natural childbirth and began her breathing. She was calm, far calmer than William, who paced backwards and forwards at the end of her bed. Ashton had already volunteered to distract the expectant father during the early stages. Peggy looked very relieved when he arrived and took Will back to the house. Zoe replaced him, quite obviously trying to impress John with her new research into childbirth. I was consigned to mopping the patient's brow and giving her sips of water. When John and Zoe went to give William an update, Peggy gripped my arm. I'd expected her to ask something about the birth or to tell me something was happening. Instead, she asked me to distract her by telling her about Belgium and later about the children in Sheffield. She sat listening, occasionally interrupting with a wince as a contraction took her attention. After one particularly strong one, her face became serious.

'I wish my mum could be here.' She squeezed my hand. 'She'd probably drive me mad if she was here, but,' she bit her lip, 'I miss her, and my dad. They were really looking forward to having grandkids.' Smiling to herself. 'My dad would have been trying to make me laugh with his corny jokes and she'd have been telling him not to be so daft.' We were both quiet for a while until another contraction. 'I'm sure this little thing's doing karate in there!'

Three hours later I went up to the house to get drinks for us all. In the house William was still pacing, up the corridor and then up the stairs and down again. Ash, Tom, Giles and Troy were playing cards and Matthew was baking. I said nothing but my raised eyebrows gave me away.

'Yes, I can cook too!' He held up his hand, revealing a protective rubber glove. 'Even used Peggy's kitchen rules.'

By sunset, Peggy was almost fully dilated and singing her birthing song. The natural childbirth book Peggy and I had consulted was at least twenty-five years old, so neither of us were sure if all the breathing techniques and advice were current. John seemed only concerned in helping to make Peggy feel calm. Half an hour later, I was sent to bring William. He began to tell her how much he loved her and how well she was doing. She snarled at him. He tried to soothe her.

Peggy roared back, 'Shut up! I'm in transition, I can say what the fucking hell I like!'

William looked shocked but then spoke to John quietly. 'She's in transition, right?' John nodded, barely able to contain his smile. William looked reassured. I would tell Peggy later how I swore in three languages before my youngest was born.

There were no complications. Arthur Thomas Hale was born at seven twenty in the evening. His parents cried. He cried. I cried and John heaved a sigh of relief. Back in the house, William gave weight and length details, still crying. Tom cried too after William explained that his son had been named after Tom and his brother. After the news was received William quickly returned to Peggy, to sleep in the chair beside her bed.

I was on my way back to my own chalet when I saw someone, a girl, running across the dark paddock towards me. She was screaming. When she drew nearer I could see it was Lucy. She was filthy, her face red and smeared with dirt, tears staining her cheeks and her forehead was cut.

'It's Bianca!' She screamed at me. 'She's fallen down the mine shaft and I can't get her to speak to me. I think she's dead!'

16. THE GHOSTS OF CHRISTMAS PAST

With our most powerful torch we could pick out Bianca's pink anorak. She was a long way down. She appeared to be lying face down, her anorak hood covering her head. She was unresponsive to our calls and from where we stood we had no idea if she was still alive. We had a rope ladder. It was something the girls had brought with them when they moved in, along with all kinds of climbing paraphernalia. Troy had raced into their chalet to collect it on our way to the mine. The ladder was far too short. Pale and shocked as she was, Lucy wanted us to lower her down to her sister, but John told her that she would be more use staying where she was and giving us advice about climbing, when we needed it. She didn't argue. I think she was afraid to find Bianca dead.

'Let me go down!' Troy volunteered. 'I'm the lightest so you can haul me back if you have to, and I've done a bit of abseiling on school camps.'

William agreed. 'Once we know what's what, we can always go down ourselves to bring her back up.'

Lucy instructed us on how to fasten Troy into the safety harness. She looked cold and Matthew took his jacket off, insisting that she wear it. We watched Troy slowly lower himself, walking backwards down the wall. He wore the hikers' headlamp he'd found in the Laughton holdall and talked to us all the way down, giving us a description of the remains of a rusted iron ladder, similar to the small fragments at the top of the drop. We waited anxiously for him to reach the bottom.

'It's a ledge here! It's not the bottom. Bianca's on a ledge! She's lucky she didn't fall further. It goes a long way down.' He was silent. We assumed he was checking her pulse. 'There's another tunnel at this level.'

'Never mind that!' Matthew snapped. 'Is the ledge wide enough for more people to come down?'

'I think so. There's about a yard on each side of Bianca before the drop.'

When Troy reluctantly climbed back it was John's turn to go down. He wanted to check that we could move her. She could have been bleeding, something he'd want to treat before any attempt to move her. Although lifting Bianca carried some risk we would have to get her off the ledge and out of the mine at some point.

John gave her a quick examination. He told us that she was bleeding and unconscious, but she was alive. At that point I helped Lucy to sit on the floor, resting her head against the wall. Troy sat beside her, wrapping his arms around her tightly. John did what he could to stem the bleeding, then waited for Matthew to descend. It was obvious from the moment the elder Thornton strapped on the harness that he'd done this before. There had been a short debate between Matthew and William as to who should go, and rather than Matthew claim that he was more experienced, he'd pointed out that William was stronger. Although the line was anchored, Matthew said he'd feel a lot safer knowing that the strongest person was up the top.

The ledge proved more precarious than expected. The edge was crumbling, and we almost lost our new doctor when his foot slipped over the edge. Matthew steadied him before he fell. They fastened the harness around Bianca and we carefully hoisted her up. John walked his way back up the wall and I helped him to carry Bianca to the Gator Utility vehicle. He drove her back to the hospital with Lucy sat beside her, holding her hand. William half walked, half ran back through the paddock to catch Peggy up with what had happened. Matthew and I were left to collect up all of the climbing gear.

'I might bring this stuff back and take another look down there,' he said, as he carefully put the pieces back in the hold-all, winding the ropes and placing the harness on top. 'Troy's right, there's a newer tunnel at the lower level and it's got wooden supports and a wooden ceiling. It looks like it goes a long way into the hill. That second tunnel could be a great bolt hole if we needed one. When my brothers get back we'll take a better look at it.'

We left the mine to walk back to the house. The sky was already getting lighter. A single star was visible in the East. I wondered if it was actually Venus. It would be dawn soon.

Bianca was in a serious condition. She'd lost a lot of blood and needed several stitches, which was John's first task, while she was out cold. Her arm was broken, which he reset with William's help, and he did what he could to check for further injuries. Unfortunately, without X-ray or scanning equipment he couldn't be sure that there were no further internal problems. He allowed Lucy to sleep on the floor beside her sister's bed, in her sleeping bag. The next morning Bianca woke and spoke to Lucy, then she slept. I could tell that John was concerned, but there wasn't much he could do except keep her comfortable and warm.

Zoe insisted that John should get some sleep. After looking in on Peggy who was back in her own bed relishing every moment with young Arthur, John followed Zoe's advice. Poor Peggy had

261

a stream of visitors all wanting to see the baby. After lunch, I pleaded with everyone to give her time to rest, and William needed his sleep too. After feeding Bianca's chickens and checking the alpacas I was heading to my own cabin when I came across Matthew, with the contents of the Laughton's holdall spread out on the grass around him.

'Just thinking I'd need a few more things before I take Luke and Mark down there. You don't happen to know where I could get climbing gear from, do you?'

'We could start by checking the Laughton's old place.' I sat beside him. 'That holdall had Lucy's name on it. Their parents probably had their own.'

✽ ✽ ✽

The inn where the Laughton's had stayed was a pretty place, with its white rendered walls and cottage pane windows, looking westward from the road below Froggatt Edge, to the woods which hid the valley of the River Noe. The steadfast geraniums in the tubs and boxes still struggled to present their final show of the year. Across the road, the tiny car park was empty except for a single vehicle which was probably the Laughton's. Inside the inn, only the dust on the wooden tables and chairs of the dining room showed the passage of time, and the scattered pamphlets and notebooks belonging to the Laughtons bore witness to their stay. Two mugs of what might have been green tea still waited on the table by the window. Up the creaking wooden stairs, we found that most rooms were still locked, except for the one clearly occupied by the girls, the twin beds unmade, and the double bedroom next door, full of the Laughton's own belongings. It was a forlorn scene, a hairbrush on the windowsill, toiletries on the dressing table, shoes at the foot of the bed, a novel and reading glasses on the bedside table and Mr Laughton's brightly coloured jumper cast off over the back of the chair.

'Ah!' Matthew spotted two other holdalls neatly stacked beneath the window. After inspecting their contents, he carried them both down the stairs and out to the Rover, while I idly looked around the room. The small desk was covered in papers, print-outs and photocopies, newspaper cuttings, photographs and notebooks. It was rude, I know, but one photo caught my eye. It was taken outside the African museum in Tervuren, just outside of Brussels. I recognised the building in the background, with the tiered lakes in the foreground. I knew it well as it was close to the school where I had taught. Two figures were standing on the terrace above the lakes, their faces slightly out of focus, their bodies clothed in dark overcoats. One wore a fur hat which reminded me of Russian diplomats in old Cold War movies. It would have been difficult to identify either man, except for the patterned burgundy red scarf and the silver-grey hair of one of them. It was Anton. I felt sick, my mind whirling.

Matthew was pounding back up the stairs. Impulsively, I grabbed the photograph and a few other items near it and stuffed them into my anorak pocket.

'All done!' He burst in. 'Ready?'

I managed to smile and started to leave the room.

'Couldn't find their car keys downstairs. Should we look around here?' He immediately headed for the bedside tables.

'Not necessary!' I kept walking towards the door. 'We've already got all the vehicles we need.' I didn't wait to see if he agreed, but went quickly down the stairs, out the front door and headed for the Rover. He followed, carefully shutting the door behind him. 'I'll bring the girls back when Bianca's recovered, and they can check through their parents' things.' I told him as I climbed into the passenger's seat. I let him drive because I was still unnerved by what I'd found, and I needed to think. Why had these total strangers got a photograph of Anton? What possible link could there be? Perhaps Anton's presence was totally accidental, and the picture was just a happy snap, taken on a visit to the park? Perhaps. I hadn't had time to read anything else on the table, so there was that possibility.

As we drove back I couldn't quite shake off the strange coincidence of that photograph. So to take my mind off the problem I began asking Matthew about his family. He was happy to sing the praises of his three brothers. All of them were different and he attributed that to their different fathers. 'My mother wasn't the greatest at choosing good partners. She had a weakness for poor, charming guys who took advantage of her. They always left her poorer, financially and emotionally. She hid her pain well, and my younger brothers hardly noticed the changes to our lives because she'd got such a big heart herself, but I noticed. I saw the toll it took. The reset she had to do every time one of them left.'

'It must have been harder for you, being the oldest.'

His fingers played on the steering wheel as he drove. 'She never made a big thing about me being responsible for the others, it just felt like I should be.'

'Something about being a big brother, I guess.' I thought of David as I spoke. We were both carrying on the conversation without looking at each other, both watching the road ahead. 'My brother was pretty critical of me as we were growing up. He'd always wanted a little brother but when it counted he was there for me. He ...' I couldn't bring myself to say any more.

'You know with this pandemic the worst thing for me is not knowing. I know my mother is dead but my youngest brother,

John, who was still living at home, he just disappeared. None of us know if he's alive or dead.'

I told him it was the same for me.

After that Matthew artfully steered the conversation away from our sombre musings. We discussed our favourite films, we agreed on a few and loudly but good naturedly disagreed on others. We tried hard to remember the first film we ever saw in a cinema, and who we were with at the time. We shared stories of old friends and youthful shenanigans that now seemed like they belonged to a lifetime ago. And we laughed. We were still laughing when the electric gates opened, and we drove up to the house.

* * *

For the next few days I threw myself into additional chores, helping Peggy, who insisted on cooking at least one meal a day, and chopping vegetables for Troy, who decided to make enough soup to last the winter. It filled a whole freezer! I just hoped we hadn't left ourselves short of veggies for other meals. Peggy laughed and said if that was the case it would be soup with everything!

It took almost a week before Bianca was able to sit up. She was listless and I could tell that John was still concerned about her. With the exception of Lucy, Giles was her most frequent visitor, bringing little gifts whenever he came. He'd scoured the county for surviving stores of chocolates and fruit-filled jellies, which were her favourites. Lucy divided her time between her sister and sharing Bianca's chores with Troy. In the evening Lucy and Troy either kept Bianca company or sat together in the house reading. Bianca's accident had brought a quiet to the house, punctuated only by the delightful noises made by young Arthur.

For some time, whenever Ashton had visited our neighbours, he'd taken Troy and helped him learn to drive. So when Bianca brightened and felt well enough to request that we celebrate Halloween, Troy volunteered to deliver the invitations. He always took Lucy with him and the pair would also pass on news about Bianca and young Arthur. A few days before our party, we had another celebration. We had never made much of our birthdays, but this was a special occasion. It was Troy's sixteenth, and to make it super special I drove back to Wincobank to collect Marie and as many of the boys who could fit into the Rover, which included Stan, who had once slept in charity bins but now had his very own bedroom in the Concord Park farm's apartment block. Marie had unofficially adopted the innocent, disabled young man when she first met him at the shopping mall. Stan lost two teeth during his stay in Sheffield, knocked out when a black hat got impatient with him, but he still beamed at everyone and offered hugs to anyone who was close enough.

Due to the large number of orphaned boys and older citizens at the Concord Park farm, it received more help from Birmingham than the other farms and was the last one to be populated. The volunteers who stayed there were chosen for their understanding about the special needs of the community as well as their willingness to acquire and pass on all their new farming skills. While the sports centre, with its pool, was still off limits, an extensive water collection system and tanks had been set up to help with irrigation. The golf club had become the temporary sleeping accommodation for the twenty-two farmers. Along with Marie and ten of her boys, all the other volunteers were either young orphans or older people who had lived in the area. The farmers had already obtained access to the land directly across the road from the sports centre. It had been ploughed and planted with potatoes. Other winter vegetables were located close to the golf club and further away I could see sheep and a few cows grazing.

'Pigs next Spring!' Marie said proudly, pointing to a half-finished brick building on what was once, perhaps, a tennis court. It was certainly an asphalt base that they were building on. 'Good old Commander Stanforth sent some volunteers to build it. They're coming back for Christmas.'

Stan asked Marie if he could show me their new accommodation block. The lad had already shown signs of an improved sense of self-worth. He positively crowed telling me about it. The building was solely for the use of the orphans, he said proudly. It wasn't a new building but a block of apartments at the corner of Bellhouse Road and Shiregreen Lane. Marie thought it might have been for older people. She'd been with the army when they removed what remained of the occupants and gave them a decent burial in the cemetery down the road.

'Better than a lot of folk got,' she sniffed, as we looked around the one apartment that had been redecorated a light grey. It was hers. She shared it with Stan. He showed me his own bedroom, currently with nothing but a sleeping bag on the floor. 'He's getting the bed for Christmas, but the daft thing can't wait 'til then, so he sleeps here anyway. Once the whole building is finished we'll fill it with youngsters, easily. A lot of 'em are still floating around the city. Caxton's got 'em occupied but he knows they need something they can call home. That's why this place has to succeed. Caxton told me there's not many young 'uns left. The plague killed off most of 'em.'

Marie surprised me with her own vehicle, a VW Amarok, a gift from Caxton. So, we could easily get them all to the Halloween party. Charlie, who took care of Stan during their time in Sheffield could already drive, so he followed us with most of the boys. Marie, Stan and I led the way. It was the first time that someone beyond our close neighbours, Caxton, and the itinerant

Ken, would find out where the farm was.

'Charlie's a good lad,' Marie offered me a shortbread biscuit as we drove. She'd learnt how to make them at one of the many new workshops that Caxton had supported to help people return to some form of normality and build some sense of community spirit. 'Best thing I did,' she chuckled. 'My lads love' em.'

It was better than I'd expected. 'You should go into production.'

Stan got excited when he saw who was waiting at the gate. 'Troy Boy! Marie it's Troy Boy!' He leaned out of the window and yelled. Troy came over and climbed into the back with him. I'm not sure who was the happiest. Stan hugged him tightly. When we stopped, Troy took Stan over to meet Lucy, who looked a little alarmed when Stan threw his arms around her and kissed her firmly on both cheeks. He told her that French men always did that. Troy introduced Lucy to the other boys and led them all off to the school hut, which is where they were going to stay.

'Troy's turned into a lovely lad,' Marie said, watching them go. Then she dug me in the ribs. 'You've done a good job with him.' I showed her to my cabin, which now had a second double bed replacing the bunks. She insisted that she wanted to meet the newest farmer, so we went to the house together to find Peggy and Arthur. By this time the pleasant little chap was quite used to people peering down at him and then being unable to resist picking him up. Peggy joked with Marie that sometimes she thought the baby had become a communal child. 'No shortage of baby-sitters then, love!' Marie teased.

By sunset most of the guests had arrived and deposited the additional food for celebrating. Many also brought baby gifts. William was volunteer bar tender for the night and as Bianca had specified a buffet, everyone helped themselves to the food. Keith, our resident trout and bee expert, provided some chunks of honeycomb as an alternative dessert, and brought his violin and teamed up with the operatic Cliftons, who played the guitar and piano. Thankfully no one sang until Keith shocked everyone with his version of 'YMCA'. The rest of the night was a selection of jigs and reels. Vince Carter called for a progressive barn dance, placing my arm firmly in his as he pulled me to the dance floor, the concrete area we normally used to park vehicles on to wash the mud off them. I could hardly refuse, and I was pleased that most people followed. Bianca, who was still confined to a wheel-chair giggled to see Lucy dragging Troy after her. The shortage of women didn't prove an obstacle. Some of Marie's 'Lost Boys', as Tom called them, danced together and so did Mark and Luke, newly returned from Sheffield. Luke borrowed my neck scarf and fastened it around his head, curtseying to Tom on his way around the dance floor. It was fifteen minutes of hilarity.

Matthew and I helped ourselves to more wine and sat to watch the next set of dances, including the usual 'boot scooting' line dance, when Tom continued to turn the wrong way and had his hands up when everyone else's went down.

✻ ✻ ✻

The following day Bianca took sick. She asked for me to visit her.

'Hello pet, John said you aren't feeling well.' I put my hand on her forehead. It was cool.

'I need to ask you to promise me something.' She gripped my hand. 'Promise me that I can be buried in Giles' family graveyard. It's so beautiful, and I'd be able to look down on this place if I wanted to see what you were all doing.' I was shocked, and my stomach began to make knots.

'You're going to tell me that I'm going to live, but I don't think I am.' Bianca explained. 'When I was down in the mine, I saw my mother's face and she told me dying wasn't hard. They're waiting for me, you see. So, I won't be sad to die, because I won't feel the pain anymore, and I'll be with them.'

'What pain?' It was hard to find my voice.

'It was so tiny at first.' A little smile played on her lips as she touched her head. 'I didn't notice it. Then, when my mother came again, in here, at the side of my bed, she said the pain was going to get worse, but I shouldn't worry because it won't last much longer.'

I gripped her hand. 'Have you told John?'

'No, but he can't help anyway. No one can.' She closed her eyes. 'Promise me.'

'I promise.' I kissed her cheek, but she didn't open her eyes. I was frightened. I had to find John. He was in the house, but when he saw my face he rushed out. On our way to the girls' cabin I told him what she'd said.

'She never mentioned anything about a pain or even about her mother.' He examined her. She was sleepy but her temperature and heart rate were stable. He beckoned me back outside. 'We need to get her to a surgeon. I'm not sure, but it could be a result of her fall. It could be a blood clot, or any number of things. I'm not an expert.'

It took half an hour to drive to Sheffield. We put the back seat down, then put her mattress and Bianca in the back. Zoe and Lucy came with us. I just hoped that Caxton would be easy to find. We had to risk it.

The drive seemed to take longer than usual. I remembered noting all the familiar landmarks but feeling detached from everything I was viewing. This couldn't be happening, I kept thinking, it just couldn't be happening. Lucy and Zoe would keep telling Bianca where we had reached or asking her how she was feeling. John and I hardly spoke. When we reached the Town Hall, we left Lucy and Zoe in the car to keep an eye on Bianca. We found Caxton fairly quickly inside the building. He registered the anxiety on our faces in silence as John explained the situation.

'Sorenson, get me Birmingham! Tell them it's urgent.' Caxton gestured for me to sit down in a chair. 'Doctor, when they come on the line I want you to explain everything to them. I'm hoping they can find Macintyre, he's the only surgeon around right now.' We waited for a long time. At first, I was content to sit, but eventually I had to get up and walk about.

Finally, Caxton was called into the communications room, behind what had once been the general information desk in the foyer. A moment later, he beckoned John. I began to follow but he stopped me at the door. 'Let them talk first. You can talk to him afterwards.'

I never got the chance. As soon as Mac heard what was happening he asked to speak again to Caxton. John came out and sat next to me in concentrated silence. I felt the whole world was caving in around us. Again, nothing happened for a long time, at least it felt like that to me. Finally, Caxton came out. He didn't stop walking but headed to the stairs. 'Where's the girl now?'

John rushed to his side. 'In the Rover, we parked outside. I told them it was an emergency.' I tried to keep up with them both.

By the time we reached the entrance, four of the remaining

soldiers were already gently lifting Bianca onto a stretcher. On the steps outside, Caxton explained what was going to happen. 'They're sending a helicopter. He looked at John. 'I would send you along doctor, but Macintyre will be waiting at the other end. So, I'm sending my adjutant, Sorenson. He has medical training and will only require your medical notes. Only room for one extra passenger and Bianca.'

At first, I thought the doctor would protest but John seems to have thought this futile and time wasting so he simply nodded his understanding.

A small though insistent voice from beside the car said, 'I'm going. She's my sister.'

The helicopter landed in the Peace Gardens and the passengers were loaded quickly. John and I said our goodbyes and then walked to a safe distance before watching the whirring blades of the helicopter lift the precious cargo into the air. We continued watching until the helicopter was nothing more than a small black dot in the sky. I offered up a little prayer in my head as it disappeared from view.

'Don't drive straight back.' Caxton suggested. 'Come over to the Leopold Hotel. You should all stay the night.' I might have declined his invitation, but I could see Zoe's eagerness behind her worn out face and John looked drained, so it was agreed that we would stay.

That evening our minds were all focused on the unknown events happening in Birmingham. I'm sure it wasn't part of his duty, but Sorenson hurried over to the hotel as soon as the helicopter returned him to Sheffield. He said he'd seen them receive Bianca and her sister at the hospital before commencing his own business at the administration headquarters. He was sure that we'd be informed as soon as anything happened.

17. SEASON'S GREETINGS

'Tell me about the two girls,' Caxton passed me a knife and fork while we waited in the breakfast line. Zoe and John had already eaten and were exploring the new Sheffield. We were still waiting to hear from Birmingham and Caxton was doing his best to distract me with food.

'The Laughton family were on a working holiday in Derbyshire when it all began, and they carried on living at the local pub when everyone else either left or died. The parents were climbers, quite famous I think, and they were writing a book about Derbyshire climbs.' I watched as my plate was filled with English breakfast goodies.

'And you say they didn't come back after the city was cleared of Pelham and his gang?' He talked over his shoulder as we searched for a seat. The plastic plates and long tables all reminded me a bit too much of school dinners, but it was an improvement on sitting on the floor.

'That's right.' I sat opposite him. 'I know some people died while Pelham was in charge here and a few were put in out of the way places, but they all seem to have come home. The Laughton's were not among them. Pity Pelham didn't keep a list of who was buried in the mass grave.'

'But he did.' He bent towards me. 'Pelham was a lot of things, mostly useless and even devious, but the one thing he was good at was records. I know because I've been ploughing through mountains of his records, everything from camp menus and food supplies to confiscated personal belongings.'

'So, we could check if the Laughtons were here?'

'Better than that, we can check their arrival date, where they were put, and if anything happened to them while they were here.' He sat back, looking pleased with himself. 'All I need is their names.'

I'd arranged to meet with Zoe and John at eleven to begin our drive back to the farm. Caxton had left me to attend to some other things, promising to check on the Laughton parents and also to keep us up to date on Bianca's progress. I hadn't expected to see him again, but he was waiting at the Rover when I arrived. He had a large wicker laundry basket with him.

'I've drawn a blank with the Laughtons, I'm afraid. The amazing Sorenson can't find any trace of them after they arrived. They were brought in the same night as the other families you mentioned, the Boyles and the Nevins, next on the list in fact, but after that, there's no trace. I'm sure Sorenson will find them eventually. At least we know they got here.' He stopped, as John and Zoe approached. 'Still no news from Birmingham, I'm afraid. Now before you go, I've got another gift for you.' He leaned on the Rover.

'If this incident with Bianca has taught me anything, it's that we need to communicate. So,' he turned to Zoe and pointed at the laundry basket.

'Dirty laundry?' Zoe screwed up her face.

'Go and listen!' He winked at us and grinned at her.

Cautiously, she approached the basket. Suddenly her face creased with amusement. 'Pigeons!'

He explained to us. 'When Zoe and I were talking yesterday I found out that her dad had raced pigeons, in fact her whole family had been involved. One of her ancestors had been a carrier pigeon trainer in the first world war. So, I thought, how could we be in touch in an emergency? I came up with them.' He pointed. 'Six white and six grey to begin with. I'm sure the colours will all mix up in time. The greys are trained to arrive back here and it's your task to train the whites. When they're ready, they can come back to us so we can contact you.'

It was the topic of conversation all the way home. Zoe couldn't remember all that her father had taught her, but enough to get started. Caxton had asked Clare to locate books on the subject. As soon as she got home Zoe was commandeering Troy and Matthew to help build a coup. In the meantime, she housed her precious little creatures in one of the enclosed stables. Galahad wasn't too impressed, and Gypsy sniffed and scratched at the door, but other than that, everyone else was fine with our new livestock.

Less than a week later, Caxton himself arrived with news of the Laughton girls. He told us that Bianca had undergone two operations, courtesy of Mac. The first relieved pressure on the brain and the second removed a blood clot. John had all the details Caxton told us if we wanted to know more. She was apparently sitting up in bed and driving her sister mad by always winning at cards. Mac expected the girls to be back before Christmas. He told us that Mac expected a full recovery. That cheered everyone, especially Troy. He also brought a very short note from Mac, crisp and sanitised, I assumed that was because he had dictated it to Sorenson. He was well, busy and missing me. It was enough.

Caxton didn't come alone. Doctors Peter Chang and Iminathi Nkozi had arrived in Sheffield together. Chang was the son of a Singaporean-Chinese businessman. He had taken a one-year contract in a Cardiff hospital, which ran out two weeks before the sickness had begun. Iminathi had been studying in London until the first cases appeared. She'd tried desperately to get back to South Africa, to her parents, but couldn't, so she went in search of her cousin, who was a first-year doctor in Bristol. He had already been dead for a week, according to the hospital records where he had been taken, when she finally found him. Iminathi and Peter had eventually met on a deserted station platform in Warwick, popular with itinerant travellers because a convent nearby supplied bedding and hot food for anyone passing through. They'd decided to go north. The nuns had advised them that north appeared to be safer than going south. Eventually though they found themselves in Chesterfield. Now both of them wanted to stay in Sheffield and help. I could see John was happy to meet other doctors.

'Eventually, one of them will have to go to another town,' Caxton explained, 'but for the moment, we're fortunate to have two doctors.' They all stayed for lunch and Iminathi begged to nurse young Arthur whose toothless grin amused anyone who held him.

'Sorenson's drawn a blank with the Laughtons, I'm afraid. We've searched every goddam list that Pelham invented. I've sent a request to Birmingham for information, but I'm doubtful they'll come up with anything. It's a real mystery.' Caxton and I were walking through the woods by the river, watching Gypsy roll in the mud and generally line herself up for a bath. 'Is there anything else you can tell me about them?'

'Not really, I only met them once. They seemed quite normal.'

'They didn't ask a lot of questions or try to stir up people?'

I laughed. 'No, they were just normal people! Why do you ask?'

He shook his head. 'No real reason, just trying to get a feel for who they were, if there was a possibility that they could have been a threat to Pelham or his administration in some way. Where did you say they were staying?'

'I don't know, somewhere near Curbar Edge, Buxton way I think.' When Caxton asked about the Laughtons' lodgings, my mind went back to the desk with the photograph of Tervuren Park. For mountaineers, Belgium would pretty much be a black hole. That area to the south of Brussels is forest, not climbing country at all. I hadn't had time to look at the other documents I stole, I decided I had to do that and perhaps go back to the inn to collect all the things on the desktop.

That evening, rather than continue the Monopoly game I'd been involved in, I complained of a headache and went back to my cabin. I'd stuffed Bianca's bag, containing her parents' papers behind the fireplace screen in my tiny sitting room. The chimney had become obsolete when the gas fire was installed in Arthur's time. I took it out, carefully removed the invading house spider and emptied the contents on the bed. I started by sorting it all into similar types of information, newspaper articles, photographs, handwritten notes, and a miscellaneous pile that included restaurant napkins, maps, random sketches and a whole collection of tickets for buses, trains, museums and even dry cleaners. Nothing jumped out at me, unlike the photograph. The items seemed to span a long period and covered half of Europe and the United Kingdom. I used clothes pegs to keep the piles together and put them back in the bag, behind the fireplace. I took out the photograph, which was still in my pocket.

'Who are you meeting Anton, on that cold Belgium day?' I asked the picture. 'The trees are bare and both of you are wearing heavy overcoats. It's winter, Tervuren Park in winter. I can't ever remember going there with you, even in good weather.' He wasn't going to answer. News reports in the early days of the pandemic had already described Brussels as largely deserted. The virus had swept through the area rapidly on account of the city being a business and political hub of Europe. Anyone who could leave had left, and the rest had died where they dropped.

I made up my mind to go back to the inn and to bring back as much of the Laughtons' research as I could. Towards the end of November, I got my chance.

Fay and Inga were organising a Christmas get together. They reasoned that it should happen about the twelfth of December, so that families could spend Christmas day together, privately. By now everyone knew my culinary ability, so I'd been co-opted on the drinks committee. Giles and Vince would be in charge, and I was tasked with checking around the neighbourhood for any 'interesting' alcoholic drinks. It was easy to put the inn on my itinerary. Unfortunately, Matthew had also been assigned to help me carry the booze.

'I promised that I'd find Bianca's pyjama bag for her. I'll get the bottles and look for the bag.' We had just pulled into the inn car park. 'Why don't you head over to Calver? We've got three pubs on the list there and we'll do Stoney Middleton together.'

Matthew didn't argue. He got straight back into the Rover and took off. I went inside the inn and lifted all the aperitif bottles down and popped them in the plastic tubs Vince had supplied. Then I checked the optics for any interesting variants. We'd already cleaned out the Millstone and two other Hathersage pubs on our way to the inn. The dining room seemed undisturbed.

The maps and walk pamphlets were scattered across the table by the window. Upstairs, I located Bianca's pyjama bag. I'd noticed it the last time. It was like a pirate's treasure chest made out of soft foam-filled material and perfect, I thought, for smuggling the items I wanted. In the parent's bedroom I got a shock. The desk was clear. I checked the drawer and even the bedside cabinets. The whole collection of notebooks and maps were gone. I was stunned. I should have taken more when I could. I was staring at nothing, feeling cheated when I noticed the fireplace. Someone had lit a fire. The fireplace had been clean when we last visited. It didn't take too much brain power to connect the dots. I moved the ash around and found some unburnt fragments and the top corner of a notebook. They went into the pirate's chest. By the time Matthew came back I was ready to help carry the bottles to the car.

A couple of days before the party, which was to be held at the Rutland in Bakewell, Giles told us that we'd be having some special guests from Sheffield. Along with the two doctors and Caxton, each of the farms had sent representatives. To Luke's delight and Zoe's disgust, Heather was among them. For me, it was wonderful seeing Sheila and Clare again. We talked for most of the early part of the evening. Marie had come too. She had decided to accept Tom's invitation to share Christmas with us. Troy was delighted.

There were shouts of congratulations and clapping when the Boyles, all wearing Santa hats, announced that Diane was pregnant. Young Harry told the room that he was going to help the doctor deliver his baby brother. From their faces I could see that Diane and John might have something to say about that, when the time came.

The only baby in the room, Arthur, had grown tired of being passed around a room of adults and entertained by face pulling and nonsensical language, and had gone to sleep in his bassinet in the quieter area, just outside the ballroom. His mother was tired too but enjoying the chance to mix with people beyond the farm.

Peggy and I were sitting together taking it all in when she leaned towards me and spoke quietly. 'Don't look now but I am seeing our friend Mr Caxton and Matthew in deep conversation over there, and they seem to be looking your way.' She grinned cheekily as I handed her another fruit juice. 'It's like being in a romantic period movie, you know, where the heroine is being discussed by prospective suitors and the camera shows them gazing at her.'

I closed my eyes then looked to the ceiling. 'Will you please stop reading romantic novels!'

She bent even closer to me. 'They've been standing in that alcove for ten minutes talking, and both of them seem to be discussing you.'

I hadn't noticed them. I watched them discreetly while pretending to watch the dancing. She was right about them being deep in conversation, and about their glances in my direction. While Peggy enjoyed period romances, I preferred spy novels and political intrigue. Where she saw repressed lust, I saw chicanery, conspiracy and secrecy. What were they discussing about me? They seemed to know each other more than I realised, but how well did they know each other? It seemed unlikely given that one was a diplomat and the other a soldier, but they did seem very familiar with one another. I could not say why exactly but the more I watched them, the more uneasy I became.

Later in the evening, after continuing to ponder why I was the focus of such interest, it began to dawn on me that maybe they knew I had stolen documents from the Laughtons. I started to feel guilty about having them in my possession. I needed to get answers about the photograph. I decided to open up to one of the few men I could trust with a secret, Giles Montgomery.

'Have you gone through all the Laughtons' items?' Giles asked me as we sat in his beautiful, oak-panelled sitting room the next day. I was glad he hadn't started with a whole string of reassuring rubbish about an over-active imagination or gently telling me not to worry. He could see I was worried and that I might have good reasons for feeling like that.

'Not yet.' In the day I never seemed to have enough time alone to examine what I had, and in the evening, I was too tired to try.

Giles was studying the photograph. 'Do you know the other person?'

'No, I don't. I only recognised Anton from his hair and that burgundy scarf. I bought it for him. We joked about him wearing it when he drank so you wouldn't see the wine stains.'

He put the photograph beside him on the coffee table and frowned. He looked deep in thought. I waited. 'Would you like me to take a look? I can't promise that I'll find anything, but I do have some time on my hands. As they say, 'All is safely gathered in' and I'm getting bored with writing my journal and doing jigsaws. So, I'd quite like a different kind of puzzle.'

I took everything I had back up to the grange that afternoon, and when I left he was already listing each item and trying to date things.

On my return to the farm I stopped in the middle of the thicket between the grange and the farm. Across the slope of the hill, I could see the younger Thorntons repairing the roof of the larger barn. Zoe and Heather were below, watching them, occasionally passing things up in a bucket attached to a rope. Both girls were interested in the same young man. I felt sorry for Zoe because

Luke had certainly shown a preference for Heather at the Christmas party. According to Caxton, far fewer women had survived than men. That was in every age bracket, he said. Yet, here were two pretty girls vying for Luke's attention. It didn't seem fair somehow.

Later that evening I found Zoe alone in the pigeon loft. She'd been crying but she did her best to hide the fact.

'Luke's told me he's thinking of spending Christmas with Heather at Crookesmoor!' She looked out into the night, pushing away any signs of moisture on her face. The light of the torch caught a tear on her hair. 'I couldn't say anything. Luke looked so happy that she'd invited him.' I put my arm around her. 'It's just that he's so nice, and sometimes it's lonely here. I know I've got Troy but he's like a little brother to me. I was hoping that because we were both together here, Luke might want to, you know. What should I do?'

Oh, Christ kid, I don't know, would have been the honest answer, but I tried to channel Peggy. 'If Luke wants to be with Heather and she feels the same, there's not much you can do, except keep letting him know you care and you're happy for him.'

'But I'm not happy, for either of them!'

I sighed. 'Jealousy is a waste of time.' I patted her hand. 'You know, you should visit some of the other farms. Perhaps you might find that Luke isn't the only apple in the barrel. I'm due to visit them in the New Year. Why don't you come with me?'

The suggestion cheered her up and the following morning she was very chirpy. 'You're right, there's probably at least one other decent guy around. By the way I've asked the doctor if he could train me to be his nurse. He said he'd like that. So, I'll be in the hospital chalet from now on!' I was pleased she'd found something new to interest her.

With a good store of food and just a little to drink, we welcomed Christmas. Keeping the Boyle's tradition, we displayed our gender neutral, homemade gifts and waited anxiously to see what each of us would get. Swaps were allowed, according to Tom's rules, and there were quite a few of those. Mark landed Zoe's carefully embroidered bookmark and Peggy got a wooden chest, perfectly designed for small hand tools, that Tom had been making for months. William wouldn't exchange the beanie that Lucy had carefully knitted for several months and wore it everywhere. The swap satisfied everyone. Tom landed my crocheted Dr Who scarf that he insisted on wearing for the rest of the evening. I was enchanted when I saw my gift, a very old leatherbound edition of 'Jane Eyre'. I remembered seeing it in Giles' library.

He looked a little bashful. 'I'm sorry, I didn't actually make something. I tried macramé but there were holes where there shouldn't have been. By the time I'd followed all the instructions I'd forgotten what it was supposed to be in the first place, a plantpot holder or something.'

I walked him back to the stile between the grange and the farm. It was icy cold, but the clear sky was filled with stars. He stopped at the stile and told me about his investigation into the Laughtons' research. 'I've been through everything and I'm pretty sure it has nothing to do with you directly, although your friend did feature in a few of the newspaper cuttings. The cuttings covered a variety of topics over a couple of years including his opening for a hospital and personal piece about his hunting lodge in the Ardennes. He seems to have been a person of interest, but why exactly, the cuttings did not reveal, at least not to me.'

'The man with him is a little more interesting. He's often pictured in the background and in colder conditions he always wears the Russian karakul fur hat. Obviously when he was in Alice Springs, he didn't, but I'm pretty certain that it was him in Australia. They both pop up in varied places. Your friend is usually photographed in Europe, but the Karakul fellow seems to be attached to quite a number of high-level meetings, at the EU, at the World Health Organisation and the United Nations. He is never in the foreground, always lurking in the background. I couldn't find any mention of the Russian hat man's name. Apart from the photographs, there were a lot of articles and reports covering a very diverse range of topics, everything from the environment, to eugenics and cat breeding. Sorry I couldn't be more help.'

I couldn't help feeling a little disappointed, if not entirely surprised. 'You've been a great help. I just wonder why they were collecting all of this information, and how Anton is involved.' I dug my fists into my anorak pockets. I was icy cold.

'They were both journalists Lexi so perhaps this was all just for some future articles they were writing. Anyway, the whole lot is in my safe for now.' He saw me shiver. 'You'd better get back inside. You'll freeze out here.

The two chickens were well and truly on their way to being cooked when I returned indoors, and I set the table with Ashton. He'd been making Christmas crackers, which was a surprise to everyone. I just hoped that he hadn't included party hats. With a gust of cold air Troy raced in and Peggy was on the point of complaining about the draft until Troy interrupted her.

'There's a helicopter landing in the alpaca field!' He saw Peggy's annoyed expression. 'Just thought someone ought to know.' By the time he'd finished his sentence I was down the steps and heading to the gate. The plain grey sides of the helicopter gave no indication of where it came from or who it belonged to, but I recognised it as one of the helicopters from Sheffield. John and

Zoe were right behind me, and somewhere behind them Troy and William were following.

Mac was the first to jump down to the grass, followed by Lucy, and then someone helped to lower Bianca, who was in a wheelchair. Mac looked almost the same as when I had last seen him, except his beard and hair had been trimmed a little neater. Without waiting, the blades began to turn, and the helicopter rose as they wheeled Bianca towards us. I didn't know who I should throw my arms around first. I didn't make the decision. Mac left Lucy to push her sister to the waiting group and rushed to throw his arms around me. We were laughing and crying and so overwhelmed, neither of us having the words, just being together, seeing the joy in each other's eyes. Around us people were hugging the girls and starting to wheel Bianca to the house. I reached out for Lucy and hugged her too, but I couldn't let go of Mac. He was doing his best to acknowledge everyone's greetings, but he held on to me tightly

There was a danger that the meal might overcook because the whole household wanted to welcome them all. The greetings, the delight, the cacophony of everyone talking at once woke Arthur, who, by the time-honoured rights of babies everywhere, demanded to be the centre of attention. The Laughton sisters both cuddled him, and Mac complemented his parents on producing a fine-looking boy.

The round of hand shaking, hugs and tears began again when Giles arrived. The tears were mostly from Bianca who was still pale, but blissfully happy, sitting at the table next to her favourite Uncle Giles. Lucy and Troy were side by side. It was a marvellous afternoon on what was our second Christmas spent together at the farm.

About four o'clock, when in the past we would have had the TV on, perhaps digesting Christmas pudding and the king's speech,

Tom suggested a bracing walk to see the wonderful work that Mark and Matthew had completed up at the mine. As we all 'rugged up' Giles apologised and said he'd started to get a headache earlier in the day and felt he should go home. He refused John's offer of medication and wished us all the happiest of evenings.

The tramp to the mine did two things. It certainly wore away some of the lethargy caused by overeating that had been creeping over us all, and it showed us just how industrious the two older Thorntons had been. Lucy and Bianca had been reticent to re-enter the mine at first, but the battery-operated fairy lights decorating the entrance relaxed them a little. The floor was now concreted and flat, leading all the way to the dreaded hole, now also decked in fairy lights. A new metal spiral staircase, wound down to the ledge, now made safe with reinforcements and also concreted. Bianca wouldn't go near the hole, so Peggy stayed with her, while we climbed down to the lower level and into the tunnel.

'We've just completed the first chamber,' Mark's voice was apologetic, 'but you can get the idea. It's safe all the way through.'

'All the way through?' Ashton was already walking beyond the illuminated area.

'All the way through to the grange!' Matthew clarified. 'It comes out in the back of an old shed on Merton Grange land. We'd hoped to show it to Giles.'

They'd made a wonderful job of renovating and making it safe. Mark insisted that this was only stage one, but with a few alterations, what we had already was a secure bolt hole and somewhere to stable our more precious animals, if we had to do that.

That evening, most people went to their beds early, Mac and I among them. I'd been telling him all night how happy I was, until the words were not enough. I knew he would have to go back to Birmingham, his job there had only just begun. I knew I would miss him terribly. He told me how he was constantly home sick, 'farm-sick' he called it, and that I was never out of his thoughts. As he slept, I watched the smile playing on his lips. I wanted the night, and all the nights after to be as perfect as this one, knowing that in a few short days he would be leaving again.

While he slept on, I got up early the next day, crunching through the frosty grass, to the stile between the farm and the grange. I wanted to share my joy with Giles, and I wanted to take him to the shed on his land to show him the mine tunnel that linked his place and ours.

ABOUT THE AUTHOR

H. G. Merritt

H. G. was originally from Sheffield, and has lived in several parts of the world, but now calls Gippsland, Australia home. As a lover of Derbyshire, it was inevitable for her to choose that part of the world as the setting for a post-apocalyptic novel.

www.ingramcontent.com/pod-product-compliance
Lightning Source LLC
Chambersburg PA
CBHW021040030726
47496CB00006B/1629